Dead Broke

ALSO AVAILABLE BY TRISTA RUSSELL

Chocolate Covered Forbidden Fruit

Fly on the Wall

Going Broke

Pocket Books
A Division of Simon & Schuster, Inc.
1230 Avenue of the Americas
New York, NY 10020

First Pocket Books trade paperback edition January 2008

POCKET and colophon are registered trademarks of Simon & Schuster, Inc.

For information about special discounts for bulk purchases, please contact Simon & Schuster Special Sales at 1-800-456-6798 or business@simonandschuster.com

Designed by Elliott Beard

Manufactured in the United States of America

10 9 8 7 6 5 4 3 2

ISBN-13: 978-1-4165-5383-0
ISBN-10:   1-4165-5383-5

Dead Broke

TRISTA RUSSELL

Pocket Books

New York   London   Toronto   Sydney

Dedicated to Braelyn

I could have given you a name with a fancy predefined meaning. However, I gave you a name that you will give meaning to. I pray that your father and I will raise you to be such an example that others will take your name because of what you have made of yourself.

Love,
Mommy

Dead Broke

"We all have our time machines. Some take us back, they're called memories. Some take us forward, they're called dreams."

—Jeremy Irons

Tremel

WITHDRAWAL SLIP #1
ENDING BALANCE: $827.76

You always taste so damn good," I whispered as I trailed soft kisses from her lower lips up to her eyes.

Sarai blushed. "You say the sweetest things, Mel."

"That's because you are the sweetest thing, baby." My tongue entered her mouth, and with soft suction she pulled me into her welcoming heat. The enticing wetness and her soft moaning caused a pulsation all over my body.

We were in Bimini, Bahamas, on a private stretch of beach behind a house we rented for the week. The plan was to watch the sun go down, but the moment I looked over at the way her pale pink sundress wrapped around her brown body, I knew exactly who I wanted to "go down." The pink fabric was very thin and I could see that she had on no panties or bra. Her nipples hardened from the cool ocean breeze.

When our kiss was done, the sky had lost its candle and the pink-and-orange heaven was slowly penetrated by darkness. I laid my bare back onto the sand as Sarai knelt between my legs. She pulled her dress over her head quickly and reached for my anxiously awaiting stiff dick.

She moved her face closer to it and opened her mouth. With tiny licks around the very tip she teased me, and then ran her tongue from shaft to tip until there wasn't a dry spot in sight. Her eyes never left mine as her soft wet lips took me in. She squeezed her lips around me and moved up and down. As she came up again I fell out and Sarai said, with the sweetest grin, "I won't even remember this."

"What?" I assumed that the sound of the waves had interrupted what she had said because it didn't make sense to me.

"I won't remember this," she repeated, with the same sexy smile.

"Remember what?" I was now up on my elbows. "You won't remember what?"

She burst into uncontained and almost possessed laughter. "Sarai." I called her name, hoping to get her to snap out of this playful stint and back down to the blow job that I was in desperate need of. "Sarai." The more I called out to her the farther away she moved, until she was waist-deep in the dark ocean water.

From thirty feet away she spoke but I heard her as though she was nibbling on my earlobe. "Tremel, if I don't remember, you remember for me." The noise from the large wave coming up behind her slowly melted into the sound of a police siren on the movie I fell asleep watching.

I slid my hand over the far side of the bed, checking my surroundings. I hoped that something had changed and my sad reality was just a nightmare. But just like the last time I dreamed about Sarai, she was still nowhere to be found. However, this time I was happy to be in her bed instead of a jail cell. That's right . . . I said jail.

On the night Sarai was shot it turns out that I did all of the wrong things in front of the wrong people the night I selected to reenter Sarai's life. Around ten o'clock that evening two hundred people witnessed my angry poetry performance onstage at Vocalize, which was dedicated to her. Five minutes later fifteen of those people also saw Sarai rush out crying. Two of which were in the ladies' room when she screamed that I was trying to ruin her life. To make matters worse, at midnight I also slipped the security guard in her building $300 to open her apartment and allow me to wait for her. And last, but certainly not least, because Damian was wearing gloves, my fingerprints were the only ones on the gun, and the gun just happened to have been stolen a week before from someone in Boston, my new hometown. Ain't that a bitch?

So as far as the Miami PD was concerned, they could get back to Dunkin' Donuts, their work was done. I was an angry black man with a gun and a motive: a cheating ex-girlfriend. I couldn't win for losing, and no one even pretended to want to hear my explanation.

Luckily, I've been out for two weeks now, thanks to Damian's drunken confession to a stripper in Texas two days before he set out to Guadalajara. Now the closest he'd ever get to Mexico is through the smell of the breakfast burrito one of the federal agents ate while waiting for him to show up at the border . . .

Those weeks in jail killed everything for me. As a newly signed artist, my CD sales not only stopped, but my shit did a U-turn when news of me shooting my ex-girlfriend and being arrested surfaced. Stores sent my CDs back to the warehouses in droves. I hired the best attorneys the $26,000 in my bank account could afford. And since the only person in my family with $75,000 to post as bail money was my uncle Norman, I just got comfortable in my cell. After the fistfight he and I had during my Christmas visit, my mom knew not to even ask him for air on my behalf.

Since my release I've been staying at Sarai's place. Not a day goes by that she isn't in my thoughts, my tears, and my heart. I can't stop feeling that maybe if I hadn't come by that night, she'd be lying here in her bed, full of life. Instead I'm not able to drag myself out of bed. It was the last place I held her, smelled and touched her hair, made love to her, and was good to her. Major parts of me regret coming back *that* night. Then again, if she was all alone *that* night . . . she would've gone through everything alone. Something tells me that my presence made what happened a lot easier for her.

The phone rang. I instantly glanced over at the clock: 3:16 a.m. I cleared my throat and reached for the phone. "Hello."

"Hello, Mr. Colten?"

"Yeah," I said as I rolled over.

"This is Nurse Graham." My heart paused right along with her voice "We need you at the hospital right away."

I sat up as my soul sunk. "Is there something I should know?"

"I am not permitted to say." She continued: "Dr. Bowen just asked me to get you here as soon as possible."

"Okay, thanks." I hung up the phone and remembered the last late-night call from the hospital. It happened on my second night out of jail. They thought that they were losing her. Sarai had flat-lined several times, for reasons they couldn't explain. Dr. Bowen was called in from home, the nurses were rushing around getting special equipment, and the PA-system operator was shouting "Code blue, code blue in room 207."

I slowly stepped into room 207 and saw my sleeping beauty lying there like she had been for almost a month. Her bedside was surrounded by the hospital staff but I pushed through them and clutched her hand. "Why you playin' games with these people?" I whispered in her ear. "You got everybody earnin' their salaries to-night." I kissed her on her cheek and said, "All right baby, you got me here, so stop it." *Blimp, blimp, blimp* . . . the heartbeat monitor suddenly sprang back into action and all of her vital signs slowly fell back into place . . . but she didn't, wouldn't, and couldn't wake up.

Soon the nurses and Dr. Bowen left us alone. I ran my hand down the side of her face with a smile and asked the same question I asked her the night I knew I would fall in love with her. "Why do I have to push your buttons to get you to act right?" She never answered, but I sat there until morning wishing she would.

• • •

As I entered the hospital I felt something different this time. I was unsure if I could pull off the same thing I did last week without tearing up, or getting angry when she didn't talk back. The elevator door opened to the second floor and introduced me to scary silence. As I walked by the nurses' station most of them avoided eye contact and others just looked away altogether. Absolutely no one spoke to me. This must be it, the time that I'd have to say good-bye to her . . . my last visit.

I stopped a few doors away from room 207 when I saw orderlies rolling out some of the machines I was used to seeing Sarai connected to. I couldn't take another step, and suddenly I didn't give a shit about anybody seeing me cry. "Damn," I whispered to myself as my hands rushed to my head. What would I do now if I couldn't just watch her sleep? Where would I visit her? I'm not about to take my conversations to a cemetery.

Somehow I got my feet to start moving again and through my footsteps and tears I could hear Dr. Bowen ask, "Who is the president of the United States?"

There was a faint whisper of an answer, "Unfortunately, George W. Bush."

"Do you know where you are?"

"Come on, after a million nurses, you, and this damn catheter?" She coughed. "Stevie Wonder could tell me that I'm in the hospital." She went on, "My question to you is, 'What am I doing here?'"

"Your question will be answered shortly." Dr. Bowen continued, "What is your name?"

"Sarai Emery." She giggled weakly, "How many times are you going to ask me that?"

He chuckled. "Until I believe that you're actually talking to me." Dr. Bowen watched as I walked through the door in utter amazement. My eyes were wide open and so was my mouth. My body shook and I nearly dropped to the ground. Sarai was sitting up in bed with her back toward me talking . . . talking. She was sitting up . . . talking. Something I never expected to see again in life, much less tonight.

"Do you know this man?" Dr. Bowen pointed at me as I approached.

When Sarai turned to look back at me, it was as though she looked right through me and at the bare white wall behind me. "No." She looked back at the doctor. "Should I?" I felt the blood freeze up throughout my entire body and my eyes couldn't leave her, I couldn't even blink. Damn blinking, I couldn't breathe.

Dr. Bowen saw my expression and seemed embarrassed and hurt for me. "Mr. Colten, why don't you wait for me in the hallway?"

I don't remember getting there but I made it to the hallway and sat on the ground outside of the room with my head in my hands and heard him ask, "What is today's date?"

"Umm." She thought awhile. "I'm not exactly sure, but Nat's party is next week, so it should be mid-May, like May twentieth or something like that."

"Okay." He paused. "That's not quite today's date, but tell me the last thing you remember before you woke up a couple hours ago."

"I remember talking to my two best friends, Nat and India, at a bar and driving home to see my boyfriend, Damian, and then going to work." She paused, concerned. "That was yesterday . . . I think."

"No, that wasn't yesterday," Dr. Bowen said.

"Was I in a car accident?" She tried to rationalize. " 'Cause I don't remember driving home from work."

"No, there wasn't a car accident." He paused. "Let me have you open up your mouth, I need to take a look at you."

For twenty minutes he examined her to be certain that all was well physically. She had all of her faculties and no part of her body was numb. During this time many nurses gleefully peered into the room, not believing that the coma girl was up, talking, and asking for a meal. One nurse looked down at me with joy. "You must be going out of your mind."

"I am." I continued in a mumble, "She said she didn't know me." What the fuck . . . *She said she didn't know me*, I repeated over and over in my mind. I continued listening in on what Dr. Bowen had to say. "You were shot, suffered severe trauma, and your body went into shock, leaving you comatose." Dr. Bowen took a deep breath. "Today's date is April fifth, 2005." He sighed. "What you're remembering happened at least ten months ago."

"Whoa." She took a deep breath. "Now, what do you mean shot? Who shot me?"

"Well, Ms. Emery, the detectives will be able to tell you more about the incident, I'm just a doctor."

"Detectives? The incident?" She was in disarray.

"Okay, wait!" Sarai was astonished. "So I've been in a coma for ten months?"

"No," Dr. Bowen explained. "You've been out for about twenty-seven days, but it seems you may have lost some of your long-term memory. When we conduct tests in the morning we'll learn more. In the meantime let me check out your wound."

"So this bandage covers the gunshot?"

"Yes. You were shot just below the heart, you are an extremely lucky young woman." He examined her injury. "So how are you feeling?"

"Sleepy, very sleepy, but you're telling me that I've been in a coma, so I don't want to go back to sleep."

"No, you seem to be doing fine," he reassured her. "Tiredness is a natural stage of recovery, get some rest. I promise that you'll wake up in the morning."

"Doctor," she called out to him. "I need to make some phone calls. I cannot believe none of my friends are here."

"They were, but it's pretty late now," Dr. Bowen said. "How about you make those calls in the morning, I'll have a nurse sit with you until you fall asleep so that you'll have some company."

She sounded scared. "I'm a little worried because my dad is sick and my brother . . . I need to talk to him."

He cleared his throat. "Your concern is understandable. I'm sure your friend Miss Blake will be able to tell you everything in the morning," he said. "However, it's important for you to rest tonight, you have a big day ahead of you." He continued: "Take these pills and when you wake up I'm sure you'll be surrounded by all of your friends."

He took a few minutes to review her chart, jot some things down, and give special instructions to the nurse who would sit with her, but before he could make it into the hallway, Sleeping Beauty was out like a light again. "Mr. Colten." He looked down at me and extended his hand. "Let's talk."

"Funny, I was about to say the same thing." I stood to my feet.

"I'm sorry, I should've told you that this was a possibility."

"This." I cut him off. "What exactly is *this*?"

"Retrograde amnesia," Dr. Bowen said as he pressed the elevator button. "Let's get a cup of coffee."

I followed him to a room behind the main doors of the emergency room and sat in a chair across the table from where he placed his coffee mug. "Coffee?" he asked me.

"No." I had one question, but I was terrified of the answer. "What should I expect?"

"Well, with retrograde amnesia, people lose memories from the time just prior to the injury. This time period may stretch from a few minutes to several years. It seems as though Sarai has lost the last ten or eleven months."

"Well, I met her ten months ago, so that basically rules me out of her life?" I asked, but didn't give him a chance to talk. "That's fucked up."

"I know." He sipped from the mug. "But we have no way of controlling how our bodies work. We all store different memories at different levels." He smiled. "However, when a retrograde amnesiac recovers, they recall older memories first, and then more recent memories make their way back, until all memory is recovered."

That was just the kind of news I wanted to hear. "So you think that she'll fully recover?"

"I can't say at the moment, but after we run some tests tomorrow, I'll have a more definite prognosis."

I kept thinking about the way she looked at me, the stranger in her room, and it tugged at the very core of my heart. "So what do I do or say to her?" Then I thought hard about it. "Or should I just stay away?"

"No, I wouldn't suggest that." He leaned back into his chair. "Just be patient, things may come back to her bit by bit, don't force it. Start out by having someone that she recognizes, like Miss Blake, reintroduce her to you."

From that moment on I realized I had a world of memories that now only belonged to me. Like how absolutely gorgeous she was at Nat's party; I couldn't keep my eyes off of her and created situations where she'd have to talk to me, even though her man was in the room. Thoughts of how she dissed me that night and how I got revenge on the poetry stage later. Damn! I thought of our first date when I turned her apartment into a Café de Mel and cooked crabs. Man, the look on her face when a few crabs got away. Memories, memories, memories.

My mind went to our first kiss and how much we both wanted it to continue, but we tried to be polite and not overdo it. I reminisced about the first time I eased my chocolate lightning into her soft and moistened piece of earth. She quivered and gave off a sexy moan as she accepted me. It was the first of many times that her body was my ticket to paradise. Now I stand alone on an oasis and she looks at me, through me, blankly, and asks if she should know me. In her mind she is still in love with Damian, but in my heart she still belongs to me.

Long after Dr. Bowen left, I sat in that room wondering how anyone would tell her that Savion, her twin brother, had put a gun to his head and ended his life just minutes before she was shot, and that he mailed her a long letter begging her forgiveness. In it, he said that watching his personality, emotions, mentality, and his body die of AIDS had stifled his will to live. His body was in the morgue for a week before I realized that in his world there was just Sarai and their Alzheimer-stricken father . . . so there would be no funeral arrangements made. Though I was in jail, I had my mother use my money to pay an Atlanta funeral home for a small service and cremation; they shipped Savion's ashes to Miami. Had Sarai died, I would've buried them together.

Because I was, and still am, so much in love with her and everything and everyone in her life, I used some of the last of my money to extend her father's nursing-home care by four months. So guess who's going broke this time?

After walking the entire hospital and finally calling Nat with the news, I tiptoed into room 207 shortly after 8 a.m. and thanked the heavens that Sarai was still asleep. Just as she had once said about her father, as long as she couldn't see me, her not remembering me couldn't hurt me. I sat on the cold uncomfortable chair and studied her face. Even though her hair was pulled into the messiest ponytail I had ever seen, her beauty shone through like sunshine after a hurricane.

I smiled at her and the voice of Lauryn Hill's "Can't Take My Eyes Off of You" flooded me and came out in a melodic whisper, *"You're just too good to be true, can't take my eyes off of you."* Would she ever love me again? I had to make her love me again.

"Nice voice." Sarai's words startled me.

"Oh, snap." I had just noticed that she was staring back at me. "I'm sorry. Did I wake you?"

"Yeah," she said. "It's all right, though." She struggled to laugh.

I was nervous, I didn't know what to say or do. I didn't know what I should act like, so I stood and walked over to the bed. "Is there anything that I can do for you?"

"Breakfast would be wonderful," she said.

"Umm." I didn't know how to break it to her. "The doctor wants you on liquids only this morning because of all of the tests they need to run on you today."

"Liquids?" She gave me that I-don't-give-a-damn look. "You woke me up and now you won't feed me? What kind of a nurse are you?"

"I'm not a nurse." I laughed.

After a brief but prickly bit of silence she asked, "So what are you, the hospital's entertainer, or are you paid to watch the sick throughout the night?"

"Neither."

"So?"

"So?" I asked back.

"So, who are you?"

"Well." I cleared my throat and strangely my mind went blank too. "I called your friend Nat, and she should be here in less than an hour."

"Okay, but that still doesn't tell me who you are." She asked as she slowly sat up, "And how do you know Nat?"

"We used to work together at Northern Miami Middle."

"Oh, okay," she said, but she still seemed confused. "But why are *you* here?"

I wasn't about to embarrass myself. "Well, if you must know, she had something important to do last night and asked that I come by and look out for you in case you woke up." I smiled. "And you did."

"I am so sorry that she put you out of your way for me." She seemed sincere.

"Not a problem at all." God, I missed her.

Sarai sprang a question on me. "So you two are seeing each other?"

"What?" I asked. "Who two?"

"You and Nat?"

I made a face. "Noooo."

"Whoa. What's all that?" She stopped me. "Time out, please don't act like there is something wrong with my girl."

"No." I interrupted her. "No, that's not how I meant it. She's a great girl, but no . . . we're just friends. Plus, I think Nick is bigger than me, so I don't want any problems."

"Okay." She smiled. "I remember you coming in last night, I'm sure that the doctor discussed this amnesia stuff with you."

"Yeah, briefly."

"Did we meet before or are you just doing Nat this favor?" she asked.

"No, we've met." I really didn't want her to ask me anything else.

She seemed puzzled. "So we know"—she corrected herself— "excuse me, we knew one another?" Damn she had gone past tense on me.

"We knew one another very well, Sarai."

When I spoke her name she swiftly looked over at me as though the sound of her name rolling off my tongue and through my lips was familiar. "What is your name?"

"Tremel." I extended my hand but didn't wait for her to reach for it; I grabbed her cold hand and held it. "I'm Tremel Colten." I sighed. "You used to call me Mel."

"It's nice to meet you." She turned my hold on her hand into a handshake. "Do you know Damian as well?" Her eyes lit up as she said his name and dropped my hand.

What the fuck? "Yeah." That was all I cared to say.

She looked around the room quickly. "Is there a phone in here?"

"There *was* a phone, the doctor removed it." I continued: "He said that it is important that all of your verbal communication is done person to person over the next few days." I sighed. "A lot has happened to you, a lot that you don't remember, and for your own good he wants your best friend to be the one to update you on what's what and who's who in your life. The wrong phone call can expose you to too much at one time."

"I wonder why Nat didn't ask Damian to sit with me." She shrugged her shoulders. "Is he on his way too?"

I was disappointed. "I don't think so."

"Well, Tremel, is it?" She wanted to make sure that she was saying my name right.

"Yes."

"What else can you tell me?"

I was already exhausted with this. "What do you want to know?"

She was blunt. "Who shot me?"

As much as I wanted to say, *That punk muthafucka you asking for is the coward that left you a quarter of an inch from death or paralyzed from the neck down,* I fought myself not to say, *I almost died trying to protect you and all I get is a handshake? I wished that I was the one lying here instead of you, and you're asking me about him?* I looked at her and said, "You don't really want to know."

"Ms. Emery, welcome back," a nurse said loudly as she walked into the room, followed by two others rolling a few gadgets into the room. She grabbed Sarai's chart. "How are you feeling?"

Sarai looked away from me. "Hungry."

"Uh-oh, doctor's orders don't call for that," the nurse smiled. "How about some juice, though?"

"Let me get a gallon of your best stuff, then," Sarai said, and we all laughed.

"Dr. Bowen performed the initial physical examination on you last night, but we need to do a more detailed vital and reflex check before you begin undergoing all of the testing today." She flipped through the chart. "Girl, you are a miracle. You can see, hear, talk, you sittin' up, and you'll probably be walking around as soon as we get some food up in you." She hung the clipboard on the foot of the bed and moved closer to Sarai's face. "We need to remove the catheter. Nurse Wiggins, would you shut the door, please?"

When the nurse lifted her sheet Sarai shifted uncomfortably and glared over at me as if to ask me to leave. She wouldn't have to tell me twice. Honestly, whether she remembered me or not, catheter removal wasn't my thing. I began tiptoeing toward the door. "Ms. Emery, would you like for your fiancé to stay?" Nurse Wiggins asked Sarai while pointing at me.

"Fiancé?" She giggled. "No, he's a friend of a friend of mine."

A friend of a friend? What the . . . ? Nat and I concocted the story of me being her fiancé so that I could visit, give my input, and be in her room as much as I could. But now that she was awake all she was doing was hurting my feelings. I left the room and then decided to leave the hospital altogether. I was angry. I knew that I shouldn't be, but I had been dumped before and this pain was no different. Even though she truly couldn't help not remembering me, it was still her face, her smile, and her voice that didn't know mine.

> "There ought to be a law stating that when you meet a man he issues you a card with the exact measurements of his dick before you give him your number, or before he gives you his."
> —SARAI EMERY, *Going Broke,* bank statement one

Sarai

1 ½

Natalya walked into my hospital room with a dozen roses, a smile, and enough tears to cry the river Justin Timberlake was singing about, and I had the nerve for my first thought to be on what I remembered our last conversation being about: "Nick and his insufficient funds." Suddenly the words came to me as though I was saying them right then, *There ought to be a law stating that when you meet a man he issues you a card with the exact measurements of his dick before you give him your number, or before he gives you his.* I still believed that. However, though I was in a hospital bed, I had sense enough to know that now wasn't the time to think about it.

"Oh my God," Nat said, shivering as she rested the flower-filled vase on the table adjacent to the bed. Her right hand rushed to her mouth in disbelief. "I can't believe this." She walked toward me cautiously, but when I smiled, her arms opened wide. "I cannot believe this." Still in tears, she took me in her arms. "I've missed you so much."

All thoughts of Two-Inch Dick Nick subsided when I realized that I had my best friend, my ace, my homie, my damn girl back at my side. Though the doctor said I'd been out for a month, being awake for two hours without her felt like two years. "Nat, I . . ." My eyes welled up and my heart leaped with joy. This coma shit had made me soft. "I love you."

"I love *you*." We held each other for about five minutes, but our tears continued on for a while. Seeing her familiar face, hearing her voice, and knowing that after whatever had happened to me she was still around, meant the world to me. She was the only medicine I needed. Finally seeing someone that I recognized warmed the cold blood within me and gave my heart the freedom to beat regularly again.

We stopped crying but began staring at each other and giggling uncontrollably; she started it, and I just couldn't help it. She spent some time asking me how I was feeling and I assured her that I felt physically fine.

"So where is India?" I asked.

"India?" She looked at me strangely. "What do you want with her?"

"She gets on my nerves, but that heifer could've come with you to see me."

"She . . ." Nat looked at me peculiarly and quickly looked away. "You and India had a falling-out a few months ago." She laughed nervously. "You finally had enough of her snobbish ways."

"Good." I smiled. I wasn't too shocked, I was actually glad to be rid of such a burden. "What finally did it?"

"Girl"—she spoke slowly—"all we have is time. We have a lot of catching up to do."

"When is Damian getting here?" I blushed. "You need to do my hair before he comes." The mention of his name brought excitement that I had forgotten existed. "I wanted to call him, but that man said that the doctor said something about me not calling people."

"What man?" Nat asked as I pointed at the door and said, "The one that you asked to come and watch me last night." I couldn't remember his name. "He said that he used to work with you at the school."

Nat asked with a dreadful look on her face, "You mean Tremel?"

"Yeah." I lowered my voice. "Who in the hell *is* he?"

Nat stood up from my bed and looked away. "I spoke to Dr. Bowen briefly on the phone this morning, and when I got here I spoke to a few of the nurses; they told me about the amnesia." She sighed. "What is the last thing that you remember?"

I thought for a while. "Our quote unquote urgent meeting at the Clevelander when we discussed Nick's lack of—"

She interrupted me. "We're getting married."

"Married?" I asked.

"Married." She showed me her engagement ring. "Yep, not until the end of the year, though."

"Oh my God." My hands flew up to my mouth while I admired her ring. I was speechless, not because the ring was beautiful—which it was—but because I couldn't believe that she was about to vow, until death, to spend the rest of her sexual life in two-inch, two-minute misery. "Wow." That was all I could say.

"He asked me over the Christmas holiday."

I had to say, "I'm happy for you."

"Thanks."

"The doctor told what the date was last night, so I guess your birthday party is over, huh?"

"Yep." She smiled. "I'm officially thirty, soon to be thirty-one." She added, "We're getting married on New Year's Eve, at ten at night." She reached for my hand. "If you're feeling well enough by that time, I want you to be my maid of honor."

"Oh my God." I was thrilled. "Are you serious?"

She looked down at me with a smile. "Yes."

"Yes, yes, yes." I pulled her into another embrace. "Of course."

Over the next hour I asked a host of questions and wasn't happy with many of the answers. Nat said that it was all for my own good.

She promised to reveal more as time went on, or as I began to remember more. All she was willing to say to me was that I had been shot right under my left breast, during a bank robbery. She also informed me that Damian was in federal prison on drug-related charges. However, the real shocker was her telling me that Damian and I weren't together anymore; my heart was telling me different.

My father, thank God, is the same, no better and no worse. Savion, no one has heard from, that's no shocker, he'd call soon. Naturally, I am very concerned about my twin's well-being, but something in my spirit says that I shouldn't fret. Finally, she told me that I had succumbed to the temptation to cuss out Mr. Motes at WBIG and lost my job. What in the hell was I doing in these ten months? Had I lost my mind? I lost a friend, my man, and a job . . . maybe it's best if I don't remember anything.

"So this Tremel guy," I asked. "How do I know him?"

"You met him at my party." She smiled.

"I did?" I tried hard to recall something, anything, but not even a piece came around.

She stared hard into my face. "He's very nice, an extreme gentleman. He is a good man. You don't remember anything about him at all?"

"I sure don't," I said matter-of-factly, and right on cue in walked Mr. Very Nice but Unfamiliar.

"How are you feeling?" Tremel asked me.

"I'm still hungry." I grinned at him. "You here to feed me?"

"If I feed you, these nurses will kill me." He walked over to my bedside and rubbed Nat's back. He gazed into my face so long and hard that it became uncomfortable. During his absence of two hours he had changed clothes, shaved, and smelled like he had just sampled the best fragrance Macy's had out as a tester. Whoever he was he was looking mighty fine. His skin was the same color that I remember giving the barks of trees in my coloring books when I was five years old. I never wanted them to be too dark, in fear of them appearing too old, and not too light because that would be a waste of crayon. So

I would lightly brush the page with my brown Crayola, only pressing down hard enough to leave a sun-tanned toasted-brown shade.

Tremel's wavy jet-black hair was cut low to match his newly shaven goatee. His lips—man, his lips were full and sexy, kissable and suckable. And under his beige polo shirt I knew was a bulky chocolate chest, and though his blue boot-cut jeans held him loosely, it hinted at what lay beneath . . . thick thighs, captivating calves, and a whole lot of tight bronze brownness was going on. He was truly something serious to look at, especially for someone who'd been un-conscious for a month.

"All right, Ms. Emery." Enter the bossy nurse. "It's about that time." She smiled. "Time for testing, testing, and more testing, honey."

"So will I meet my steak dinner waiting when I get back?" I was dead serious.

"Chicken I can work out for you, but you're on your own with steak, homegirl."

For the next five hours I underwent blood work, X-rays, and a CT scan, but all I could think about were the unanswered questions I now had about pieces of the missing ten months of my life that Nat did tell me about. Why exactly did my relationship with Damian end? How can I get in touch with him? Did he know about what hap-pened to me at the bank? Where in the hell is my brother? How is Daddy really doing? And how much do I owe the nursing home?

There were huge holes in the information that Nat trusted me with. She was never any good at looking at anyone and telling a bold-faced lie. There were things that she wasn't telling me and I wanted to know who I had become.

The orderlies wheeled me back to my empty room after five in the afternoon; by this time I felt like an Ethiopian . . . I was starving. "Can you please see to it that they bring me my dinner right away?" I said to a man as he helped me get back into my bed.

"I'll stop by the nurses' station on my way back down."

"Thank you so much." This was an emergency. "No more drip, drop nourishment, I need to bite into something."

"I know what you mean," the man said. "I'll get somebody to hook you up," he added as he made his way out of the room.

I was all alone with my thoughts again, but I really wanted to be alone with the thoughts that I couldn't think, which were about what happened in the past ten months. I sat back, closed my eyes, and tried hard to recall leaving the bar, going home, seeing Damian, getting mad because he had jacked off before I arrived after being away on a business trip for a week . . . I was pissed, but the brotha slapped it up, flipped it, and rubbed it down for me in the shower later on. Okay . . . let me stay focused . . . I went to work . . . I went to work . . . I went to work . . . and that was the last moment of my life that I could recall.

"Did someone order room service?" Tremel asked as he brought in a hospital tray piled with food and some snacks I'm sure the nurses would've discarded had they glimpsed them. "I heard that you were back in your room and thought that I'd bring you this peace offering in return for waking you up this morning."

The brotha was right on time. "Oh, my word!" I exclaimed. "You can wake me up every morning if this stuff is as good as it looks." My eyes brightened.

"Don't make promises you can't keep," Tremel said as he rested the tray down on the cart and rolled it in front of me. "Some of this stuff has to stay between you and me, though." He grabbed a lot of the sweets, potato chips, and cookies and put them in the top drawer of the tall nightstand next to my bed, but oddly enough he left the box of Whoppers on the tray. I love Whoppers, and anyone that knew me well would know that.

I picked up the little box. "I love Whoppers."

"I didn't bring them coincidentally." He smiled. "I aim to please."

His words sent chills up my spine. "Thank you."

"Compliments of the chef." He removed the chrome lid from the plate and revealed baked chicken, pale macaroni and cheese, corn, and a dinner roll. He laughed. "I had no pull in the kitchen, but the vending-machine man hooked it up."

"You are an angel." I was so hungry that the dish looked like the finest lobster and porterhouse steak dinner around. "Thank you so much."

"I waited around until after your testing to see that you got something in your stomach." He placed a knife, fork, and napkin in front of me and said, "I'll leave you alone to enjoy your dinner." He turned to walk away.

"You're not going to join me for dinner?" I asked.

He was very modest. "I don't want to get in the way."

"Of what?" I interrupted. "I have no phone, they don't want me to watch TV for a few more days, and I have no roommate." I looked around. "You're my only link to the outside world." Then I added, "And you brought me Whoppers, so I take it that you know something about me."

"I really do." His gaze pierced me.

"Unless, of course, you have something else to do, or someplace to be." I was hoping that I didn't sound too desperate for conversation.

"There is no place else I'd ra . . ." He paused and those sexy lips bent into a smile and his eyes glistened. "I have no place to be."

He sat and watched me devour everything on my plate in ten minutes. This wasn't the time or place to be cute with it. Shit, I sucked that food down like I was an anteater with my snout stuck in soil. The red Jell-O for dessert was like crème brulée, and the fruit punch was my glass of Cabernet Sauvignon.

"So tell me about you," I said once I was done.

"What would you like to know?"

It didn't take long for me to figure out what I wanted to know about him. "Whatever I knew before."

"You knew a whole lot," he said. "Where should I start?"

"Just like the Bible." I smiled at him. "In the beginning."

"We met at Nat's birthday party." He sat back in his chair and took a deep breath. "The party was also a masquerade party, so we all wore masks. Mine was white." He paused. "All of the men were given locks, and we had to find the woman who had our key. You all, the women, were wearing makeshift belts or necklaces with keys on them." He smiled. "You were looking good. No, you were looking great! I couldn't see your entire face because of the mask but I didn't even need to, your smile was enough." His words were taking me there. "You had on a purple one-sleeve shirt and black pants."

"I remember buying that shirt," I said. "It took me trying it on three times to win me over."

"It was a great choice, you were stunning," he continued. "I was watching you from across the room, then approached you from behind and asked if I could turn my key in your lock."

"Did it work?" I was curious.

"No." He laughed. "I had already found the right key on another chick, but I wanted a reason to come over and talk to you, even though your man was in the room."

"What did you say?" I was all ears.

"I just asked to try your lock." His tone of voice changed. "You allowed me to, but it seemed like you didn't want to be bothered."

"That's it?" I had to know.

"No."

"C'mon, stop holding out on me." I giggled. "I need info."

"Well, I watched you dance and we talked a little after that, but when you found out that I worked as a janitor, you threw the nice-girl routine out of the window and sent me packing."

I was embarrassed. I didn't know what to say, and because he said nothing else, it made it even harder to know what the right thing to say might be. I knew that I was shallow, but I didn't think that I came across as a snob . . . not until now. "I am so sorry."

"No need to be," he said with a grin. "We still managed to become friends, but just not right away." He stood up, dragged his chair closer to my bed, and pulled a deck of cards from his back pocket. "Let's play blackjack." He dealt us both two cards and said, "Don't worry about the past, it'll come back to you, and if it doesn't, then you need to find a way to make your new memories unforgettable."

"Well, I don't know how to play blackjack."

He smiled. "Then consider this your first new memory."

"We do not remember days, we remember moments.
This richness of life lies in what we have forgotten."
—CESARE PAVESE

Tremel

WITHDRAWAL SLIP #2
ENDING BALANCE: $434.20

"My world does not revolve around your big black dick.
It takes more than facedown and ass up to impress this
  chick.
Therefore, I won't be defined by my fat juicy pussy.
There is more to me than your eyes will ever see.
And you will not make me a slave to my punanni.
So, you played me!
You splayed me!
Bitch, yeah, you betrayed me!
Kept me up late, begged me to keep the faith.
Had me neglecting my man, my boo, my soul mate.
You even told me that you were willing to wait.
You fed me major bullshit from a heaped-up plate.
So with the fat juicy pussy I didn't hesitiate.
Remember when my juices made you drool?

My shit had you acting a goddamn fool.
I worked this pussy on you like a power tool.
And my head? Oh yeah, my head was old school.
I couldn't help what I was feeling.
You took my heart and sent it through the ceiling.
Moments later, with me, you were through dealing.
You told me to act like I knew my pussy was good.
Came on strong, like you really understood.
But it was all a game, a muthafuckin' crying shame.
A weekend of promises built on nothing but lies.
Now I spend weekdays wondering why.
No I miss you, flowers, or a midnight call.
I phone you to hear, 'I love my wife after all.'
After all?
Hold up, after all the shit I had to compromise?
After all the time you spent between my thighs?
Ha! Ha! Ha! Au contraire.
No one ever said that life was fair.
If you ever learned the real reason why I fucked you
then you'll see who it was really beneficial to.
You thought I was about to be a cheap trick.
You ran game to the wrong educated, street-smart,
sophisticated, ain't-'bout-to-have-that-shit chick.
Because my life does not revolve around yours,
or any other big black dick."

The room rocked with applause, I hadn't heard Vocalize roar like that since the last time I performed. "Damn, your sister is on fire, man."

"Yeah, she recited that piece for me yesterday," Lorenzo said. "I was like, show me where that brotha lives." He laughed.

"Yeah, that sounds like something personal right there," I said. "Been there and done that." I thought about the many times that writing and reciting my poetry saved my life or saved me from doing something pretty stupid. "That stage is the perfect medicine."

"Oh yeah?" Lorenzo asked, then added, "So when you getting back up there?"

"I don't know." I changed the subject to the matter at hand. "How much is she asking for rent?"

"I think two hundred a month." Lorenzo scratched his head. "Well, I told her that I was bringing you with me tonight, so she'll be over here in a minute to discuss that with you. Our uncle C.J. had a friend who was supposed to move in, but apparently they backed out." He added, "She normally recites at that poetry club in Fort Lauderdale, but I talked her into coming to South Beach to show off tonight."

"And show off she did," I said as I watched Charlize walk toward us. She resembled Gabrielle Union, the same slightly slanted eyes, crisp cardboard complexion, soft rounded nose, rosy cheeks, and had the same audacious presence and I-run-this-shit attitude. Lorenzo Daniels and I used to work together as school custodians. Coincidentally, I ran into him at the hospital a few days ago; his wife had a baby. We got to talking, and without telling him too much I told him that I needed a place to stay. With Sarai being released from the hospital tomorrow, my number one objective was not to have her uncomfortable around me. I couldn't expect her to live with a man she had only known two weeks. Therefore, I needed to relocate for a while.

"Hi, Renzy!" Charlize said with a smile as she approached the bar where we were sitting. Her brown eyes aimed at me and immediately the word *hello* melted into a smile. "You must be Mel?" She extended her hand.

"I must be." I returned her smile and accepted her soft smooth handshake. "And you are Charlize?"

"I must be." Charlize's faultless aligned bright white smile showed up once more. Her long black hair . . . be it weave, human, or synthetic, had it going on, and her makeup was flawlessly applied and gave off an intriguing bronze glow. "Lorenzo tells me that you might be interested in the room that I have for rent."

"Yes." I hadn't even seen the place, but I was desperate, and if it really was $200, then she had herself a new tenant. "But I can't say how long I'll need it for. It could be two years or it could be just two months, but I would need to be in it by tomorrow night."

She joked, "Got kicked out, huh?"

I was a bit hesitant. "Naw, I just need a new place until some things pan out."

"Well, I'm asking two hundred a month. There is a bedroom set already in the room, and it's also equipped with a twenty-seven-inch television."

"Sounds good to me." My other options were returning to my family in Ohio or homelessness. I wasn't about to do the cardboard thing. "I'll take it." I handed her an envelope with $200 in it.

"Huh?" She was shocked. "But you haven't even seen the place."

"I've seen you." I continued, "You don't look like a woman with a nasty house."

"Thank you." She blushed. "You're very right about that."

"Just tell me the rules of the house." After renting a room from an elderly woman once for more than a year I was sure that I could endure anything, but I just had to know exactly what I was getting into.

"First of all, I'm allergic to dogs and cats—"

Lorenzo interrupted with explosive laughter. "She's scared of dogs and cats." He put his drink down. "Why you sittin' here lying, Charl?"

She playfully shoved her brother. "It's my house and I can say whatever I want."

"Allergic?" He chuckled. "I'll be back, I'm going to say hi to a friend of mine." Lorenzo stood up and walked away.

"Well, allergies or not, have no fear, I don't come with pets."

"Good." She then asked, "What *do* you come with?"

"Clothing, a laptop, a few bottles of cologne, books, and a keyboard."

Her eyes popped open. "You're a musician?"

"Yes." I cringed, fearing that she might be bothered by my 2 a.m. urges to get up and search for the perfect melody to accompany lyrics that came to me in a dream. "Will my keyboard be a problem?" I had to know.

"I have a Steinway baby grand and a cello."

"All right!" I was relieved. "I've never run into a black female cellist before."

"Me neither." Charlize laughed. "Wait a sec . . ." She moved closer, looked at me closely, and squinted. "Do you sing?"

"Yeah."

"Mel," she said, completely astonished. "You're Tremel?" She covered her mouth. "TreMelody?"

"Yeah, that's me." Sometimes I hated to admit who I was, since my singing career seemed to be over before it truly started.

"What a small world!" she exclaimed. "I have your CD."

"Really?"

"Really!"

I never knew the right way to respond when people mentioned my CD. "Thanks." I moved along with the conversation. "How long have you been playing the piano and cello?"

"The piano since I was eight, the cello I taught myself when I was twenty-two."

"What, last month?" I asked. "You look like you're twenty-two now."

Her eyes lit up again. "Thank you."

"So just how young are you?"

"A landlord never tells." She blushed hard, so hard that for the first time there was a hint of a dimple on her right cheek.

"Oh, my bad, I didn't know that that was top-secret government information."

"That's right, I have Secret Service men guarding my birth certificate." We both laughed.

"Well, landlady, would you like a drink?" I was hoping that she'd turn down my offer, because I had only had twenty dollars on me and Lorenzo and I had already drunk seventeen of it away.

She glanced at her watch. "I wish I could, but I have an eight o'clock appointment, and I have to be on top of my game with this particular client." She placed a card in my hand. "Here is the address, I'll be at home tomorrow anytime after five."

"Cool." I slipped the card into my pocket.

"Cool."

I was surprised at how quickly we were able to handle things. "So this is a done deal, you don't need references or anything?"

"Lorenzo would never recommend a man stay with me if he didn't know, trust, and like him." She continued, "He is my background-check system." She slung her purse up to her shoulder and looked around for her brother. "Well, tell that crazy brother of mine that I had to go."

"I will." I extended my hand to her. "I'll see you tomorrow."

She slid her soft palm into mine briefly. "Have a good night."

"You too." With that said, she was gone.

Walking back into the apartment this time was difficult, because it could be the last time I was truly welcomed there. The chances of Sarai remembering me are good, but it's been two weeks and she hasn't recalled anything new so far. I collapsed onto the bed, her bed, and the white ceiling above played a movie of memories, memories of our relationship from start to this godforsaken intermission. And for close to an hour I smiled back at my leading lady. When the credits began to roll my eyes closed and I once again made love to Sarai in my dreams.

The warm shower water crashed onto my head, slowly rained down my neck, trickled onto my back and chest, down to my stomach, playfully tickled my dick, then it embraced me as it slid down my thighs, calves, and toes. This was weird! Whoever thinks about the way water moves over their body? Who? Me! I was trying to think of everything and anything to postpone reality.

It was the morning that Sarai was being released from the hospital, she was coming home . . . to her apartment . . . the one that she has no clue that I live in, or no recollections that I had ever set foot in. This woman doesn't even know that I know where she lives. I spent the last two days packing. I gotta get the hell up out of this woman's place. I refer to her as "this woman," simply because currently she's not "*the* woman" that fell in love with me. She's "this woman" that doesn't even know me.

Over the past two weeks Nat and I managed not to tell Sarai much of anything that she didn't already know. However, to put her mind at rest about certain things, Nat called Sarai's father, and Sarai talked to him a few times. Just hearing his voice did her much good. Instead of getting down about things, Sarai focused on her physical rehabilitation. Her muscles, amazingly, had gained strength quickly, and by the fourth day she was walking to the restroom unassisted. Now she wanders up to the nursery twice a day to coo at the newborns.

I didn't spend too much time at the hospital. I purposely arrived right before visiting hours were over so that I could steer myself away from the long conversation I wanted to have with her. She was nice and polite to me, but my name was still blank whenever she called it. Almost like a teacher calling the roll on the first day of school, she says it and looks around to see which kid responds to it, then gives them a "nice and polite" grin.

To Sarai, I was just a friend of Nat and Nick's, and someone that she now knows that she met at a party which she cannot recall. Therefore, when the doctor suggested that someone stay with her for at least a week, it was no secret that Nat was moving in and me, the stranger, I had to find a new place to go. Whenever she smiled I wanted to kiss her, whenever she stretched I wanted to hug her, and whenever she appeared tired I wanted to drain her of whatever energy was left by making love to her.

With a little over $400 left to my name, I am pitiful. I've been looking for jobs, but instead of answering logical questions during interviews, I have to spend the entire time trying to convince the interviewer that what he or she saw on the news a month ago was wrong. My belongings were already boxed up and waiting for me at the door, and as I left for the day, I left for the week, month, or however long it took for love to call my name.

· · ·

Each time before I visited Sarai I recited the same little prayer all the way up the elevator. "Please let her remember me. Lord, please let her remember me." I walked into the room to find a doctor, one I had never seen before, standing in the room with Sarai. "So, do you need anything?" he asked.

"No." She glanced at me, offered a smile, but quickly gave the doctor her attention again. "Actually, I don't even know because I haven't been in my apartment yet, so I don't know what I have and don't have right now."

He rubbed her back. "Well, don't hesitate to call me if you need me." The short stubby man looked like he was getting pleasure by just touching her. "If you like I'll stop by your place tonight to check on you."

"Well, Nat will be with me for the next few days." She smiled. "So I should be fine."

"All right." He moved his hands to her shoulder. "Don't take too long to get to my office, though." He smiled "We need to make sure that you're okay from every angle." He started walking toward me where I stood by the door.

"Thanks for stopping by, Dr. Baker."

Dr. Baker? My heart fluttered. Oh hell nawh. He had some nerve coming to see her. I had heard the story about this short, slimy, pudgy muthafucka. Though he was her doctor Sarai looked up to him like an uncle, but the moment she got down on her luck, instead of lending her a helping hand, he propositioned her for sex and became her first paying client. As he brushed past me I followed him into the hallway and asked, "Excuse me, are you Dr. Baker, the gynecologist?"

"Yes." He smiled and offered me his hand. "Yes, I am."

"Nawh, partner." I didn't even look at his hand. "She may not remember you and what you did to her, but I always will." I walked up on him. "And if I ever see you anywhere around her again, I will give you something you'll never forget."

"I beg your pardon?" He seemed offended. "What are you talking about?"

"I'm talking about you paying for pussy." I thumbed my nose and continued: "Remember that? Huh?" I wanted to slap his taste buds to one side. "You better hope that she never remembers that shit, because if she does . . . I *will* find you."

He backed away with an attitude. "You must be mistaken."

"Mistaken?" I lowered my voice. "You telling me that I have the wrong short, fat, black, pathetic gynecologist with the last name Baker?" I asked, but he didn't need to answer. "Sorry if I have it wrong, but I tell you what, if you see that short, fat, black, pathetic bitch, you tell him just what the fuck I said, Dr. Baker." As I said his name I flicked his name tag.

"Who in the hell are you supposed to be?" He looked me up and down like he could really move something.

"I'm the muthafucka you wanna be." I stepped back from him. "I don't have to pay."

"Oh please, does she even remember you?" he said slightly under his breath.

"That's cool," I confronted him. "Just as long as you never forget who the fuck I am." I turned my back to him and walked away.

"Hey, Mel." Sarai gleamed as I entered the room. For the first time since she was awake her hair wasn't pulled into a ponytail, but hanging down and slightly curled under at her shoulders. She was wearing jeans and a black shirt. "Is Nat on her way?"

"I thought she'd be here already."

"No," she said, and pointed at the suitcase by the door, "but I'm packed and ready to get going." She continued: "I was hoping to be out of here two hours ago."

"Where do you need to be?" I joked. "You're acting like you have something to do."

"I do." She offered me the warmest smile she had done in weeks. "I need to call the Chinese place down the street from me to get some real food in me." She scratched her head. "I can't remember the name of that place, though"—she frowned—"but what's new? I can't remember much of anything."

"Actually, that was a running joke." I chuckled. "You never knew the name of that restaurant, just the phone number and the delivery driver's name."

"Liu," she said with much excitement.

"Yep, good old Liu."

"Good, at least I'm on the right track there." She glanced over at me and stared awhile before she spoke again. "You know, I've been sitting here day after day fighting to remember things, but lately I've found myself making up things to fill in pieces of the puzzle and to satisfy myself." Sarai continued after a heavy sigh: "How do you think that I will know if I am really remembering something or if it's just me playing games with myself?"

It took all I knew not to reach out and comfort her with an embrace. "Well, I'm no expert, but I think that when you're purposely embellishing on something it's more of a mental feeling, but when you truly remember something you should feel something emotional, something heartfelt."

"That's what I thought." The corners of her mouth turned upward. "Thanks."

"Anytime." She had no way of knowing just how much I meant that word, so I repeated it. "Anytime."

"Have a seat." She pointed at the chair by the window. "I was actually thinking about you earlier."

I was in seventh heaven. "Really?"

"Yeah." She looked over at me. "It's so nice of you to come and check on me, and even keep me company since I've been here." She sighed. "Thank you."

"You're welcome." I was concerned about not seeing her as much once she was released. At least at the hospital I could just show up, her room door was open, I could just walk in. But after today, reality will bite, she doesn't have to welcome me into her home. "It's been my pleasure coming here and spending time with you."

"I feel like I owe you something."

"Well, maybe that's because you do." The words came out of my mouth before I could zip it shut.

There was a hint of a blush on her cheeks. "Oh yeah, what do I owe you?"

I wanted to say that she owed me a hug, a kiss, her body, heart, and soul, but I settled for: "You owe me a few smiles." How lame?

She gave me one right then and there. "I can do that."

"I know"—I sat back in the window seat—"and you do it so well."

There were a few seconds of uncomfortable, yet unavoidable silence between us, but that was countered by Nat bursting into the room with, "All right, it's time for the real world, girl."

"I was ready for the real world two hours ago." Sarai sarcastically looked at her watch. "It's four o'clock now."

Nat said, "I had to be sure that your apartment was in order." What she really meant was, *I had to be sure that the man you don't remember was out of your apartment.* She continued: "I couldn't have you returning to anything less than what you remember."

"Well, it's still going to be weird as hell living there without Damian."

"Oh, to hell with Damian, girl." Nat took the words right out of my mouth. "Sarai you have to stop that."

"Stop what?" she asked angrily. "Nat, excuse me for losing my memory. Excuse the fuck out of me for me still thinking that I have a man in my life that loves me more than he loves himself." She was fighting tears. "This is all very confusing for me, very scary, and it's nothing that I can help or just stop."

"I'm sorry." Nat wrapped her arms around her best friend. "It's going to be all right," she promised her. "It's going to be fine." She rubbed her back. "And there are people"—she looked back at me— "there are people that love you more than life itself, you just have to get to know them again."

I could see why Sarai kept and considered Natalya as a best friend. She truly wanted nothing but the best for her. She went to bat for Sarai every chance she got when the staff seemed like they were slippin' because Sarai didn't have insurance. She combed her hair, read to her, washed her off, and even though Sarai is up and somewhat back to normal, she continued to so the same things daily. She was just the kind of best friend every woman should be and have. We all left the hospital together, but at the light where Nat made a right, I went left. It was a "welcome back," celebration for two, not three, not me.

I pulled up to the pastel-green, trimmed-with-ivory North Miami Beach house shortly after seven and knocked on the door.

"Who is it?"

"Mel." I cleared my throat. "Mel."

"Who?"

"Tremel," I added. "I'm renting the room."

"Oh." I heard the lock move, the door crept open slowly, and then there was Charlize, dressed in a gray sport bra and matching jogging pants. "Come in." I stepped into the living room and a sweet aroma softly attacked me. The room was dark, and in the middle of the floor was a pillow, and encircling it were five or six lit jarred candles. "Sorry about the darkness, I just got through meditating."

"Thanks for telling me." I laughed. "For a second I thought you were having a séance."

"Oh, hell no, I ain't calling up no evil spirits in here," she joked. "I have enough crazy-ass living folks in my life, no need for the dead ones."

"I hear ya!"

"Let me show you the house." She closed the door and hit the light switch. "This is the living and dining room." There was cream-colored tile that stretched from the door to the far end of the living room, where her shiny black Steinway baby grand piano sat in front of a window by the black dining-room table set for four. The living room was embellished with black leather furniture, a sixty-three-inch plasma TV, and a fully stocked black minibar with three stools in front of it.

"Follow me," Charlize said, and then showed me the laundry room, kitchen, and my room and bathroom right across the hall. We moved to the back of the house. "This is my home office," she said as she opened up a door, turned on the lights, then swung the door fully open. "I only turn the lights on in here when I have to clean." It was a large peach room with a partition between two massage tables, and there had to be about fifty candles on tiny shelves built onto the walls all around the room. "I'm a professional masseuse."

"Damn!" I said as I looked down at the plush cream-colored carpet. "This is nice."

"Thank you." She smiled. "My office hours are from eight to four on Tuesday, Thursday, and Saturday." She closed the door. "I work at a spa on the beach on Monday, Wednesday, and Friday." She ushered me down the hallway. "This is where I make music." She opened up a door to a small room; strangely, the walls were black and so was the carpet; there was nothing in it except a black stool that was about two feet tall and a black music-sheet holder. What else? No windows, no fan, or anything except a black velvet cello case. "If you ever hear me playing, just knock and wait for me to open the door."

"Okay." I was looking at the room, bewildered. "I will." What in the hell was this chick into?

She must've noticed the look on my face because as she closed the door she tried to explain. "I just like feeling like I'm in another world when I play, so I—"

I interrupted. "You don't need to explain. I'm a musician too."

Charlize smiled and turned away. "All right, I'll let you get a peek at my room." A few steps later and we were in a burgundy-painted room with gold carpet. Her king-size mahogany sleigh bed was adorned with a burgundy-and-gold comforter and five or six matching pillows. "I'm a pillow freak," she said.

Gold sheers draped down from a circular contraption above the bed and were pulled back behind the headboard on both sides. It gave the room a very erotic touch. Before my mind wandered off, I decided to end the tour. "Thanks for showing me around. I guess I'll start bringing in my stuff."

"Do you need help?" she asked.

I looked back at her and smiled as I left the room. "What kind of man would I be if I asked you to lift my boxes in here?"

"You'd be a man who recognizes a strong woman when he sees one." She winked at me.

"Well, strong woman, thanks for the offer, but I only have a few boxes, I should be all right."

"Okay."

I brought in my boxes and then spent two hours removing their contents and putting them in their new homes. Everything still smelled like Bath & Body Works' Sweet Pea, which Sarai's apartment always smelled like because she bought the lotion, shower gel, and body butter in gallons. I sniffed everything with my eyes closed just to feel like I was still there with her, but when I got to the pair of black-laced thongs, which didn't just happen to fall into my box, I opened them up with both my hands and reminisced on the first time I had seen her in them.

We were at Macy's in the Aventura Mall, I wasn't in the best of moods because it was close to 9 p.m. and we had been in there since six. She had tried on every black dress in the damn store, and just when I thought she was on the last one, Sarai yelled, "Baby, it's too tight around the chest, can you get me one in a size ten, please."

"Damn," I whispered to myself. "I'll never come here with you again," I said as I snatched the size-ten halter-top dress from the rack and marched back over to the dressing room for the hundred-millionth time. "Here," I said with an attitude when I tapped on the door, more than frustrated.

"Thank you." She cracked the door wide enough for me to see that all she was wearing was those black-laced thongs. "I'm sorry, just give me two more minutes," she said to try to encourage me against getting upset.

"Two *more* minutes?" I pushed the door open a little more so that I could see the way the lace clung to her skin like a tattoo. "You know I've never been a two-minute man."

"Huh?" She was confused.

My dick was already hard. "There is only one thing you can do to make me come shopping with you again."

"What's that?" She hung the dress up on the clothes hook and started unzipping it. And before she could even look my way, I was in the dressing room locking the door behind me. "Mel, you can't be in here," she whispered.

"Says who?" I asked.

Her back was to me. "Baby, they have security cameras all over the place." She pointed at the mirror. "There is probably one behind this."

I looked in the mirror, pulled her toward me, and watched as her naked back pressed against my shirt. "Well, they're just gonna have to watch, 'cause I've suffered long enough out there watching you wear all of this sexy shit." In the mirror she could see her reflection with me caressing her from behind. As I kissed her neck my hands slid from her waist up to her firm nipples. I pinched them softly and then raked the palm of my hands over them slowly.

It was an incredible turn-on to look in the mirror and see her eyes fluttering, her mouth slightly open, her tongue sensually licking her lips, and those damn black-laced thongs. After taunting her upper body, I moved south. My right hand journeyed down, down, down into her panties. "Baby, don't do this to me in here." She begged too softly for me to believe she meant it.

"Shh." I kissed her behind her ear as my finger wiggled and then slipped in between the top part of her warm and moistened pleat. She closed her eyes in pleasure; it was her habit. "Open those eyes," I whispered to her from behind her. "I want you to watch my hand in the mirror." Through the lace I could see my brown fingers encompassing her outer realm. When I reached her pussy's heart I placed it between my pointer and middle fingers and pulled on it a few times before I applied pressure right above it and quickly moved my fingers from side to side in a vibratory fashion.

She was doing as I asked, watching my hand, so I gave her a better view. I moved closer to the mirror, placed one of her legs on the small cushioned bench in the corner, and pulled her panties to the left side with my left hand. "Look at that pussy," I said. "It's beautiful." It was. It was always clean-shaven, wet, fat, and juicy-looking . . . like it was puckering for a kiss. I looked at it in the mirror intensely; her clit was swollen and now only seven inches from the mirror. "You are so perfect," I said to her as we both watched my middle finger disappear into her cave.

"Oh, Mel," she said while fighting her eyes from rolling back. "Damn, baby."

Though we were whispering, the squish-squashing noise my finger made with her tightness could easily give us away to a horny or inquisitive passerby. She leaned back hard into me as I inserted deeper each time I ran my finger back into her. Soon I was massaging her button with my left hand and diving into her with my right. "Make that pussy talk to me, baby." And she did, she ground her waist around and fucked my hand like it was a big dick. The heat from her pussy could steam up the mirror; she was hot.

"Attention, all Macy's shoppers," the lady on the intercom said. "The store will be closing in fifteen minutes. Please finalize your purchasing decisions and see the store clerk nearest you." Sarai's eyes finally closed, she couldn't watch anymore. "Once again, the store will be closing in fifteen minutes. Thank you for shopping Macy's of Aventura."

I continued playing with her while I undid my pants and stepped out of them. I placed her knees on the bench and bent her over. "I'm not alive until I'm inside of you," I said to her as I readied my access pass for her gate. I slid into her inviting warmth and felt every hair on my entire body stand on end. "Oh, oh, oh, shit," she said, louder than she should have. By the look on her face I knew how good it was to her, so I grabbed her shirt from the clothes hook and brought it to her mouth. She knew what that meant . . . I was about to beat it, beat it, beat it, beat it.

She bit down on the shirt while I looked down to watch my car pull up to her bumper, reverse, slam on brakes, and go from zero to sixty in less than a second. Fuck pulling up to the bumper; I was trying to total her car out and I hoped she had shock absorbers. I raised one of her legs up and jammed her hard and fast over and over and over again. The announcement for the store being closed came and went without me coming. Finally, I grabbed her waist with both hands and took one last stroke before coming.

After a minute of heavy breathing, laughing, and trying to cool off, we were dressed and running toward the only store exit still open. The security guard looked at us peculiarly. "Didn't find what you were looking for, huh?"

"Actually, we did." I smiled as we exited, looking unkempt and wrinkled. "But it didn't have a price tag on it."

I smiled at the lacy black thong underwear and tucked them into the top drawer of the dresser. When I emerged from my room with eight broken-down boxes to put in the trash, Charlize had the place smelling like we had a third roommate, a gourmet chef, living with us. As I passed the kitchen she said, "Hey, Mel." I stopped and back-tracked to find her in front of the stove. "I don't cook every night, but when I do you're welcome to taste my masterpiece."

"Thanks." I couldn't help but notice her other masterpiece, her apple bottom, in those tight jeans. "Where can I put these boxes?"

"Ummm." She looked over at me but her eyes didn't leave my arms; I was only wearing a wife-beater. "Put them in the laundry room, the trash truck won't be around for a few more days." Her eyes traveled the length of my body and then back up to my arms, where she smiled and said, "I'll have dinner on the table in about five minutes if you care to join me."

"Sounds like a plan." I was hungry, and had no idea what I was going to do for food that night. "After I drop these off in the laundry room, I'll go wash my hands and meet you at the table."

Over our dinner of medium-well steaks, yellow rice with vegetables, and dinner rolls, we had an interesting conversation about whether or not Shaq would take the Miami Heat all the way this year. On her third glass of Riesling she giggled. "You know, don't think that I'm weird, but ever since Shaq came to Miami, I have been having dreams about him."

"Huh?" I nearly dropped my fork. "Dreams like what?"

"Oh my God." She blushed. "I can't believe that I'm telling you this."

I picked up my glass of white wine and took a sip. "You haven't told me anything yet."

When she smiled and pulled her hair to the side, she revealed that dimple of hers again and I had to look away. "The dreams are pretty wild," she confessed, and clammed up. "Maybe I'll tell you another time."

"Well, how many dreams have you had?"

She thought a minute. "At least one a week, and he's been here for a minute."

"Wow." With my fork I pierced the last piece of steak on my plate. "Well, whenever you wanna share, you know where to find me." I pointed at my room.

Her eyes lit up and I caught her looking at my arms again. "Yes; yes, I do."

"Actually, I prefer collard greens, macaroni and cheese, and potato salad."
—TREMEL COLTEN, *Going Broke*, bank statement two

Sarai

2½

You don't miss the water until the well runs dry. My water hadn't run dry, it just wasn't cold enough. The hospital was the Sahara Desert and my apartment was the big pitcher of water I had been waiting two weeks for. Gone were the days of thin hospital gowns, food that required no taste buds, and bedpans. When I walked in, my apartment looked nothing like I wanted or expected it to, it was good to be home.

"I guess we have to sort out all of this," Nat said, and dropped a box full of mail in front of me. "Where would you like to start?"

I could imagine how long going through all of that junk would take. "Just dump it," I suggested.

"No," Nat said, "I'm sure that some of this stuff is important."

"Yeah," I said sarcastically, "like this." I bent down and reached for a letter with my bank's logo on it and tore into it. I snatched the page out and unfolded it. "What?"

"What?" She followed me.

In confusion, I looked over at her. "I don't have this much money in the bank."

"How much?" she asked.

I smiled sinisterly as I thought of the bank's mistake. "Over forty thousand." I looked over the sheet of paper again to be sure that it said Sarai Emery on top. "I should go withdraw all of it now before they catch on."

"Relax, girl." She giggled. "It's not wrong," Nat said as she lugged my bag to my room. "It's yours."

I quickly rationalized. "Oh, this must be Damian's money."

"No," she said, and quickly rushed back into the room, "you gave him every dime he ever had in your account and then some." Nat looked at me seriously. "That money is all yours, Sarai."

"Mine?" The most I've ever had in my account was about five grand, and that was after claiming someone's kid on my income tax. "How and when did I get all of this money if I don't even have a job?"

"You made some sacrifices, judgment calls, and investments," she said. "Trust me, it's your money."

I couldn't believe it! I mean I wasn't a millionaire, but this was more than all right with me. I had money! "Damn, looks like we can hit the malls tomorrow."

"Malls nothing. Your ass doesn't have insurance, remember?" Nat reminded me. "Those hospital bills will be rolling in soon." She walked toward the door. "I need to get those other bags from down by the elevator."

"All right, I'll start going through this stuff." I dragged the box of envelopes over to the sofa and sat down. "Trash, trash, trash . . ." I said to three consecutive mail pieces. "Bills, bills, bills." I sounded like Destiny's Child as I flipped through more letters. "What do they want?" I stared at the envelope from the Policemen's Benevolent Association. "Damn, I should have never sent them anything; now they're stalking me for another twenty dollars." I rolled my eyes. "Trash!" I grabbed a bunch of sales papers and tossed them. I picked up the next envelope and paused. "Correctional facility?" I came to my senses. "Oh, my goodn . . ."

Nat entered the room with her suitcase in tow. "I forgot to tell you that you have a new neighbor," she informed me.

Still staring at the envelope, I halfheartedly answered, "Oh yeah?" Thinking quickly, I hid the envelope between my thighs so Nat couldn't see it. "What are they like?"

"What is *he* like," she corrected me. "*He* is a trip, but fine as all outdoors." She lowered her voice. "He's out there right now."

I wanted to get up and check him out, but I couldn't afford to reveal an inch of the envelope. "What do you mean by he's a trip?" I pretended to be interested.

"You ever"—she spoke in a whisper—"look at a man and get a serious feeling that he's no good?"

"Yeah."

"Well, that's what I mean." She added, again in a soft voice, "He's a high school basketball coach, tall, lean, the perfect body, hand-some face, sex appeal for days. I can tell that he fucks *all* the time, or that he has to at least be fuckin' somebody . . . anybody. But good women like us give him the time of day and our phone numbers anyway." She huffed. "Bastard." Her whisper was now almost as loud as the knock on the door. Both of our eyes popped open. "Who is it?" she asked.

"Craig," the voice said from behind the door.

Her eyes bulged out. "That's him," she mouthed, and bent to study her reflection in the door of the microwave.

I giggled and asked in a low voice, "What are you doing?" I smiled. "You just called him a bastard."

"I know."

"Plus, you're engaged," I reminded her.

"I'm getting married, not buried." She ran to the door and opened it. "Hi." So phony!

The voice spoke. "I think you left this by the elevator." He handed her the blue-and-gray umbrella she shaded me with while getting out of the car.

"I sure did." She smiled. "Thank you."

His tone was cheerful. "Would you like for me to lift this box in for you?"

Nat looked out. "Oh my God, I had totally forgotten about that one." She was embarrassed. "Yes, please bring it in."

Within a few seconds I was looking at the kind of man you see when you "somehow" wander onto an African-American porn Web site. I mean, this brotha was tall, at least six four, medium brown, about two hundred and thirty pounds, and a face similar, but I swear more handsome, than Boris Kodjoe's. "Hello," he said with a smile in my direction. "Where would you like for me to put it?" I'm sure that Nat and I were thinking the same nasty shit when he asked, but we both refrained from laughing.

"Umm . . ." Nat was lost for words.

"Right there." I pointed at the love seat but was really looking at his arms. "Right there will be fine."

With ease he laid the box down. "There you go."

"Thank you, Mister . . . ?" I left his last name up to him.

"Mister Johnson." He made his way over to me on the couch. "But if you're going to be living right next door to me, you can call me Craig." His smile revealed a small gap between his two front teeth, but oddly enough, it didn't take away from his audaciousness one bit. "And you are?" He reached for my hand.

"Miss Emery, but since there is only a wall separating our bedrooms, you get to call me Sarai." I extended my hand and suddenly wished it would fall off: I still had my hospital bracelet on. *Bling! Bling!*

He shook my hand, and gawked at my wrist. "Are you all right?" He stared peculiarly at the band.

"Yeah," I lied. "A bout with the flu." What was I supposed to do, tell him that I had amnesia? Error! That is *so* not cute.

"Feeling better?" he asked.

"Loads." I looked down at his calf muscles slyly: they were chunky. "I feel a lot better."

"So"—he looked back at Nat—"both of you live here?"

"No," she chimed in. "I'm just here being a nurse for the week, trying to get her back on her feet." Nat asked from the kitchen, "May I offer you something to drink?"

"No thanks, I'm in the process of unpacking, and if I don't get back to it soon, then I'll put if off again like I have a million times before."

"When did you move in?" I had to know.

I could tell he wished that I was standing up so that he could see just what I was working with, but I was guarding this letter between my thighs with my life, plus I was tired. "About a week now," he answered.

"Well, welcome to the eleventh floor." I grinned.

"Thanks." He gazed down at me with the sexiest smirk. "It was a pleasure meeting you, Sarah."

I hated when people called me that. "Sarai." I pronounced it "Sa-rye."

"Nice meeting you." Craig continued on, saying my name carefully: "Sarai."

"Likewise, Craig." We shook hands again.

When he was gone Nat and I looked at each other and laughed softly, then she made her way over to the couch with two glasses of cranberry juice. "What do you think he has in his dicking account?"

It had been some time since we talked like this. "Hmm, he looks like he could very well be a millionaire."

"So, I take it that you would sleep with him?" Nat asked.

"Yes," I answered with no hesitation.

Nat frowned. "I would too." She corrected herself: "I mean, back in the day I would've, but now no." She sighed. "Why do we women subject ourselves to such drama, though?"

"Oh God." I pretended to be frustrated. "Here you go getting philosophical and shit."

"Hear me on this, Sarai."

"You and your logic," I interrupted. "I swear if I didn't know better, I would think you smoke weed." I laughed. "'Cause people who smoke weed swear they think of the most theoretical shit in the world."

"Seriously, our intuition tells us when a man means us no good, is a player, is a loser, et cetera, but we cancel that out because he's fine, or because of how much money he has, or . . ."

I added, "Or beçause he has a big dick."

"Shut up, I wasn't about to say that." Nat pushed me playfully. "I was about to say a nice car."

"Men do the same thing," I informed her.

"Yeah, but the difference is that that is their end goal." She spoke on: "You see, women and men both start the pursuit with similar intentions. We start out wanting a man's body, but somewhere in the middle we yearn for their hearts and souls." She was on another damn level. "We get caught up, and before we know it they're through with us, because their end goal was always just physical, but we went and got emotional."

"So their mission is accomplished." I thought I would agree in order to humor her. "And ours undone?"

"Correct. See, you feel me." She was thrilled that I understood. "We are left incomplete and spend forever chasing that which would make us whole."

"Did you just say, and I quote, 'that which would make us whole'?" I couldn't help it, I burst out laughing before she could say another word. "Who in the hell are you, Shakespeare?"

She threw a pillow at me. "Keep thinking it's a game." She stood up. "I'm going into your room to call the other half of my wholeness." She jokingly stuck out her tongue at me and disappeared.

"I'll be in the bathroom," I called out to her, and quickly shifted the envelope from my thighs to the inside of my shirt and raced to the bathroom in the hallway. I tore open the envelope with such force that I nearly ripped the paper inside. I sat on the toilet-seat cover and read:

Sarai, Without a doubt, I know that I am the last person in the world you want to hear from. When I heard the news that you

were awake and all right I knew what I had to do . . . beg for your
forgiveness. I cannot live with myself thinking of what I did to you.
If I could bring onto myself what I brought to you, I would, ten
times over. Forgive me, please. Damian/Dwayne

I read the letter over and over, slower and slower, and enunciated
word after word to be certain of what it said, but I still didn't fully
understand it. After about twenty minutes into the brain teaser Nat
knocked on the door to make sure that I was all right. I promised
her that I was, but I honestly wasn't sure. I was sitting on the toilet
like Sherlock Holmes searching for a clue to what I couldn't compre-
hend when suddenly images of a party flashed through my mind.
I remembered the Mardi Gras–and–masquerade theme, the beads,
the masks, the people, and the look on Nat's face when the first of
the guests arrived.

I was swaying to the music next to the entrance when a guy in a
Phantom of the Opera mask approached me and the scene of how we
met miraculously played out just as Tremel said it had two weeks
earlier while I was in the hospital. His key didn't match my lock, and
he walked away, but by then I already wanted to know more about
him. However, with Damian nearby, I couldn't act on it. The night
continued to fall in line in my mind.

Damian had to leave to meet with some Bahamian traffick-
ers and I was now lonely. I remembered the jealousy that mounted
up within me when I saw Tremel on the dance floor holding a sexy
Latino señorita too close. Inappropriately enough, they were dancing to Ginuwine's "Pony." *"If you're horny let's do it, ride it, my pony.*
My saddle's waitin', ride it, my pony." To drown my sorrows I ordered
a martini and turned my back to them, but minutes later he joined
me at the bar and my envy spoke up. "I saw you out there. I take it
that you like arroz con pollo?" I was wrong for dissin' the Spanish
chick like that.

His answer to me was, *"Actually, I prefer collard greens, macaroni*
and cheese, and potato salad."

I recalled the entire evening, even up to the fiasco of finding out

that the handsome stranger's name was Tremel Colten, then learning that he was a janitor and later having no words for his broke ass.
Damn, I could be mean.

Like it or not . . . memories were slowly coming back to me, and
I wasn't walking toward them . . . I wasn't running either . . . I had
rented me a car and was burning out the engine trying to get back to
where I'm supposed to be in my mind.

> "Memory . . . is the diary that we all carry about with us."
>
> —OSCAR WILDE

Tremel

WITHDRAWAL SLIP #3
ENDING BALANCE: $16.87

Hey, how are you feeling?" I asked nervously into the telephone receiver.

"I'm fine, thank you." Sarai giggled. "I just wish certain people would stop treating me like I have the plague."

I heard Nat in the background. "I am not treating you like that."

"Hold on," she quickly said to me, then responded to Nat. "Yes, you are, I can't do anything and I can't *go* anywhere." She added angrily, "I can't even watch TV like I want to."

"Well, excuse me for looking out for you," I faintly heard Nat say. "The doctor said that you should wait another week before watching the news and certain other programs."

She wasn't doing a good job covering up the phone. "So what that the damn pope died while I was in a coma, I'm not Catholic, so I really don't give a shit. I'm Christian, Jesus died for me a long time ago." She continued. "All I want is to see if Erica Kane is being good to Jack. What's so wrong with that?" As Nat went on and on in the distance Sarai got back to me. "You there?"

"Yeah." I was laughing. "Sounds like you two are having fun."

"Oh yeah, loads and loads," she said sarcastically.

"I've been calling every day to check on you, but—"

"Let me guess," she cut me off. "The warden didn't think I should venture to the phone?"

"No," I confessed, "not at all; it was me, I always asked her not to bother you."

"Really?" She sounded disappointed.

"Yeah." I couldn't tell her why.

"When I didn't hear from you I thought that you had forgotten me," she said softly.

I smiled. "I'd never do that." She didn't know just how serious my statement was. "I could never forget you."

"Good," she continued cheerfully. "Especially now that I remember you."

"What?" I asked anxiously, and when she didn't respond fast enough, I grew rather persistent. "What did you say?"

"I remember you."

"Remember what?"

"Meeting you at the party." She was excited.

"Are you serious?" I had to know.

"Yes I am, Mr. Phantom of the Opera."

I was overjoyed. "What else do you remember?"

"I can recall a few other things that happened around that time, but nothing major." She then added, "At least not yet."

"Well, that's fantastic." I was a little disappointed that she didn't remember more, but the fact that she had remembered something about me was better than nothing. "So, was I a gentleman that night?"

"Very much so." I could hear her smile. "I wasn't much of a lady, though, and I apologize for—"

"Shh." I quieted her. "We've already lived it once and I've forgiven you twice."

"Thanks."

"When did you remember *this*?" I couldn't stop talking about it.

"The first day I got home."

"That was last Thursday!" I exclaimed. "And you're just telling me now?"

"Well, I don't have your number or anything."

Damn, my cell phone was turned off two days ago when I refused to pay the $304 bill. "Oh, okay."

"Is the number on the caller ID your number?"

"No," I said quickly. "I'm at work."

"Still with the school system?"

"No." I had finally landed a job a few days ago as a delivery driver for a florist. "I'm working as a driver." I left out the gay-ass delivering-flowers part.

Truth is I stumbled into this flower shop to ask directions to an interview I was already late to. The old Cuban man that owns the place had his nephew doing the driving, but an hour before, the police raided his nephew's apartment and he was arrested on some charges like running an Internet child-pornography ring. So the old man said, in straight-off-the-raft English, "I no have license. You drive van, please." Mr. Jimenez was dead serious. "I pay you, I pay you cash, one hunrey dollar a day, my friend, please drive van." At the time most of the money I had left was used to put gas in my car to get to the interview. God works in mysterious ways. "It's my third day on the job," I told Sarai.

"Good for you," she said.

I changed the topic. "So what are you girls up to?"

"We're up to our necks with each other," she joked. "I need to get out of the house."

I had to seize the moment. "How about dinner tomorrow night?"

The line went silent. "What?" she asked.

"Was I out of line?" Damn, I felt dumb. "Did I say something wrong?"

"I can't believe you just asked me that."

Shit! I wish I could hit rewind. "Um, sorry, I didn't know that it would be all that."

"All what?" she asked. "I just can't believe that I might finally get out of this apartment." I could tell that she was smiling. "I'd love to get out of here, and dinner with you tomorrow night would be the perfect reason."

"Cool." I was relieved. "How about seven?"

"Seven it is." She then added cheerfully, "What about my warden? How will I get past the bars?"

"I'll handle her." I quickly remembered our first date. "But if I can't then I'll just bring dinner to you."

"That's sweet," she said. "Let me get your number just in case something comes up."

I hesitated. "Well, my cell is off."

"Okay, just gimme your home phone, then."

I rattled off Charlize's house number like it belonged to me. Sarai had me in a trance and I wasn't even trying to get out.

"Thanks." She sounded so sweet. "So am I right in assuming that you still prefer collard greens, macaroni and cheese, and potato salad?"

I chuckled a bit. "Yes Sarai, you're right to assume that I *still* prefer you." It was like meeting her again for the first time.

I drove all the way home with a smile. Nothing could get me down. Shit was finally going my way . . . *my* way. Sarai's frozen memories of me were slowly starting to thaw, and she'd consented to a date with me. What could possibly go wrong? Nothing! When I entered the house there was no one in the living room. No *one*, but *something* was present . . . music. I heard Charlize's bow softly brushing against the strings of her cello and I immediately stopped to listen. She was playing from her "special" room and there was a slow, low, growling note followed by dozens more before she took it up a few notches higher and faster; it was beautiful. I was impressed, she could really play.

In an effort to be spontaneously creative I walked over to the piano, lifted the top, and tested a few keys. It was in tune. I closed my eyes and allowed my mind to feel what she was playing, and from the next room I accompanied her melody perfectly by tickling the piano keys. At first I felt her hesitate and almost stop. She didn't know if I was aware that she was playing . . . until she felt my vibe and realized that I wasn't leaving her behind . . . I was behind her . . . playing with her.

Our duet continued for about fifteen minutes before I decided to leave her alone to work. Eager to thank her and somewhat apologize for interrupting, I ventured down the hall to the door and turned the knob with a smile. "Sorry if I . . . whoa." To my surprise the small black room was lit with four jarred candles and brown-skinned Charlize was sitting erect on a stool in only her brown skin; she was completely naked. The only thing between her and me was the cello between her legs. I couldn't see her most "private" area, but her faultless plump breasts were exposed on either side of the neck of the musical instrument and I was in awe.

Seeing me, her mouth dropped and so did the bow as she scurried to cover her chest. "I asked you to knock anytime I was in here."

I didn't know what to think or say. "I'm sorry." I couldn't stop staring at her. "I was—"

"Please close the door." She was livid. "Just close it."

I did as she said, then tried to tell myself that I wasn't seeing things. I walked back to my room in a daze and sat on the bed. "She was naked!" I smiled and quietly reminisced on what she looked like. Charlize had it going on! I'm sure that she was embarrassed and I didn't want to be face-to-face with her anytime soon. "She plays in the nude?" I laughed. "That's weird as hell."

My plan was to stay in my room the rest of the evening to avoid the uncomfortable cloud of tension that I assumed would be looming over us. However, two hours later she smoked me out of my hole when she started cooking. The aroma seeped under my room door, rose into the air, and made a beeline up my nostrils. I knew that smell . . . homemade spaghetti with meat sauce and garlic cheese toast. I fought the scent for over an hour before cracking my door to see if the coast was clear and leftovers were available.

"I know that you're starving." She must've heard the noise the door makes when it's opened too slowly.

Damn! "Oh; no, I'm straight," I said down the empty hallway that brought her voice to me. "I was just going to the bathroom," I lied.

"I'm fully clothed, you can come out now." She giggled. "Plus, there is plenty left."

My stomach would go without my body if it had to. "All right, I'll check it out when I'm done."

"It sucks eating my birthday dinner alone."

"It's your birthday?" I asked.

"Yep, and I'll fix you a plate." The sound of her chair rubbing against the tiled floor told me that she wasn't taking no for an answer.

"Okay." As I washed my hands the vision of Charlize's brown naked body illuminated only by candles occupied my mind. When I made it to the dining table I tried hard to keep a straight face.

"I hope that you'll enjoy it," she said, and placed the plate of food before me along with an empty wineglass. "Red or white?"

All I could see was brown . . . her brown skin. "Huh?"

"Red or white wine?"

"Oh." I finally understood. "Red." I stared at the plate to avoid looking her way. "So today is your birthday?"

"Yep."

"Why aren't you out celebrating?" I asked.

"Going out tomorrow night." I heard glee in her tone. "A little date."

"Well, happy birthday," I said. "I wish I would've known; I would've gotten a cake or something."

"Thank you," Charlize said with a grin, and walked to the wine cabinet as an unwelcome silence rolled in. She returned from the bar with a bottle of Syrah, poured some into my glass, and rested it on the table before she sat in front of me and her unfinished meal. She was now dressed in a light pink cotton around-the-house shirt-

and-pants set, yet all I could see was brown skin. She looked amazing, and I'm sure that she saw the glow of admiration glued to my ignorant face.

We couldn't go on silently the entire night. "So how is the job going?" she asked.

"Things are good." I finally looked her in the face. "It's something for right now."

"It's better than nothing." She held up her glass, suggesting a toast. I raised mine and said, "Happy birthday, Charlize."

"Happy birthday to me," she sang.

After our glasses kissed, I felt compelled to apologize. "I m very sorry about earlier. I had totally forgotten that you asked me to knock whenever you were in there."

"It's okay." She sipped her wine. "Maybe I should've told you about my habits."

I was intrigued. "Tell me."

"When I practice at home I do so in the nude." She never looked away from me. "It allows me to feel the vibrations throughout my entire body."

I was officially turned on and didn't know what to say. "That's deep."

"Each body part responds to the raw vibrations differently and every note is a new sensation." Charlize brought her glass to her lips again. "I don't like anything to stand between me and my music."

"That I saw," I said sarcastically, and we both laughed briefly. "Naw, but really? Do your thing, everybody has something that works for them." I wanted her to be at ease. "Just like everybody doesn't have dreams about Shaq."

"Thanks for not being freaked out." She smiled. "I thought you were packing your stuff and heading out in search of a new place."

"Shit." I shouldn't have said another word. "If anything, I may want to lengthen my lease now." That was one of those things you should think but should not speak. Therefore I followed it up with a smooth, "No offense."

"None taken." She blushed and started twirling spaghetti around her fork. In midtwirl she looked over at me and blushed. "God help us if you have the same habit."

At about 3 p.m. the next day I loaded up the van for my third round of deliveries. I made it out to the beach with the three arrangements in search of the closest address. The first array, a bunch of sunflowers, made an elderly lady's birthday complete. She kissed me on my cheeks so many times that you'd think that I was the one that bought them for her.

My second stop, to drop off two dozen roses, was to a boutique called Size Too. The lucky lady's name was Esmeralda. With a smile I walked into the small store and the two young Hispanic ladies behind the counter looked at me, each other, and then back at me.

"Esmeralda?" I asked, looking at the one in the tight green shirt.

"No." She pointed at the other girl. "That's her."

"Esmeralda!" I looked at her in her pink strapless summer dress. She was hot! I knew that the sender would be getting some tonight. I rested the vase on the countertop and slid the clipboard toward her to sign for it. "Let me have you sign down here."

"I don't want it," she said.

I had to make sure that she was talking to me. "Huh?"

"I'm not accepting it." She spelled it out for me. "I cannot believe that he's doing this."

"He is wrong for what he did," Green Shirt said. "Fuck those flowers."

"I know." Esmeralda sighed. "I can't believe that he thinks that that shit would work."

"So you don't want 'em?" I asked.

"No," she said with an attitude. "I don't care what you do with them, but don't leave that shit here." She crossed her hands over her chest. "Tell him to send them to the bitch I caught him with."

Green Shirt interrupted. "You should call her and tell her about these flowers." She paused. "I bet she'll come out here and . . ."

"And what? She'll get her ass kicked one more time. Fuck all that."

Esmeralda rolled her eyes like a sistah. "Just take them and give them to someone else. Shit, give 'em to your girl. I'll tell him that I got 'em, then ripped all the petals off and flushed them down the toilet." She added, "I don't want him getting his money back."

"Sounds good to me." I wasn't about to beg her to take the flowers. "Just sign it so that my boss doesn't trip."

"Okay." She grabbed the pen and did as I asked.

As I walked back to the van and secured the arrangement in the back, I knew exactly who I would give it to—my date for the evening. However, as I drove down the street I noticed the sign that read PLATINUM DAY SPA coming up at the corner on my right. If the light turned red, I'd stop by; if it was green, the flowers go home with me and then to Sarai. Green, yellow, red! "Damn." I turned in to the parking lot and saw that Charlize's car was parked by the side of the establishment.

I quickly walked in with the roses and asked the receptionist to see to it that the belated birthday girl received them and to tell her that they were from her roommate. Well, as soon as I was heading for the door . . . "Tremel?" I heard behind me. I spun around. "What are you doing here?" Charlize asked.

I smiled. "Well"—I was caught—"happy belated birthday." I pointed at the roses.

"Oh my goodness." Her eyes lit up and her hands rushed to her mouth. "Are you serious?" Her voice went up an octave. "These are for me?" she asked the receptionist who shook her head up and down.

"It's just a little something," I said. "Sorry that I didn't know that it was your birthday yesterday."

"Well, I didn't tell you." She admired the flowers and then walked over to me at the door. "So you had no way of knowing. I'm going to be spoiled by the end of the day. My uncle C.J., from Sacramento, is in town and he just left here, he brought me flowers too."

"So, how old are you now?"

She blushed and opened the door to take our conversation outside. "I don't tell my age."

"Why not?"

She answered in a louder tone due to the heavy traffic and the sea breeze. "Because it somewhat gives people what they think is the right to expect you to do certain things or act in a certain way."

"Well, I don't expect anything from you," I said in a half-joking way. "C'mon, give me a clue."

She thought for a second. "I voted in the last election."

"What does that mean?" I asked.

"It means that I'm at least eighteen." We both laughed. "It's Friday, so what are you getting into tonight?"

I'm not sure just how big my smile was but I'm sure that it could be spotted from space. "I'm going out with an old friend."

"An old female friend?" she asked.

"Yeah."

"Wow." She touched my shoulder and popped my collar. "Mr. Lover Man."

There was a bit of awkward silence, until I remembered. "You're going out tonight too, right?"

"Yeah." She looked out onto the street. "The big birthday week-end." She sighed. "I can't wait to see what he has up his sleeve."

"I need to get going." I jingled my keys. "Have a great evening."

"You do the same." Then she blushed again. "Thanks again for the roses, they're beautiful."

"No need to thank me," I said. "That's the least I can do after yesterday's fiasco." I winked at her and started walking away. "See ya later."

"'Bye."

The moment I drove away from the spa I had a weird feeling about the flower incident. Somehow I wished I would've held out and given them to Sarai; she deserved them. Especially with money as tight as it now was for me. Thinking of the way she would've smiled, the look in her eyes, and the "oh Mel, this is so sweet" that I was almost guaranteed to hear was eating me alive. I was now hoping that something would go wrong with the next delivery so that I could claim it as a gift to her.

I passed the address twice without realizing that the ten-story office building was where I needed to be. I parked the van in front, snapped on my hazard lights, and tried to make it quick, but the receptionist insisted that the sender wanted the flowers delivered directly to suite 504, the number on the tiny envelope.

On the elevator on my way to the fifth floor I checked myself out in the mirror on the back wall. I was looking good in my blue jeans and gray polo shirt, but I wasn't dressed for this office atmosphere. Every man was in a suit and tie, and every woman was doing her damn thing in panty hose and heels. So much for casual Friday! With the floral arrangement and a clipboard, people had to know what I was there for, so when the doors opened I didn't feel too out of place. I searched for the suite number, and when I found it I got nervous because it was one of the only doors I passed that didn't have a narrow window, allowing a preview of what or who was behind the door.

After taking a deep breath, I turned the knob and was almost relieved when I saw a meeting room with about seven or eight brothers all dressed in serious business attire seemingly having a roundtable discussion.

"Good afternoon." I smiled as I walked in. They all turned and greeted me. "I don't know which one of you this is for, but I was told to deliver it here."

"Oh, you're right on time," one of the men said. "Bring it on over here."

As I walked closer to the table the features of the man sitting at the far end of the table became clear to me. I couldn't believe that we were in the same room and my hands weren't around his neck. It was Julian Odom, the man that was responsible for my career with Jump Records, the same man that found a clause in my contract and swindled me out of a future when I went to jail for something I didn't do. "Tremel Colten," he said and leaned back in his chair with a smile.

"Fuck you," I said under my breath, and then loudly followed with his first and last name. "Julian Odom." I rested the floral arrangement on the table and slid the clipboard toward him. "I need a signature."

"Whoa!" Julian laughed. "*Somebody* doesn't like his job."

I snickered and without looking at Julian said, "No time for pleasantries, I just need a signature from one of you."

"No time for pleasantries?" Julian huffed. "Now, is that any way to treat all the men that were paying your goddamn bills?"

"I know that's good and goddamn right." Another man eyed me. "You should be in here singing for us."

"Sing for you, my ass." I spat the words at him. "Fuck this!" I didn't know what this was all about, but I was already tired of it. "Keep the clipboard, and enjoy the fuckin' flowers." I turned my back and left the room to the sound of grown men chuckling like l'il bitches.

I stormed out of the room and ran into an older gentleman walking toward the door in a three-piece suit. "Oh, did my delivery get here?" he asked.

I was too pissed to be polite. "Yeah." I kept walking.

"Hey." He caught up with me. "Here is your tip." He waved a hundred-dollar bill in front of me; it was like candy to a six-year-old.

"I don't have change for that." I was still truckin' to the elevators.

"I don't need change," he said. "It's all for you."

I slowed down. "A hundred dollars?" I had to ask.

"Yeah," he said. "Thanks for bringing it."

I took the money before he changed his mind, and I don't know when it happened but soon we were walking slower and side by side. "My friends weren't out of control in there, were they?"

"Your friends are assholes," I said as I pressed the down button.

"Oh, sorry about that, it's been a long week."

"No problem." I tried to calm down. "It's just that I know one of them and we parted on bad terms and he had some slick shit to say." I thought about the situation. "I just got out of there before losing my cool, ya know?"

"Yeah; yeah, I know," the man said, but quickly turned his tone to a whisper. "But maybe Julian and the other men in there have good reason to be so angry."

"What?" I stuttered. "What? Who? How did you know who I was talking about?"

"Well, Julian and I arranged this meeting." He smiled. "We were hoping that we could use you to get a message to your girlfriend." He smiled.

"What?" I was confused. "What message and who are you?"

He held out his hand. "I'm Conrad Johnson." I wasn't shaking his hand, so he slid it into his pocket. "The men in the room . . ." He paused. "Well, I thought it would be interesting for you to meet some of the men that fucked Sarai. Julian was her first client and also her very last." He chuckled. "It wasn't your voice, but the depth of her mouth, all tongue and lips, that landed you into Jump Records." He smiled and whispered even lower. "I mean, you can sing, but that bitch sucks dick like a—" Before whatever the word was could come out of his mouth, I was pulling my fist away from his face twice and watching him fall to the ground in shock right when the elevator doors opened.

"Tell that bitch we want that money she stole or there will be hell to pay," Conrad screamed as he watched the elevator doors close.

Adrenaline had me high, up until I got to the van and remembered what Julian had said: *Now, is that any way to treat all the men that were paying your goddamn bills?* My bills? I thought he meant that they were all a part of Jump Records. Shit, when I first saw him, for a moment I thought that it was a clever ploy to re-sign me. This bitch was saying that he was payin' my bills through paying my girl for her pussy. I couldn't even start the van, I didn't want to start it. I wanted to go back up there and kick everybody's ass. I couldn't believe this.

Almost instantly my anger got transferred. It was no longer toward Julian, the men in the room, or the man by the elevator . . . but resting heavily on Sarai: she had had sex with all the men in that room while she was supposedly in love, involved, and intimate with me. They had all seen her naked, she sucked them off, they handled her roughly, came in or on her . . . they had all fucked her . . . all so that she could pay *our* bills.

She'd confessed some pretty terrible things to me the night I found the pictures of her and my uncle, but she never mentioned even knowing Julian Odom. I quickly thought back to us returning from Cleveland after spending Thanksgiving with my family. I tore through the pile of mail looking for a letter from Jump Records when I found the pictures my uncle had sent to me of him with his dick inches deep in my girlfriend. They were supposedly sent to show me that she was no good, and because she didn't know that he was my relative she did it all for the love of money. I left her that night, but before I did she came clean about everything and everybody she had done . . . well, so I thought. No wonder she had no doubts when we sent my demo to Jump; she had already cleared the path. "Damn!" I shouted, and put the van in drive. I traveled about three blocks before I pulled into a Taco Bell parking lot to get my mind right, but that just wouldn't happen . . . and after an hour and a half I knew that it would never be right again.

I returned the work van, snatched my pay envelope out of an old rickety drawer, hopped into my truck, and left without saying good-bye to Mr. Jimenez. Being in contact with another human being right then would leave me doing time, but this time I *would* be guilty of the crime. I felt like strangling someone . . . anyone.

It didn't help when I walked into the house and saw Charlize all dolled up and in a great mood. "Hey," she shrieked as she walked toward the kitchen from her room. "What's up?"

I just stared at her, through her, past her. I wasn't trying to be rude; not only did I not *want* to say anything, but I *couldn't* say anything. I just walked to my room and shut the door. I collapsed onto my bed and then the real hurt crashed onto me. Images of Sarai in bed with Julian invaded my mind. I heard her moan with pleasure and visualized her riding, kissing, and sucking him until he spat off into her face. "Slut."

I was back at square one. I had dealt with this feeling when I first learned that Sarai had slept with my uncle for money. However, at least at the time she didn't know that Norman was my uncle, but this was a whole new ball game. She knew exactly who Julian was and had slept with him because of who he was and how he could be beneficial to me knowing that it would in turn be favorable for her as well.

"Bitch," I said to myself about the woman who was expecting me to pick her up in less than fifteen minutes. "Fuckin' bitch," I whispered.

There was a light knock, and before I could say "gimme a minute," the door was slowly opening toward me. In walked Charlize. "Hey, I just wanted to thank you again for the flowers." Without looking her way, I could tell that she was smiling. "They were beautiful." I didn't say anything, and didn't bother sitting up, I just continued to stare at the ceiling. "Why aren't you getting dressed? I thought you were going out tonight." As she walked closer she saw the pain written on my face. She asked, "Tremel, are you okay?" Because of my lack of participation in having a conversation, she plopped down on the bed and shook my body. "What's wrong?"

"Nothing." I almost shouted at her. "I just need to be alone."

"What's going on?"

"Nothing." Didn't she hear me the first time? "I'm just tired."

"Liar!" she said as she looked down into my eyes. "Talk to me."

I looked over at her sexy black dress. "Aren't you about to go out?"

Charlize glanced at her watch. "He won't be here for another hour, he's running late as usual." She continued: "So talk to me."

"Charlize, honestly, I really don't feel like talkin'." I tried to tame my tone. "I seriously just need time to think."

She just ignored what I said. "So you're not going out anymore?"

"Nope."

"Well, did you at least call your date and let her know?"

I answered in a sure, smart-alecky way. "I sure didn't."

"That's not right," she chastised me. "Regardless of what you're dealing with, she did nothing that warrants being stood up." She continued to defend Sarai: "You men don't ever consider—"

"Consider what? *What*—that women are always the fuckin' victims? Consider my ass! I've had it up to my fuckin' hairline with always considering other muthafuckas." I sat up and raised my voice. "You don't know what I'm dealing with or who I'm dealing with, so just reserve your comments." I stood up and looked down at her. "Save that shit for someone else."

She swallowed hard. "You know what, I'm gonna fall back." Her words really meant, *Negro, I would tell you about your black ass, but I'll chill out for a minute and let you do you*. I could tell that she was hell-a embarrassed, confused, and uncomfortable. "Excuse me." She got up and left the room quickly. Right away I felt guilty about yelling and cussing the way that I did and went out after her. I found her in the kitchen pouring herself a glass of red wine.

"I think I'm going to need a glass of that too," I said in an apologetic tone, and followed up with, "I'm sorry about the way I spoke to you."

"Not a problem, but forget having a glass. I think you need the whole damn bottle, partner." She passed it to me. "Seems like you have issues."

"Yeah." I smiled. "Maybe Robert Mondavi can help me drown them."

"Here's to drowning." She touched the bottle with her glass and we both drank, she from her glass and me straight from the bottle. Within thirty minutes we were screwing the steel spiral of the wine opener into a second bottle, and right as I was done pouring her glass, she kicked off her heels, picked up her glass, and grabbed me by the hand. "I know what you need," she whispered seductively and pulled me behind her all the way to her dark "home office." As we strolled through the door together she looked back at me. "I'm going to help you relax a little."

I didn't know what she was up to. "Aren't you supposed to be going out?"

She smiled. "Not before I hook you up."

"C'mon," I said. "You don't have to worry about me, go out and have a good time."

"I'll worry about me, and I hope to help you." With that said, she rounded the room with a long-mouth lighter and lit many of the candles on the shelves against the walls. Afterward she walked toward me with a folded towel, the glow of the candlelight illuminating her. "All right, get undressed, lie facedown on the table"—she gestured to the massage table draped in white sheets—"and cover yourself with the fresh linen I've provided for you." She handed me the towel. "I'll be back in five minutes." She started walking toward the door.

I laughed. "I wasn't trying to get a free massage out of you."

"Really?" She turned toward me. "Then exactly what were you trying to get out of me?"

Whoa! I *could've* taken her question and run with it . . . but I remained calm. "Nothing." I smiled. "I've just never had a *professional* massage before."

"Never?" She seemed shocked.

"Never!"

"So what's an unprofessional massage like?" She had to know.

I grinned. "You wouldn't be leaving the room as I undress, and before I got naked, I would see to it that you were first." I removed my shirt and enjoyed watching and hearing her exhale.

"I'll be back in five minutes." She left.

I did as she asked, got naked, lay on the table facedown, and draped the sheets over my lower back, butt, and upper-thigh region. When she returned she turned on relaxing music, and I swear when I closed my eyes I saw the sun slowly rise. In the soothing mix I heard strings, guitars, flutes, a harp, and of course a keyboard. Before anything went down, she taught me the proper way to breathe when meditating, relaxing, or getting a massage: inhaling through your nose and blowing it out of the mouth slowly like through a straw.

Though my head was facedown in the headrest, she brought three fragrances to my nose and asked, "Which one makes you feel best?"

"The second one." It reminded me of being a boy.

"Okay, I'll be using the luscious lavender lace oil on you today and I ask that you relax and enjoy our time together." I could hear the drip-dripping of oil into Charlize's palms; she rubbed them together and then her fingertips slowly found my neck. Suddenly I felt all cares, fears, and frustrations melt away. I continued breathing, just like she had shown me. "How is my pressure?" she asked.

Pressure? It took me a few seconds to get what she was saying. "Oh, you're fine." I corrected myself: "It's fine."

"Okay, just relax." Her tone was very comforting. "I got you."

"Do you?" I asked jokingly.

"Yeah." She giggled and applied a little more of her sweet muscle to my neck. "Doesn't it feel like it?"

"Yeah, it feels like you got me." Five minutes later she was touching a sensitive area, my shoulders, and I had to fight not to whimper or moan like a punk. The feel and scent of the oil did a quarter of the trick, her touch took me another fifty pegs, but the thought of her sitting behind that cello butt-booty-ass naked took me the rest of the way. This shit was feeling too damn good. I bit into my bottom lip and lowered my head again in defeat. She won the first round! "Mmmm!" I had to let a little bit of my satisfaction out. "You're good."

"Thanks." She spoke with a smile.

About twenty minutes into the massage she was caressing my right ass cheek through the sheet. *Whoa, Nellie*, I felt like screaming. A man's ass is a peculiar thing. Though it felt good, I didn't want to get too relaxed back there and bust a fart in her face. She slowly drifted down to my thighs.

"How is my pressure?" she asked in a whisper that could easily be mistaken for a whimper.

"Damn." The word escaped as I struggled to catch my breath.

"What does that mean?"

"Mmmm," I groaned. "What more can I say?"

She giggled and continued on down my body until she arrived at my toes. She even paid them individual attention, wiggling and pulling them from the little nub to the big dogs. The girl was awe-some. Halfway up the other side of my body she asked, "How do you feel?"

I smiled down into the headrest. "Never better."

"Great, I want you to—" The phone rang and I felt the change in her touch. "I'll let it ring." And it rang again.

"That might be your man," I said.

"My what?" she said, and chuckled sarcastically.

"Your date." I reminded her.

"Oh, you're right." She rushed over to the phone. "Hello!" She paused for a second. "Yes, one moment please." Charlize walked back over to the massage table. "It's for you."

"Me?" I raised my head in shock and looked at her. "Who is it?"

"May I ask who's calling?" she asked into the receiver, and then looked in my direction. "Sarai."

Suddenly the massage had done no good; I was tensed up again and angry. "I'm busy. Tell her that I'll call her back."

Charlize gave me a weird look and then put the phone back to her ear. "Umm, he's a little busy right now and said that he'll call you back." She kept staring at me. "I'm not sure." She smiled. "Okay, good-bye."

"Thanks."

"Uh-uh, don't be thanking me," Charlize huffed. "Why did you lie?"

"I didn't lie; you do have me a little busy," I said. "So come back over here and finish what you started."

That she did; boy, she did! When she touched me again my entire body came alive . . . if you know what I mean. "So who is she?" Charlize asked after a few minutes of silence.

"My ex." I kept my answer short.

"How did she get this number?"

What was this, an interrogation room? "I gave it to her."

"Why?"

Damn! "We were supposed to be going out tonight."

"Oh, that's right, that's what got you on this table."

"No." I decided to push her buttons. "No, I think we both know what got me on the table."

"What?" She stopped massaging and asked again, "What?"

I rolled over onto my back and propped myself up on my elbows. "You know." I looked down at my chest and winked at her. "Don't play dumb."

She smacked me on the shoulder. "I hope you're kidding."

And though I was, it was too fun to stop there. "You know that you've been dying to touch my chest." I playfully winked again. "Come on and get your feel on, girl."

"You're not well in the head, Mel." She laughed.

Suddenly my feelings were a tad wounded. "Last chance." I was almost begging.

"Do you need attention or something?" She smiled and took a step toward me. "Fine, if it'll make you feel good, I'll touch your chest." She quickly jabbed me twice on my right pec, but I made the third time the last time by grabbing her hand and sliding it down my abs; she couldn't move. I leaned toward her until our lips nearly touched . . . the doorbell rang. "I . . . I better get that." She quickly pulled her hand away from my chest and was out of the door.

The next words I heard were yelled from the living room. "Mel, I'm gone, see you tomorrow." I guess those were the code words for, *You can get your naked black ass out of my office now.*

> "I'll be out of here in ten minutes, but if you say another goddamn word, I'll be out in twenty and I'll be dragging your wannabe bad ass behind me in a garbage bag."
> —DAMIAN CARTER, *Going Broke,*
> bank statement three.

Sarai

3½

It's been a whirlwind week. It's Friday, but it all started *last* Friday when Tremel never showed up for our evening out; I don't call it a date because I've grown so bitter about the whole thing to the point that I feel loser-ish. Why am I bitter? I didn't know that he was living with a woman. When I called she said that *he* was busy, but from the sound of it, *they* were busy. I wasn't trying to be nosy but the phone wasn't hung up properly . . . now either that heifer didn't do it purposely or . . . or nothing . . . she wanted me to know what was really good . . . and I listened.

Tremel was supposed to pick me up at seven. Seven! So at 8:15 I called him. And was stunned when a woman answered. I just *knew* that I had the wrong number, but in an effort to not be rude and just hang up I asked, "Hi, may I speak to Tremel?"

"Yes, one moment please," she said. A few seconds later, it sounded like she had an attitude. "Umm, he's a little busy right now and said that he'll call you back."

"Do you know how long it'll be?" It was a desperate question, but I was sitting there dressed to the nines and couldn't appreciate waiting and didn't feel like waiting any longer.

"I'm not sure," she said with a hint of joy in her voice.

"Thanks a lot." I was being sarcastic.

"Okay, good-bye." She put the phone down, but didn't hang it up. "Why did you lie?" she then asked him.

"I didn't lie; you do have me a little busy." Tremel sounded far away. "So come back over here and finish what you started."

I didn't hear anything for a few seconds and the seconds turned to minutes, but I stayed on the line anyway. During that silence here is what my mind's eye saw: I imagined her not very happy about the call, but going back to join him in bed anyway. He reached out to her waist and pulled her down to him so that he could kiss her lips to keep her from asking questions. With her back now against the sheets, he traveled down her body. During his journey he sucked her hardened nipples, pecked at her trembling stomach, and rubbed his lips through her pubic hair and then parting her thighs just enough for his head to fall between. However, she wasn't going to allow him to dismiss the phone call. "So who is she?" she asked.

"My ex." What a liar. He was willing to say anything.

Finally she pushed him off of her. "How did she get this number?"

"I gave it to her." What a bold display of masculinity. Men make me sick sometimes.

"Why?" she asked.

Right then the door of my apartment flew open; it was Nat bringing groceries up. "Girl, Publix is having a produce sale." She was ecstatic. "Two packs of strawberries for two ninety-nine." She continued: "I nearly lost my mind in there."

I couldn't hear anything anymore. "Shhhhhhhh."

"Don't shush me." She looked at the clock. "Aren't you supposed to be gone?"

"Nat, please be quiet for one minute," I begged. "I'm trying to hear something."

"Fine." She exited—I assumed to get the other stuff waiting by the elevator.

I never heard his answer to her question; the next thing I heard was Tremel saying, "Come on and get your feel on, girl." That's all I needed to hear to hang up. They were about to go at it, and I just couldn't stand to listen.

Wow! I said to myself. Here I was thinking that Tremel was an innocent, interesting, and upstanding character and all the while he was just a wolf in sheep's clothing like so many others I've encountered. "Fuck Tremel too."

Since I was already dressed, and the only way for me to get past the "guard" was Tremel, I grabbed my purse and the keys to Nookie, my truck, and made a beeline toward the door. "He's here?" Nat asked as she walked back in.

"Yeah," I lied. "I'll see you later."

"Wait." She placed two brown bags on the counter. "He's not coming up?"

"Nah, he's already late and we have reservations." As I closed the door I yelled, "Don't wait up."

In the garage I noticed a flyer to a place called Erogenous Zone under my windshield wiper. "Let's see what this is all about." I spoke to myself. When I made it past the security booth I rolled my windows down, and turning the radio up, I felt like Martin Luther King. *Free at last, free at last, thank God Almighty I'm free at last.* It had been forever since I had driven down the causeway to South Beach. Speeding through traffic, the wind in my hair, and the Miami River on both sides of me made me feel complete.

It was only 9 p.m., but on a Friday night on South Beach things start jumping early, so I was right on time. I followed the directions and pulled up in front of Erogenous Zone with a huge smile on my face. Apparently it was a brand-new establishment, and if a name like that wasn't pulling in customers, I didn't know what would. I handed my keys over to a man I hoped was a valet-parking attendant as he made it no secret that he loved my breasts by staring lustfully at my chest. So be it! I was neither afraid nor ashamed to advertise my 38-Ds in a low-cut round-collared brown shirt, with a matching skirt and open-toed four-inch heels.

Erogenous Zone sensually lived up to its name. It wasn't a club; it was more of a lounge. However, once inside, I quickly determined that it was not just any lounge: this place wasn't for the weak. For starters, the walls were crimson red and the ceiling orange. The two colors, orange and red, have been scientifically proven to stimulate the sexual organs. The place was elegant, but the soft tropical mist in the air ushered in dirty thoughts.

The lounge was broken up into four temptingly arousing quarters, each with its own bar section with about ten stools. However, on each side of each bar were two twin-size beds draped in bloodred sheets accompanied by pink-and-orange throw pillows, night tables, lamps, love seats, two chairs, candles, and a few vases of freshly cut red roses. It was basically a scene reminiscent of a sexy bedroom, but it was actually more lounging space.

The section's name hung high above the bars in big red neon letters: *Nipples*, *Clitoris*, *Anal*, and *Toes*. Anal? Who wanted to admit to that? A lot of people were in Toes and Nipples. However, I stayed true to my sexual practices and sauntered over to the half-empty Clitoris bar. That was my erogenous zone. That's right, I am a straight shooter, ain't nothing goin' down or in unless you licked the clit. No nookie unless you eat the cookie.

There was instrumental music streaming through the speakers; it was heavy in bass, so heavy that each thud went from the speakers through the steel of my stool and to my clit, causing a vibration and resulting in a drop of moisture. Trying to ignore it, I grabbed the menu in search of a drink. The drinks had names like the Long Lick, Rub Me Right, Dykes & Dildos, Creamy Finger, Pussy Pinched, Double Penetration, etc. . . . This place was a five-alarm fire!

The bartender, a very attractive, average-height, slim, light-brown-skinned sister with tidy honey-brown corkscrew curls, walked over. "I love your hair," she said. "Very chic!"

"Thanks." I'd had it done earlier.

She leaned across the counter and whispered into my ear. "How would you like me to lick you?"

I was shocked, not only by her question, but because her breasts were only an inch or so away from my lips. "I beg your pardon?" I almost gagged.

"That's the way we ask." She backed away a little. "What'd you like to drink, sweetie?"

"Oh, I'm sorry." The tension melted from my shoulders. "This is my first time here."

"I know. Let me guess." She giggled. "You thought I was coming on to you?"

"Yeah," I admitted jokingly. "I thought I was going to have to swing."

"It happens all the time," she stated. "But it's what the managers want, so I say it." She added while looking around, "After all, this is *Erogenous Zone*."

"Gotta do ya job," I said, smiling

"Yeah." She looked around, perturbed, then asked, "So, what are you having?"

I was too shy to say any of the names of the drinks in public and especially to a stranger. "What do you recommend?" I played it smart.

"Mmmm." She scanned the list. "I love Creamy Fingers." She paused. "Pussy Pinched is good too, but my favorite is Dykes and Dildos."

"Okay." I was game. "I'll try that."

"You're my kind of girl," she said as she walked away. I quickly searched the ingredients to see what the fuck I was in for: vodka, tequila, rum, gin, sweet-and-sour mix, and Chambord raspberry liqueur. "Damn," I whispered. This was a long way away from the wine I had intended to drink this evening. Not to mention I was still on medication . . . don't try this at home.

After a few minutes my drink arrived in all of its purple glory. She watched me take my first sip. "Mmm, this isn't bad."

"Dykes and Dildos." She winked at me. "It never hurts to try something new."

"I see." I took another sip. "How long has this place been open?"

She thought for a few seconds. "A little over a month."

"Oh, that explains why I didn't know about it."

She grimaced. "Where do you live—in Idaho? Everyone knows about *this* place."

I was a bit self-conscious. "Well, I was in the hospital for a while."

"Oh, I'm sorry." She moved away a little just in case I had something contagious.

I smiled. "I was in an accident."

"Car?" she asked.

"No, gun," I said nonchalantly. "I was in a coma for a couple weeks. Yada, yada, yada."

"Damn," she shrieked. "You all right?"

"Yeah, I'm fine. Just having some problems remembering some stuff from my past, but I'm okay." I came clean. "This is my first time out since it happened."

She seemed concerned. "And here I go fixing you the strong shit."

"Child, please." I waved her off. "Thanks for fixing me the strong shit; my best friend is staying with me until Monday, and if you didn't fix me something, I was bound to strangle her when I got home." I giggled.

For the next hour, in between the other patrons, we talked, laughed, and in that space of time I had two more Dykes & Dildos, and I had enough liquid courage in me to ask for it by name. She returned to me with another tall glass. "Whoa," I slurred. "I wasn't ready for another one yet."

"Well, the gentleman over there sure thought you were."

"What?"

Without looking at him, she said, "The older man at the end of the bar in the taupe three-button Donna Karan suit, Cartier timepiece, puffin' on a Camacho Liberty thought you needed another drink."

I glanced down at the end of the bar and he wasn't even looking my way. He was older but not old, and could go for good-looking on the right day and in the right lighting. Brotha was clean, though, and very sharp. He must've felt me looking at him because he turned and smiled but just turned away again. "Who is he?"

"This is his first time here," she said, "but I think he does some type of business with the managers." She winked at me. "You got a big fish on your line. You gonna wheel it in?"

"Please, I'm not going over there." I almost rolled my eyes.

"So you're not one of *those* girls, huh?"

"What girls?"

"Honey, I've seen broads give their souls to men in return for a six-dollar drink."

I giggled. "Maybe if I had a soul."

With her arms akimbo she asked, "Now, why would you say a thing like that?"

"I don't know." I shrugged my shoulders. "Since this memory-loss thing, I've been feeling nonexistent." I brought my glass to my mouth. "I don't know the reason why my boyfriend and I aren't together, my brother's number is disconnected, I don't know how to reach him, and a good girlfriend of mine still hasn't called." I paused. "Things just aren't adding up and I'm not remembering things fast enough."

"Fast enough for who?"

"Me!"

"Don't be in such a hurry." She started wiping down the bar. "Someone once said, 'One of the great disadvantages of hurrying is that it takes such a long time,' and I agree!" She sighed. "You don't know what you're trying hard to remember, they could be things that you need to forget." She smirked. "I don't know about you, but there are things about my life that I'd pay to forget." A coworker walked over to her and whispered something in her ear and she snickered. "I'll be back."

I looked behind me and noticed that the crowd had grown significantly. All of the seats at every bar were taken and the makeshift bedrooms were bursting at the seams with people drinking, laughing, talking, and even dancing. There were only men sitting in the anal section and they were . . . talking to one another. I put two and two together and determined that they were gay.

"It's a shame that I had to come all the way here just to see you," I heard in my ear, and turned quickly to see Craig, my new next-door neighbor, commandeering the stool next to me.

"Hey you!" I smiled at him.

"You live right next door and I can barely catch a glimpse of you."

Well, we can change that, I thought as I looked him up and down. "I'm still in recovery mode. I don't get out much."

His perfectly aligned teeth formed a cunning grin. "Whatcha drinkin'?"

I blushed and just burst out laughing. "I can't tell you." I handed him the drink menu and waited for his expression to change, and it did. He was so handsome. How can a man as fine as Craig find time to go out? He should be knee-deep in pussy at all times. "So which one of these sins are you partaking in?"

"Dykes and Dildos."

Craig winked. "Well, I hope that's just a drink to you. I would hate to have you go to waste."

Oh, you nasty, nasty boy. I stared at his lips and imagined them on my lips . . . that would be the ones with no lipstick. "Yeah, it's just a drink."

"I think I'll give it a try too." Craig waved over the temporary bartender. "Would you like another?"

All of the arrows pointed to the word *no*. "Yes, thank you."

Craig and I spent the next thirty minutes conversing over our drinks and then, with "I see you have company," my bartender friend returned.

"Yes," I said. "This is Craig, he just moved into my building."

"Hi, I'm Sydney." She held out her hand to Craig as I learned her name for the first time. At least I think it was the first time, my memory was fading, and it had nothing to do with anything medical . . . I was drunk.

"Awesome drink," Craig said.

"Thanks." She looked at me. "You need anything, babygirl?"

I could feel my head swinging. "Girl, I don't need anything, nothing, nada."

She smiled. "Are you okay?"

"I mean, yeah, but, man . . ." I laughed. "Damn!"

Her smile went away. "How many more of these did you have?" I couldn't say a word, I let my three fingers do the talking. She looked at Craig and then back at me. "How are you gettin' home?"

That was the last thing I remembered of Erogenous Zone. But even with my eyes closed, I still recognized that I was only in my panties and bra, and in a bed. I rolled over and bumped into something, something I wasn't used to having in *my* bed: a person. My eyes sprang open to find darkness, but it was *just* bright enough for me to know that I wasn't in my bedroom.

My mouth was tingling from the taste of Listerine and I couldn't tell whoever it was that I had done the unthinkable with. Instead I stared up at the ceiling and tried hard to recall something, anything, or anyone. As I rolled over to exit the bed I felt movement and then a dim light clicked on. "Are you all right?"

"Yeah." I looked over my shoulder and looked into a smiling face.

"Do you have to throw up again?"

"*Again?*" I asked. "I threw up?"

Sydney giggled. "For an hour straight."

I glanced at her clock: 5:37. When did we get here? I thought. Where are we? I rolled onto my back and asked reluctantly. "What happened?"

"We're in Miami Lakes at my apartment, we got here a little after one." Her warm body brushed mine as she rolled onto her side to face me; I quickly moved away an inch.

With her head now perched up on her hand she said, "You were gone, girl. I'm talkin' fallin'-on-your-ass drunk. That Craig guy said that he would take you home, but you kept giving me these looks like that wasn't what you wanted." She continued: "I asked to leave work early when I heard that you were in the ladies' room calling Earl." She giggled. "So I had my homeboy drive your car here behind me and you in my car, with me."

"Thank you so much." I was grateful, but uncomfortable as hell being seminaked and in *bed* with a *chick*. "Where are my clothes?"

"There was vomit on everything you had on, they're in the dryer now." She looked at the clock. "They should be done."

"I'm glad that I don't remember anything because I'm embarrassed just imagining what I did."

"Nothing to be embarrassed about," Sydney said. "It happens to the best of us."

"Ever happened to you?"

"Hell no." She laughed.

"Thanks a lot."

"Nah"—she lowered her voice—"I couldn't let you go home with Craig—"

I interrupted her. "He lives one door down from me, I would've been all right."

"Yeah"—she spoke closer to my ear—"but he just wanted to fuck you."

I thought about the sexual positions that Craig's strong arms could probably hold me in and shuddered. "What's wrong with that?" I chuckled.

Sydney moved herself uncomfortably close to me. "Everything." Before the *i-n-g* was completely pronounced, her lips touched mine. Her contact was slow yet aggressive. Gentle enough not to scare me off, but tough enough to insist that I not stop her. She parted my lips with her tongue, then wiggled it past my teeth and into my mouth. Soon my tongue pushed against hers in opposition, but my defiance was breached by the soft stroke of her hand as it rushed to my cheek and slid down to my shoulder.

At first I thought, *She's* fuckin' kissing me. And then, *She's* really kissing me. However, with her tongue in my mouth, I exhaled and I welcomed it with nervous suction. I pulled her into me . . . and I wanted to. I thought, I'm kissing *her*, and I breathed out again. I'm *really* kissing her.

Our lips were locked for about two minutes before reality hit. I've done some wild shit in my day, but never this . . . not the kid. "Hold up," I managed to squeeze out.

"What's wrong?" she asked like this was an ordinary run-of-the-mill operation.

Suddenly I felt like Ellen DeGeneres, very gay. "Wow." I looked away from her with wide eyes that said it all. "That was so *not* cool."

"I'm sorry." She lay back on the bed. "I thought maybe you . . ." She paused.

I still couldn't look her way. "You thought maybe I what?"

"I thought that you . . ." she continued, "wanted to."

I almost laughed. "What would make you think that?"

"You were coming on to me earlier."

"What?" I said with too much attitude. "When?"

"The things you were saying and doing in the car." She seemed embarrassed. "And you were groping me before you went to sleep."

"Groping you?" I couldn't believe any of this. "What?"

"Look, it's no big deal." She tried to smile it off.

"No." I was serious and curious. "Where did I touch you?"

"You grabbed my breasts and pinched my nipples. And in the car you tried rubbing between my legs," she said. "But I guess I should've known that you were drunk."

I didn't even want to remember me doing something like that. However, I didn't believe that I did something like that. "Yeah, I had to have been drunk to do something like that because I am strictly dickly." I tried laughing it off. For the next minute we lay side by side just as quiet as can be. "I think I better get going." I sat up.

"Oh yeah?"

I lied. "Yeah, I have be somewhere at nine."

With no hesitation she rolled the covers off of her and in a tight pink T-shirt and black lace boy-shorts panties she marched out of the room and returned with my clothes and somewhat of a smile. "Here you go, they're all dry."

Why did I feel like I was being kicked out? "Thanks." I got my clothes, found the bathroom down the hall, and got dressed. "Well . . ." I walked back into her room to find her slipping on some blue jeans. "I'm about to get out of here."

"I'll walk you down and show you to your car."

"Thanks." I tried not to look at her. "Thanks so much for looking out for me."

"You don't have to thank me. It's what I wanted to do." She stepped into some slippers. "I didn't want something bad to happen to you."

We walked to the elevator and then out of the complex and to my car. Thank God she accompanied me, because I would've never found Nookie in the sea of vehicles that seemed to go on for miles. "Well, you have a nice day." I didn't know how to end it, so I went for a handshake.

She smiled. "We don't have to be all weird about it." She didn't shake my hand; instead she quickly hugged me. "Drive safely, girl." She waved me off, turned her back, and walked away.

All the way home, a thirty-minute drive, I was lost in confusion. Child, please. I thought of what Sydney said I did. Whatever.

"So how did it go?" Nat raced into my room with me still in the fetal position under two blankets. "Must've gone very well, you didn't get in until seven."

I checked the caller ID when I first got in; Tremel hadn't called, so I was good to go. "It was all right."

"Just *all right*?" She laughed. "It's three in the afternoon and you're still asleep. I'd say that it was a little more than all right."

"How did things go with the photographer?" I changed the subject.

"Those pictures are going to be hot." She and Nick had taken engagement pictures, both dressed in white linen, at sunrise on the beach. "It was beautiful out there."

"I can't wait to see them."

She sat down on the bed and pulled the covers off of my head. "I'm out of here in two days, do you think I should st—"

"*O freedom,*" I sang the old Negro spiritual sarcastically. "*O freedom, o freedom over me.*" We both laughed. "*And before I be a slave, I'll be buried in my grave, and go home to my Lord and be free.*"

"All right, little slave girl, I guess you don't have a problem with me leaving on Monday."

"*At all,*" I joked. "Nah, I'll miss you, but, Nat, we just can't live together." I added, "Shit, if you continue to live here, you have to have at least one of two things."

"What?" She was curious.

"Money or a big dick."

She thought. "I have money," she finally said.

"Who said that that was most important of the two?" I joked.

Mayhem Monday came and Nat left. It was sad to see her go, but I truly needed to feel independent again. Tuesday was terrific; Wednesday I was like whoa, and then on that tempting Thursday night my life felt like it was getting back to normal . . . until the telephone rang. "Hello." I answered.

"This is a collect call from an inmate at the Miami-Dade County Federal Prison." The recording paused. "This call is from—" Then I heard his voice. "Yo, this Damian." The automated system kicked in again. "This call is three ninety-nine for the first minute and twenty cents per minute thereafter. To accept this call press five now; to reject this call please press one."

"Oh my God," I actually said into the phone, and listened to the entire message again before pressing five.

"Hello!" Damian's sexy, raspy voice spoke to me.

I was trembling as my mouth moved "hi," but the word never made it to my voice box.

"Hello?" he said again.

"Hey," I said in a breath.

Then there was unexpected silence. "How you doin', ma?"

"Good," I whispered like a tamed child.

"Damn, it's good to hear your voice." He exhaled heavily and with a crazy laugh. "I can't believe that you finally accepted my call."

"I never got a call from you." Then I remembered Nat. "Oh, it was probably—"

He rudely interrupted. "I called every day. All the calls were rejected . . . but whatever, man." He stuttered the same question again. "How you doin', Sarai?"

"I'm doing fine." I closed my eyes and allowed his voice to melt all over me. I wanted him next to me, by me, in me. I choked up, but held on to my tears. "How are *you*?"

"Livin'," he answered guardedly, like he was surprised that I even cared. "Look, ma, I just needed to hear your voice." He continued: "I had to know that you were all right."

"I'm fine." I decided not to beat around the bush . . . I had to know. "Baby, what happened to us? What happened between us? I don't remember anything, since the robbery I—"

"Robbery?" He stopped me. "What robbery?"

"The bank robbery, when I was shot," I clarified. "Maybe you didn't know about it, but I got out of the hospital a little over a week ago and have lost all memory of the last few months." I spilled my guts. "I don't even remember why we're not together, or why in the hell you're in jail." The tears finally rolled down my cheeks. "I miss you and nobody's telling me shit."

"Fuck," he said under his breath. "Sarai, don't . . ."

"Don't what?" I asked.

"Don't miss *me*," he said. "You don't want to miss me."

"Damian, don't say that, I need to know—" *Click* . . . the phone line went dead. "Hello?" I looked at my phone; the red light indicated that the line was still open. "Hello?" Soon the automated operator informed me, "If you'd like to make a call, please hang up and try again . . ." I still had a million and two unanswered questions.

"Damn, what happened?" I waited by the phone for him to call back. However, come midnight, I put those hopes to rest and crawled into bed.

The next morning, Friday, I woke up from a bad dream, at least I thought it was a dream until I realized that my eyes had been wide open and I had been staring up at the ceiling for I don't know how long. Damian's phone call had triggered a flash flood of memories: me driving back from Orlando unexpectedly, phone sex, walking into the apartment, the light switch, India impaling her pussy with Damian's dick, screaming, fighting, sucking, fucking . . . I dialed Nat's number. "Hello," she answered. I couldn't say a word, she heard me sobbing uncontrollably. "What's wrong? Hello? Sarai, are you all right?"

"No."

"What's wrong?" she asked.

I whimpered. "Did I walk in on Damian having sex with India?"

She sighed. "Sarai, take a deep breath, it's going to be okay."

"Answer me."

"I'll be right over."

"Nat," I yelled, but quickly realized that it wasn't supposed to be at her, so I fought to speak calmly. "I don't need you to come over, all I need is an answer."

She sighed again. "Yeah, Sarai, but that—"

"Thank you," I whispered, and hung up.

As though it happened yesterday, I remembered him slapping me, and when I asked him to leave and began putting up a fight, he held a gun to my head and said, *"I'll be out of here in ten minutes, but if you say another goddamn word, I'll be out in twenty and I'll be dragging your wannabe bad ass behind me in a garbage bag."* Right after that, with his nine-millimeter still cocked at my temple, he forced me to suck his dick, a dick still saturated with the taste and smell of a woman I used to call my girl, my dawg . . . my friend.

"Oh, this is why I shouldn't *miss* you?" I screamed at the walls for keeping such a filthy secret from me. "This is why I shouldn't miss you, huh, you bitch? This is why you hung up, you fuckin' coward?"

Since I couldn't call the prison and demand to speak with the inmate who should win the bitch-of-the-year award, I did the next best thing.

"Hello."

"So I guess I know why your saddity ass never made it to the hospital."

"It's six in the goddamn morning." She sounded annoyed. "Are you serious?"

"Oh, I'm dead serious, bitch," I spat at her.

"If I *had* made it to the hospital, your sorry ass would've been faded to black." India spoke vengefully.

"I try not to use the word *hate*, but, India, I fuckin' hate you. Words cannot express the things I wish would happen to you."

"All of this over some dick?" She continued nonchalantly: "Haven't we been through this shit already, Sarai?"

"Fuck what we've done before," I said. "I'm ready to do it again."

"No, fuck doing it again, you do it by your damn self. I don't want the trifling muthafucka." Then she added, "And after what he did to you, why do *you* even care?"

"Fuck what he did, what about what you did to me?"

This sick bitch found it within her to giggle . . . *giggle.* "Shouldn't you be somewhere on your knees working for a muthafuckin' dollar?" She slammed the phone down. You better believe that I tried to call back, but I got a busy signal for over an hour . . . and yes, I tried to call . . . for over an hour. So when the phone rang again I assumed that it was her. I answered but didn't say anything.

"Hello?" It wasn't India; it was a woman whose voice I had heard somewhere before. "Helloooo?"

"Hello," I answered

She sounded like the woman who had answered Tremel's phone. "May I speak with Sarai?"

I sat up in my bed, ready to confront *this* heifer too. "This is Sarai."

She took me by surprise. "Hey, this is Sydney."

"Hey." Suddenly my body was tingling from the embarrassment of our night together again.

"What's up?" She sounded chipper. "How are you?"

"I'm good." I thought about our kiss for six days, but had become comfortable with the notion of it being just another drunken mistake . . . until now. This was weird. "How are *you*?"

"I took a test in my trig class last night and feel like a new woman since I got that out of the way." Happiness rang through in her voice. "Anyways, are you missing an earring?"

"Yes," I sighed as the conversation took a turn toward what two straight women should be talking about. "Do you have it?"

"Found it under my bed on Monday." Then she specified: "A small gold hoop with a little diamond, right?"

"Yeah, that's it. I assumed that it got mixed up in my friend Nat's stuff and expected her to be calling about it."

Sydney's voice was deep, breathy, sensual, and there was a twinge of sex in every word she spoke. "I would've called you before, but I've been studying like crazy."

"No problem." It was killing me, so I had to say, "I didn't realize that I gave you my number."

"Well, I'm used to you not remembering things that you do, but at least this time you might believe that you did it," she said jokingly.

"Alcohol is a powerful thing." I put her on alert.

She seemed to reduce her tone to a whisper. "And just when I thought that I met a girl who could handle her liquor."

"Oh, I can handle my liquor."

"Yeah? But who's gonna handle you?" she asked, but quickly tracked back to her having my phone number. "Don't worry, I'm not into stalking people, I'm only calling because I'm getting off and know that you live downtown, so I can swing by and drop the earring off if you like."

"That'd be great." I paid over $600 for those earrings a few years back, and it does me no good to have just one. "Thanks." I gave her directions to my building, straightened up around the apartment, and since it wasn't even eight o'clock in the morning yet, I just washed my face and private areas, kept on my black lace teddy, but slipped my purple silk robe over it, tying the belt tightly around my waist.

In fifteen minutes the phone rang again. "Hello."

"Hello, Miss Emery?"

"Yes."

"Hi, this is Kathy from the front office, how are you?"

"I'm doing fine." How nice of them to call to check on me. "My memory isn't what it should be, but all in all, I am—"

She cut in. "Okay, we need to know when to expect payment." She paused. "We know of your hospitalization, so we were lenient with your friends, but you're behind"—she counted—"one, two, three . . . you're behind three months now; with late fees you now owe six thousand two hundred and fourteen dollars."

"Oh shit," I said under my breath. I had forgotten how high my damn rent was. Thank God I had some money in the bank. Fuck paying the hospital bills, I need a roof over my head. "I am so sorry, Kathy, I can bring it down later today after I come from the bank."

"Well, because it's so late, you're going to need to mail a money order or cashier check directly to—" My line beeped . . . it was Syndey again.

"Kathy, can you hold?"

"Excuse me?" She seemed perturbed.

I asked her again. "May I ask you to hold?"

"Sure," she said sarcastically.

I clicked over. "Syd?"

"Yeah," she answered. "I'm here, but do you mind if I just leave it at the security booth?"

"Umm." Something inside of me died when I said those words. "Yeah, you can leave it there." Suddenly I recalled the moment Sydney's lips first touched mine. Now that I could slow down the tape, I realized that at that very instant my heart accelerated, I inhaled, and I closed my eyes. *I closed my eyes!* Now, that's something I don't do when I'm out with an ugly man that swoops down unexpectedly, or with a man that has talked my ear off about himself all night, or with dudes with bad breath, gold teeth, acne, etc. . . . I keep my eyes open so that they can get the cheek or even worse . . . the back of my hand. However, if an attractive man, a man with a killer body, a man I can tell is working with a mother lode of sausage, a man who makes me smile and feel comfortable . . . when a man that I like moves in for a kiss, my heartbeat accelerates, I inhale, and then . . . I close my eyes. Bottom line, I wanted to see Sydney and that was freaking me the fuck out. "You can leave it with security," I said a second time, to try to convince myself that it was right.

"Yeah, 'cause I know that it's still early and I caught you by surprise," she said.

I lied. "Well, I did brew coffee for us, though."

Sydney laughed. "I'm not a coffee drinker."

I felt like I had to see her, just to know if I was just panicking because I allowed her lips to touch mine too long or whether there was something else tormenting me. "You know what, I'll come down and get it from you, because I wouldn't want my earring to be missing when I go to claim it later." I added another lie: "That happened to someone who lives here that I know."

"All right, don't worry, I'll just bring it up," she said, and immediately I found myself in the mirror combing my hair into as neat of a ponytail as I could. Why? What in the hell was going on with me? I clicked over and Kathy was gone.

When Sydney knocked on my door my emotions took me on a wild outing; I was happy, nervous, sad, scared, excited, disappointed, mad, but when I opened the door and saw Miss Sydney dressed for work in a tight-fitting black-and-red Erogenous Zone V-neck tee, black miniskirt, and top-of-the-calf-high black boots, I'm sure that my smile said how I was truly feeling. "Hey!"

"Hey, girlie." She reached her hand toward me for what I thought was a go for my robe, but she was extending my earring. "Here you go."

"Thanks so much." The sight of her made it easier for me to believe that I had actually groped her last Friday night. Suddenly I wished I could remember it. Why? Let's just say that it was extremely difficult for me to look away from Sydney's chest. Her breasts were about as large as mine, her dime-size nipples were hard and protruding through the soft cotton shirt. And suddenly I found myself wondering just how it would feel to run the palm of my hands over them. "Would you like to come in?" I asked.

"Nah," she said, and took a step back. "I've worked all night. I better get going. I'm dead tired."

Was she fuckin' serious? She was acting like she hadn't kissed me just last week. *Damn,* was I serious? Maybe she kissed me because *I* had come on to her . . . but she didn't have to kiss me. Plus, she had my number all this time and never called until now. If I had her number, would I have called her? More than likely, so maybe it was me that was the freak . . . and maybe she hadn't even thought about me. I needed to know, my right hand moved to pull the string on my robe. My plan was to untie it, and let her see me in my lace teddy with no bra or underwear, just pussy and tits, it was her invitation to finish what we had started, but before I could pull the belt to untie my robe, Craig's door swung open and my hands fell to my sides.

"Wow, look who's in the neighborhood," he said. "Good morning, ladies."

"Good morning." We both looked at him.

"Sarai, I have a letter of yours that was mistakenly put in my mailbox," he said. "I'm in a rush to get to school now, so I'll give it to you when I get back. Is that okay?"

"That's cool." I tried to get my mind right. "But if it's a bill, you can just keep it."

"Yeah, but payback is a mutha." He winked and laughed as he pressed the elevator button. "Did you watch the news this morning?"

"No," I said. I couldn't wait for him to leave, and that was rare because normally I couldn't see enough of him.

His mouth kept going. "There was a shoot-out about three blocks from here, a six-year-old girl was killed in the cross fire." He shook his head. "Muthafuckin' stupid-ass punks with nothing to do."

Ding. The elevator arrived and the doors opened.

"I better catch that," Sydney said, and turned away from me before I could say a word, pull the string, or grab her hand . . . anything. "Hold the door for me, please," she yelled to Craig. As she entered the elevator I saw him study her thick brown thighs and then her haughty chest. When the doors slid closed my untamed imagination left me feeling like I was in competition with Craig.

Because of what I did next I had to look up the word *insanity* on dictionary.com, where it is defined as "Unsoundness of mind sufficient in the judgment of a civil court to render a person unfit to maintain a contractual or other legal relationship or to warrant commitment to a mental health facility." It might as well have said "Sarai Emery," because ten minutes after Sydney boarded the elevator, I took a shower, got dressed, hopped in my Expedition, and drove to Miami Lakes and then to Sydney's apartment . . . this was crazy . . . I considered myself in-fuckin'-sane . . . insane.

She answered the door in a green T-shirt with tiredness written all over her face, rubbing her eyes. "What happened?" She was shocked. "What are you doing here?"

I asked her, "Did you smell coffee in my apartment?"

"What?" she asked, as though she thought she heard the wrong thing.

I crossed the threshold. "Did you smell the scent of coffee in my apartment?"

"No, I don't think so." She paused. "Why?"

"Because when I was on the phone with you, I said that I had brewed coffee for us."

She recalled. "Yeah, and I said that I didn't drink coffee."

"Sydney, I ran out of coffee about a week ago," I confessed. "I'm not even that big of a coffee drinker."

"I don't get it."

"I just wanted to see you, I just wanted you to come up," I admitted.

I took a deep breath and stepped toward her; she didn't move away. My heart was beating fast, I inhaled, closed my eyes, and moved in on her, but she moved away as she pulled me into her apartment, closed the door, and then walked me to the back of it. With our breasts pressed up against each other she said, "Will you be too drunk to remember if I kissed you?"

"I haven't had a drink all week." I stared at her lips.

Her hands touched my waist. "Would you like to kiss me?"

"Yes." Excitement moved all over my body. She inched closer and closer, until I could feel her breath on my lips. Her hands moved upward to the sides of my breasts and my breathing became heavy. "I want to kiss you so bad."

"Then do it." She smiled.

I didn't have to lean and neither did she. Somehow our lips connected and this time I didn't waste time trying to analyze why I was kissing a woman. I just allowed myself to kiss and be kissed like never before . . . it just so happened to be by a woman.

I pulled her tongue into my mouth with such vigor that I could taste the watermelon candy that she ate about an hour before. My hands, no longer timid, made their way to her back and slid down, but weren't bold enough to venture to her plump ass. She tenderly but passionately took in my lips and soon teased them with her tongue, licking me, tugging at me, taunting me. She made it known that she wanted me elsewhere and my already shivering body told her to take me.

We made it to her bedroom, on the same bed where she could've more than likely devoured me before had she tried a little harder for two minutes last week. With me on my back, Sydney crawled atop me and it was then that I finally took in just how pretty she was. Her maplewood-brown complexion, slanted eyes the color of coffee with three spoonfuls of cream, sharp nose that smoothed out at the end, and provocative pouting lips. Dare I say it, she was sexy as hell. "I've never . . ." I decided to shut up.

"You've never what?" she asked.

"I've never done anything like . . ."

"This?" She finished my statement with a question.

"Yeah," I whispered, but put my hands on her back and pulled her down toward me. We shared another long heated kiss, and with both of her legs bent on either side of me, it was more sexual that sensual. I could almost feel her heat on my thighs. Still pecking at my lips, she said, *"Je te montrerai comment on le fait."*

My eyebrows moved toward each other in confusion. "What was that?"

She blushed. "Sorry, sometimes my French gets away from me."

"Oui, mademoiselle." Those were two of about five French words I knew. "What did all of that mean?"

"I said, 'I'll show you what to do.'" She looked down on me. "But with a body like yours, you can't go wrong."

"Really?"

"Really." She pecked at me over and over again. "Really."

Before long, I was lying there in just my panties and bra, and she in the same. Her hands moved down to my bra, where she caressed my breasts with her hands and pinched my nipples between the middle of her fingers until I verbalized my satisfaction while still sucking on her lips. "Oh shit," I moaned.

Sydney pulled my bra down and my breasts popped out. *"Beaux seins."* Her speaking French, kissing me fervently, fondling my nipples, and grinding into me below had me at my limit. *"Vous êtes si sexy."*

I couldn't help it anymore; my pussy was drenched, as if there was a dick waiting. I unhooked her bra, and for the first time ever, I was staring at tits that weren't mine. She stared down into my face to see if I would back down. She whispered, *"Léchez mes memelons."*

I didn't have to have a degree in French to know that she wanted the warmth and wetness of my mouth on her nipples. I reached out and squeezed her jelly-soft round flesh between my fingers. Immediately her eyes clenched and her bottom lip folded in. I touched one of her nipples with my tongue, and by just sucking her nipples, Sydney moaned like the biggest dick of all was in the room. I took her entire nipple in and ended with my teeth grazing the very edge of it when I was done. She was beautiful, everything and anything about her had to be good, smell good, feel good, and taste good, and I knew that soon I'd taste her.

"Say '*mange ma chatte*,' Sarai."

"Huh?"

She repeated, "*Mange ma chatte.*"

"What does it mean?" I had to know.

"It means"—she smiled—"eat my pussy."

"Is that what you want to do?" I asked.

"That's what I want you to *tell* me to do."

I giggled. "Say it again, slower this time."

She pecked my lips between each word. "*Mange . . . ma . . . chatte.*"

"*Mange ma chatte.*" There was something extra sexy about asking her to do it, especially in another language. "*Mange ma chatte, mademoiselle.*"

Sydney slowly removed my panties; I was freshly shaven and the feel of her warm hands on my slick surface made more juice trickle. She was already soothing every inch of me. "Oooh, Sydney."

"*Appelle-moi Syd.*" She smiled at me. "Call me Syd." She knelt down between my thighs without ever losing eye contact with me, and the moment her mouth—yes, her mouth . . . not just her tongue, the moment her mouth made contact with my raw pulsating flesh, I knew what John Legend meant when he sang about walking on "Cloud Nine."

Syd pushed her tongue up under my clit, taunting it in an upward motion, and soon in small circles. "Damn," I exhaled, and soon I gave way to pleasure by grinding my lower body into her mouth to show my gratitude. She sucked hard on my switch but still stirred her tongue around and around it.

Say what you like, but many men have attempted the same thing and failed miserably, too busy trying to stay hard instead of focusing on what my needs were. Some men think that eating pussy simply means "apply spit." Syd neglected no part of the vehicle of my femininity.

Yes, I consider my pussy a vehicle because it possesses the abil-

ity to take me places and the driver has to have a WTF license . . .
the ability to make me ask myself, *What the fuck?* The driver of my
automobile has to know how to make sharp turns sometimes with
just one finger on the steering wheel. They must know that it's not
the length of the journey but the quality of the ride that matters. Because you can drive me across country for an hour . . . that doesn't
mean that I wasn't thinking *are we there yet?* the entire time.

Syd had her WTF license and even knew how to throw my shit
in reverse. Not only was she a driver, she was also a mechanic, she
opened up my hood, changed my spark plugs, battery, and my overheated radiator . . . soon I was spewing oil and she was loving it. Her
head shook vigorously from side to side with her hardened tongue
whipping across my moistened throbbing flesh. "Shit," I screamed,
and shuddered.

Syd asked, "You like it?"

"Yeah," I panted. "Hell yeah."

"Say, '*Je l'aime.*'"

I had no clue what it meant, but I said it like a Frenchman. "*Je
l'aime.*"

"That's right." She continued to sample my goods. "Tell me you
like it, say it again."

"*Je l'aime, Syd.*" Before I could say it again, her fingers were inside
of me and her tongue was having a seizure on my pussy. I screamed,
moaned, and felt my body jerking out of control, then my juices
burst within and slid out of me and onto her fingers and to her waiting lips.

Sydney worked her way back up to my face and for some reason it
was now okay to ask a question I could never build up the nerve to
ask anyone . . . even if the answer was blatant: "Are you gay?"

She smirked down at me. "I just do as I please."

I needed clarification. "So you're bi?"

"I consider myself limitless." She moved closer to me, and with
no hesitation I drew her saturated lips into my mouth, and within
minutes I was between her thighs, where I *really* took her *lips* into
my mouth.

"The existence of forgetting has never been proved: We only know that some things don't come to mind when we want them."
—Friedrich Nietzsche

Tremel

WITHDRAWAL SLIP #4
ENDING BALANCE: $152.29

I've never tasted anything like that before." I threw down my fork in defeat . . . I was full of chicken breast stuffed with grilled shrimp and homemade dressing. Emeril Lagasse has nothing on Charlize; the girl can burn. She cooks so well that she had me eating things that my momma couldn't pay me to eat as a child. "All I can say is if you keep cooking like that, you'll never be lonely. You can get and keep any man."

She laughed. "Well, I don't know about that. I have to get one first."

"Damn, I thought you had that one guy in the bag," I joked. "I thought you were in the end zone, thought it was a touchdown."

"Please." She rolled her eyes. "He has to throw the ball first."

"Oh, okay." I never asked her about her date last Friday night for two reasons. One, I tried to kiss her just seconds before the guy arrived and she stopped me. Two, because she had an attitude with the strength of a category-five hurricane the entire next day. I figured that it was because of either him or me, so I decided that her Friday night was her business.

Since the "almost" kiss, we've reverted to being roommates with no problems. There has been no talk of it, no strange looks, smiles, or anything. And that probably had a lot to do with the fact that we've cut back on our alcohol intake during dinnertime. Neither of us wanted to end up doing or saying anything dumb. I still cannot believe that I tried her like that . . . but being angry with Sarai had a lot to do with it.

I haven't called Sarai. There is no use; I can't argue with her about something that she won't even remember, and I can't allow myself to get close to her again, because when she does remember, my intentions are for us to go toe-to-toe. Until then, she doesn't even know what she's missing. However, I still can't sleep without thoughts of her having sex with Julian dancing in my head.

"Have you heard from your ex?" Charlize asked with a smirk.

"Huh?"

She reminded me. "That's who you said the girl on the phone was."

"Oh," I recalled. "Nah, she won't call and I won't be calling her."

"So what's up with all of that?"

"You know." I remained calm this time. "It's nothing, nothing that even needs to be discussed." I fastened my beware-of-drama seat belt before I continued. "What's up with you and Mr. Friday Night?"

"Mr. Friday Night?" She laughed. "Same ol' same ol'. Like I said, he's not throwing the ball to me."

"What do you mean?" I asked.

"I don't know." She looked away. "He's dealing with a lot, and it seems like until the situation clears, he won't be a hundred percent emotionally free."

Sounds like bullshit to me . . . but who am I? "Who is this dude?" I asked.

"We've been seeing each other for about seven months." Charlize reached for her purse and pulled out her wallet.

"Damn, you gonna pay me not to talk about this brotha?" I joked. "Is he *that* bad?"

"No, you idiot, I'm showing you a picture." Her laugh was infectious. "His name is Trent, but I call him Frank."

"Frank? Trent?" The names sounded nothing alike, so I had to ask. "Why do you call him Frank?"

"He's in the army." She blushed. "I guess everyone calls him Franklin, but I don't take orders too well, so I call him Frank." The guy in the picture was standing next to a dark blue Lincoln Navigator. I was peepin' the truck; it was bad, definitely fiercer than the corny joker in fatigues was. He looked close to forty. Brown complexion, low-cut black hair, serious face, but he didn't look tough . . . dude didn't look hard enough to be a private, if you asked me. "He's stationed at Patrick Air Force Base—"

"Isn't that in Cocoa Beach?" I asked.

She sighed. "Yeah."

"That's three or four hours away, how did you meet him?"

She seemed embarrassed. "Online." She tried to vindicate herself. "He comes to Miami at least twice a month, though."

"Are you happy?"

"Yeah, but when his divorce is final I'll be ecstatic." She looked down at her plate. "She's taking him through hell and the highest water ever."

"Any kids?"

"Three kids, ages eight, four, and two," she said. "They were married for seven years, but when he found out that the two-year-old wasn't his, he filed for divorce."

"Sounds like a *Maury Povich* episode." I laughed.

She got up to start the dishes. "Now *she* has a girlfriend—"

"She has a *girl*friend?" I thought I was hearing things.

"Yes, a girlfriend," Charlize clarified. "She's gay and now wants half of everything."

"Oh, this shit sounds more like *Jerry Springer* now."

I cleared the table and sat on the counter to keep her company with chitchat until she was done with the dishes. Afterward, we took our conversation to the sofa, where we both agreed that one watermelon martini apiece was cool.

For the next hour, I learned whatever she knew about Trent Franklin, but the difference in our knowledge was that she liked him and I didn't. It was something I saw in his story. No, I actually saw *through* his story. It was an unbelievably bizarre tale that seemed to cry out for someone to feel sorry for him . . . and *that* she did. I'm not calling him a liar, but as a man, I know how we embellish on certain negative things to cater to the female's soft spot.

Our conversation was sidelined by the phone ringing. She answered and then looked at me. "It's for you."

"Who is it?" I mouthed.

"I'm not playing that game," she whispered, and tossed me the cordless phone.

I took a deep breath. "Hello?"

"Hey, Mel," the female voice replied.

"Hey," I answered cautiously, not knowing who she was. "What's going on?"

She giggled. "This is Nat in case you don't recognize my voice."

"Oh, hey." I laughed. "I sure didn't know who you were."

She joked, "I should've pretended to be a bill collector and get some money out of you."

"All they ever get from me is the dial tone," I said. "How are you doing?"

"I'm hanging in there. These wedding plans are driving me mad." She paused. "The only thing that keeps me from taking the show to Vegas is because a few of my out-of-state family members have already bought plane tickets."

"I'm sure the day will turn out great." I continued: "Especially with me as a groomsman. I'll be straight out of *GQ* magazine."

"Yeah, I'm hoping that you and Sarai don't steal the show," Nat said.

"I don't think that you have to worry about that." If she only knew. "As good as you'll look, all eyes will be on you."

"Ahh, thank you," Nat cooed.

Right then Charlize stood up and whispered, "I'm going to bed." I nodded at her and took the call to my room.

"So, what's up?" I asked through the receiver, and waited on her to chew me up and spit me out about standing Sarai up last week.

"Well, I was calling because I think that it's time that we tell Sarai about Savion." Nat really sounded concerned. "She's worried about him and tries to call him. She even wrote to his address and the letter was returned. She's talking about flying to Atlanta."

"Fuck." The word slipped out. "Well, you can go ahead and tell her if you want."

"Excuse me?" Nat asked with much attitude. "I thought that *we* agreed to tell her together?"

"Yeah, I know, but—"

"But nothing." She raised her voice. "I need you for this one, Mel. Her brother, not just a brother, but her twin brother, is dead, and not just dead, he shot himself in the head. I cannot break news like that to her all by myself."

"Well, she's remembering a little more, so maybe she'll remember that he was sick and then it'll be easier to tell her."

"Yeah, but it's not like he died from the disease," Nat said. "Plus he's been dead for two months."

I tried to buy time. "Let's wait."

"No, I think that now would be a good time," she informed me. "Especially since you two are getting back on track."

"Is that what you call it?" I asked sarcastically.

"That's putting it lightly." She giggled. "Yeah! I would call coming home at seven in the morning after being with you on track if I ever did see a track."

"What?" I asked. "Seven in the morning? When?"

"Last Friday when you guys went out."

I paused and thought of lying but didn't. "We didn't go out last Friday night."

"Oops!" Nat was stunned. "Are you serious?"

I told Nat that I was strapped for cash and called and canceled our date. I didn't want to tell her what the real deal was. However, according to Nat, Sarai left the house claiming to be going out with me and came home after seven the next morning with a hangover and her shirt turned inside out.

"I'm sorry, Mel. I thought she was with you," Nat apologized. "Now I'm wondering who in the hell she was with, she—"

"Don't worry about it." I changed the subject. "Look, why don't we wait until after you come back from that cruise you're taking to tell her about Savion?" I wasn't ready to see Sarai just yet. "That gives us a couple more weeks."

"Umm." She thought for a while. "Okay. Yeah, we can do that."

After I said good-bye to Nat, my anger level elevated as my imagination ran wild with what Sarai could've been doing, and who with, until seven in the morning. For hours, I tried telling myself that I didn't care but realized how much I did care when I reached out for the phone. It was exactly 3:24 in the morning. I know this because I was staring at the clock, still not believing that I couldn't sleep. I needed to talk to her, but as my fingertip grazed the phone, it started ringing. I wanted it to be her calling, dealing with the same type of agony. So I picked up quickly so that it wouldn't wake up Charlize, but I was too late. "Hey, baby," Charlize whispered into the receiver from her room.

"Baby?" the already angry woman asked. "Who are you?"

"What?" Charlize stuttered. "Who is this?"

"You know Fire?" the woman asked.

"Fire?" Charlize sounded confused. "No, who *is* this?"

"This is Yolanda Franklin, and Trent Franklin, Fire, is my husband." She took a breath. "Do you know him?"

"Yeah." She was wide-awake now. "Why?"

"Why?" The woman assumed she already knew what was up . . . and so did I. "Are you fuckin' him?"

"Oh my God! Excuse me? This is a matter between the two of us." Charlize sounded like she was on a business call, and Trent's wife's voice was reminiscent of Lela Ali's right before the bell of the first round. "That's none of your business."

"The hell it ain't!" Yolanda screamed. "That is my husband, we have three kids—"

"Two." Charlize had the nerve to correct her. "You have *two* kids together. The third one is just yours."

"What?" the woman huffed. "We have three muthafuckin' kids and another one on the goddamn way."

"On the way?" Charlize repeated. "You're pregnant?"

"Three months, bitch."

My roommate was stunned. "I . . . I thought you were gay!"

"Gay? Gay my ass!" she screamed. "Where'd you get that from?"

"Frank." Charlize unraveled a bit. "He didn't mention you being pregnant." She thought out loud. "Three months? We've been together for seven months. Did you all get back together briefly or something?"

"No," Yolanda informed her, "we ain't never been apart, not for nine damn years."

"You're not getting a divorce?"

"I hadn't planned on it until tonight." She calmed a little. "What's your name?"

"Charlize."

"Ooooh, I see." Yolanda's voice cracked. "I saw your number over and over on his bill, but that slick fucka got you in his phone as Charles."

"Charles?" Fury finally seeped out of Charlize. "Fuckin' bastard! He told me that the two-year-old was not his and that he was divorcing you because of it *and* that you were gay now."

"That lyin' bitch," she said. "Where'd you meet him?"

"Online."

"I figured that," she said. "So when was the last time you seen him?"

"He was with me last Friday night," Charlize said. "But he left early Saturday morning because he said that you called with some drama."

Yolanda chuckled angrily. "He and his brother must be in this shit together. They told me that they were driving to Jacksonville to some football game."

"He was here. He drives from Cocoa Beach to spend the weekend with me at least once a month."

"Cocoa Beach?" Yolanda was confused. "What's up there?"

"That's where he . . . well . . . that's where you all live, right? On the base?"

"On the base?" Yolanda chuckled angrily. "Honey, we live in an apartment in Perrine." Perrine was four hours south of Cocoa Beach and thirty minutes from our place.

"Wait a second." Charlize tried to get the story right. "He's not stationed at Patrick Air Force Base?"

"Hell no, he ain't *stationed* nowhere. He's not even in the military."

Charlize needed to hear it again. "What did you say?"

I had heard enough and wanted to laugh, so I slowly hung up the phone and did just that. I wasn't laughing at either of the women. Their situation wasn't funny, but I was laughing at stupid-ass Trent, Franklin, Frank, Fire, Flame, or whatever else he liked to be called.

The next morning, as I left for work, Charlize was at the kitchen counter in her bathrobe. She looked like a different woman. Her brown sultry eyes were puffy and red, and her naturally pouting lips weren't pouting but frowning. She just stared at her mug of coffee. On Saturdays, she normally has clients showing up as early as seven; it was 9:30. "Hey!" I said as I grabbed my keys from the table.

"Hey." It was the weakest *hey* ever uttered by a human being.

"No clients today?" I asked.

"I'm not feeling well," she lied. "I called and canceled everyone."

"Anything I can do?" My left hand made its way to her back. "You need medicine or something?" What she really needed was a punching bag.

"Nawh, it's not that kind of sickness." She wouldn't look at me. "I'm all right."

As long as she wasn't telling, I wasn't asking. "You sure?"

"I'm sure." She forced a smile.

"Okay." I jingled my keys and began walking away. "I tell you what." The idea hit me. "How about I take you out tonight?" Her neck snapped in my direction and her eyes screamed, *I don't need any more bullshit in my life.* I smiled. "Not on a date or anything." I paused. "I wrote a piece last night and I wanna get back onstage at Vocalize. Maybe you can come and cheer me on, and the drinks will be on me." I laughed. "Say no if you want, but we've killed our liquor stash here and it's your time to buy." I paused. "I think I want some Dom Pérignon next week."

She managed to smile and then asked, "What time are we leaving?" She moved her head up and down. "I wrote a piece last night too. I think I need to get it out." Oh, I bet she did.

"I'll be home at about seven." I thought. "Let's leave here at eight."

"What should I wear?"

"Anything." I opened the door to leave. "But accessorize it with a smile." With that said, I was on my way to work. In between my deliveries, I wrote and memorized a short poem, the piece I lied about writing the night before.

The last three deliveries of the day were all ordered by one customer at the last minute. The first one was so far south that Mr. Jimenez called a florist down there to fill the order. The second delivery was only ten minutes away, and the last address seemed right down the street from me, so I told Mr. Jimenez to make it a great night and that I'd be seeing him on Monday.

I pulled up to the rust-colored duplex, grabbed the roses, and knocked on the door. I saw a little boy pull back the curtains. "Oooh, Momma, a man is out there with flowers."

"Jeffery, get down off of that sofa with your shoes on," the petite, young, sexy, dark chocolate-skinned woman said as she opened the door, still looking at her son. "You know better than that."

"Hi." I paused. "Misha Douglas?" I asked.

"That's me." She smiled.

"This is for you." I handed her the clipboard.

"I thought the flowers were for me"—she laughed and took the clipboard—"but I can put this to use too."

"Sorry." I was flustered. "I just need you to sign for them."

As she signed her name, she mumbled, "Fire done lost his damn mind if he thinks that that is going to change anything."

Call it coincidence, irony, or a twist of fate . . . call it something. "Excuse me?"

"Huh?" She looked at me strangely.

"I thought you said something."

"Nawh." She handed back the clipboard and grabbed the flowers. "I'm just talking to myself." She smiled. "It seems like I'm going to be doing that for a while."

I peeped into her shirt and got an eyeful of heaping mocha cleavage. "You shouldn't have to talk to yourself," I flirted. "I'm sure there are a lot of men willing to talk to *you*. Hell, I'm even willing to bet that I'll be here delivering flowers again when you find the right someone to talk to." I winked. "You have a great day, Miss Misha."

"You too." I bet she didn't realize that her mouth could still form a smile that big. " 'Bye."

I knew that she had said Fire. I went back to the truck, and sure enough, my last delivery was not just close to my address, it was my address. It was for Charlize Daniels! I opened the card. *I'm willing to explain. —Franklin.* Man, this guy was foul. Instead of giving Misha a double dose of roses, I tossed the card but decided to take the flowers to Charlize anyway. I wasn't going to pretend that they were from me . . . I would simply give them to her without a word spoken.

I pulled up to the house, and as I got the roses from the back of the van, a dark blue Lincoln Navigator parked behind me and lo and fuckin' behold I was staring at the dude from Charlize's picture. He hopped out and bolted toward me. "What up, man?" He did the head-nod thing. "I'm right on time. They're from me, I'll take them in."

"Oh yeah?" I asked.

"Yeah." He smiled, reaching for the flowers. "Give 'em here."

"Did you make your way to Misha's house too?"

"What?" Fire looked amazed. "What did you say?"

I stared at him. "I think you heard me."

"All right, delivery boy. You takin' this five-seventy-five-an-hour job too damn seriously," he said with his hand still out. "Gimme the goddamn flowers so I can go inside and handle my business."

"I got your delivery boy, bitch." I pushed the roses in his hands. "These are your flowers, but you ain't about to handle shit here."

"Who in the fuck do you think you are?" he asked.

"*I'm* handling shit inside this house." I noticed his army fatigues and boots. This bastard had issues. "And I dare you to bring your wannabe military ass back around here again."

He was at a loss for words. "Who the *fuck* are you?"

I reminded him. "I'm the delivery boy, remember?" I continued as I walked toward the house with my keys out: "I'm also the man of this muthafuckin' house."

He mumbled some nonsense, but quickly found himself inside his SUV and down the street.

Without mentioning what went down outside, I entered the house and got dressed for the night. We left at eight, as planned, and I could tell that just being out of the house was remedy enough for Charlize. She was dressed in a dark red pantsuit and heels, with hair that looked like black silk falling toward her shoulders. At Vocalize that night, she took the mike before I did. "Hey, Vocalize, this is my second time here. My name is C-Note." She forced a smile. "The piece I'm about to speak is called 'Canon in Me.'" She took a deep breath, her moon exploded, and the stars fell.

> "*My heart was a treble clef, but now my life has no music.*
> *My whole note, now a sixteenth of a sixteenth note.*
> *All for the likes of* you . . .
> You, *a forgotten folk song dressed up like a classical*
>   *masterpiece.*
> *I studied you as if you were a Beethoven-composed*
>   *symphony.*
> *Your string section made me sing, it did shit to me.*

With the harp, you came off mighty sharp.

Sexy percussion left me in a mild concussion.

But I should've known when your horn had me torn.

When your flute stopped being cute . . . I should've given you the boot.

And when your cello left me mellow, I should've found another fellow.

I was your audience and your orchestra, your instrument yet your fingers too,

I was soprano!

I was alto!

I was bass!

Yet you lied all up and down, and in my muthafuckin' face.

I was harmony and melody alike . . . I was . . .

I was your treble clef and staff: E, G, B, D, and F!

Every—Good—Boy—Does—Fine!

And Every—Good—Girl—Gets—Fucked over and over again.

Bass clef: Good—Boys—Do—Fine—Always and All—Cows—Eat—Grass!

Well, good boys don't exist, and if you find one, right now he can kiss my black ass.

Your arrangement cannot be unwritten; too many have heard you play.

Too many have heard the lies you didn't mean to say, and seen the information you purposely didn't display.

Pachelbel, famed for his Canon in D Major.

You? Your game was playing Canon in Me . . . and even made up your own key.

Vivaldi known for Four Seasons, you're known for a million bad reasons.

I studied you as if you were a Beethoven-composed symphony.

And look at where that shit got me.

My whole note, now a sixteenth of a sixteenth note.
All for the likes of you . . .
You, *a forgotten folk song dressed up like a classical*
    masterpiece."

Charlize had sisters standing before she was through. They were
waving their hands and screaming as if they were in church and
someone had seasoned the Word with teriyaki sauce. That girl was
brilliant. Though I write poetry, I am always amazed when someone
else gets so deep and complicated that it's plain to understand just
what he or she meant. And even if I hadn't overheard her phone call,
I would still know that Franklin played her in his own sweet way.
Canon in D is a magnificent classical piece, so Franklin played his
Canon not in D, but in her sweet note . . . whatever note it took to get
her to fall for his wicked arrangement.

I hugged her when she returned to the table; the room was still on
fire. "You're a genius, girl."

"No, I'm just in pain," she said into my ear over the crowd. Then
I noticed a single tear sliding down her kissable cheek.

"You'll be fine." I rubbed her back while she was still in my arms.
"You always have me to turn to."

"Thanks," she whispered.

"Shit, I can't go on after that." I tried to cheer her up. "I knew I
should've gone before you. Forget my l'il poem."

"Shut up, Mel." She wiped the tear away and stepped out of the
hug with a smile. "I'm sure when you get up there no one will remember 'Canon in Me.'"

When Twalik Abdul, the host, hopped onto the stage with the
mike and looked at me, I got nervous. "All right." Twalik smiled.
"I don't have to ask y'all to make noise because y'all already bringing down the house." There was even more noisemaking. "Our next
performer is someone who used to be a regular; he fell off a little bit,
but is back tonight." Heads started turning in my direction and I
fought to act as if he wasn't talking about me. "I hope that his return
is permanent and not just a tease." He laughed. "Ladies and gentle-

men, sistas and brothas, kings and queens, I present to some and introduce to others, Mr. Tremel Colten." Without asking, the house band played the song I used to like to enter on, Coltrane's "Giant Steps." I got up to people hooting and hollering; I just hoped that I could live up to all of the hype.

"What's up, Vocalize?" I said as I got the mike and then waited for the excitement to die down enough for me to speak again. "I'm definitely permanently in the house." I glanced over at Twalik as he sighed with relief. "It's good to be back." I looked out into the audience and really couldn't see anyone because of the light shining in my face, but I could see that red suit. My mouth preceded my good senses. "I put something together earlier, but I think I'm going to freestyle a piece as a gift to a friend."

"C'mon, baby," a strange woman's voice cracked out of the thick crowd. "Make me feel good!" the woman yelled, and was followed by chuckles throughout the room.

"I'm going to call this piece . . ." I took a deep breath and didn't know exactly where I was going with it, but I knew who I was talking to. "It's called 'Every Good Boy Does Fine.'"

> "I'm a good boy, but I won't kiss your ass.
> Because first of all, lady . . . you have too much damn
>   class.
> Don't let one off-key spoil it for me.
> You are music to my ears.
> You are my treble clef,
> and I don't give a damn why that brotha left,
> but I want to pick up the slack
> I want to give back every note you lack.
> Every—Good—Boy—Deserves—You tickling his piano
>   keys
> and daydreams about being before you on his knees.
> I see Vivaldi's Four Seasons in your eyes
> And imagine Beethoven's symphony between your thighs.
> Your body's sound track? A Mozart composition.

You count the beats while I hold you in position.
Next to you, girl, no one is competition.
You are music to my ears, but I never knew what to say.
Since he fucked up, then I consider today my day.
Your string section makes me sing.
Girl, your horn turns me on and on.
Your harp, baby, it's pretty sharp.
You'll suffer a sweet concussion
After you feel my percussion.
And your cello, oh, baby, your cello can turn me into a
*   different fellow.*
Put that sixteenth of a sixteenth note in my hand,
And you'll feel whole wherever you stand.
Do-Re-Mi-Fa-So-La-Ti-Do
Don't rape me of a chance to know
What it feels like to be your man
Put your sixteenth of a sixteenth note in my hand.
Not Every—Good—Boy—Does—Fine,
But this good man will be fine . . .
If given the opportunity to make you mine."

During the clapping, everyone's eyes raced back and forth from Charlize to me, wondering if we were just vibin' or really fuckin'. I don't know why I had done it, but I can say that I was really feeling what I said. However, I couldn't even look in her direction. I walked over to the bar, ordered two shots of Patron Gold tequila, and returned to our table to see Charlize in conversation with Lorenzo, her brother, who was now looking at me all weird and shit. I hoped that he hadn't been there for my delivery.

"Hey, man." He stood up to shake my hand. I placed a shot in front of him, shook his hand, and then gave the other one to Charlize.

"Where's yours?" she asked.

"I'll go back and get one. You guys wait until I get back," I said, and then ran back off to the bar. "Damn," I whispered, shaking my head. I didn't want Lorenzo to think that I was boning his sister because I wasn't. And even if I was, I wouldn't want him to know.

When I returned, Lorenzo was gone. "Where did he go?"

"Restroom." Her lips parted. "He should be right back."

"Oh, okay." Suddenly I was jumpy around her. "Did I do all right?"

She was staring off in the distance. "Huh?"

"Did I do okay up there?"

"You know." She smiled. "Lorenzo brought his talkative ass right after you left the table. He and Rita are going through something again, and when he starts talking about her, that's all she wrote, you can't hear nothing else." She laughed. "But the crowd went wild, so you must've done something."

"Nawh." I was a little disappointed, but glad that she didn't know what I was thinking and feeling for her.

The three of us sat for another hour having drinks. The last poet left the stage and Twalik said his good nights. The band started playing and the houselights got brighter. Twalik joined us, and within five minutes of conversation with him about the Emancipation Proclamation, we were all yawning. I mean, don't get me wrong . . . black history is very important to me, but Twalik talks about nothing else . . . ever. I've heard him talk about the Emancipation Proclamation at least twenty-five times. I just wish he'd mix it up sometimes with a commercial talking about football, movies, women, cars . . . something.

Back at the house, Charlize and I said good night, but I stayed in the living room and ventured over to the piano. Not wanting the brightness of the fluorescent lights all up in my face, I turned out the lights and lit the many jarred candles my roommate seemed to always have around. I took off my shirt, left on my wife-beater, and took a seat. My fingers hit the ivory, and after all of the musical talk in our poetry, I was sitting there with my dick getting harder and harder with every song. In twenty minutes, I was on my fifth song, "Anytime" by Brian McKnight. *"Do I ever cross your mind, anytime? Do you ever wake up reaching out for me?"* Sarai was on my mind so strong that with my eyes closed, I thought that the warm hands traveling down my chest were a part of my lustful imagination.

When I got to the last *"I miss you"* in the song, I heard Charlize's voice. "Did you mean all of the things you said onstage?"

"Huh?" My eyes sprang open. "I thought you didn't hear me."

"I heard you." Still standing behind me, she kissed my earlobe. "I heard every word you said, just like it was only you and me in the building." My fingers continued to make music as she played her new instrument, my chest. She rubbed, squeezed, plucked, and pinched my nipples.

"I'm glad that you were listening." I finally turned to see her. Charlize stood before me in a floor-length black sheer lingerie dress with matching black silk panties and bra beneath it and black heels. "I'm *very* glad that you were listening." I stood to my feet and placed my hands on her waist. "You look gorgeous."

"Thank you." She blushed. "It took me forever to build up the nerve to come out here."

"Why?" I asked.

"Well." She looked away. "I wasn't sure if the poem was just to make me feel good."

"The poem is truly how I feel"—I pulled her closer—"but this is to make you feel good." My lips marched toward hers and zeroed in, first pecking at hers playfully and then gently sucking them into my mouth one at a time. Soon I held her tongue captive and our breathing was that of two joggers.

She unbuckled my belt and then pushed my pants toward the floor and they didn't hesitate. She caressed me through my boxers and was a bit stunned at my already erect goodness and mercy. I slowly lifted the sheer nightgown over her head and tossed it to the ground as she removed my boxers.

She reached for my hands and politely put them on her breasts. "Here are my sixteenth notes."

"Feel like whole notes to me." I smiled. We were still feverishly pecking away at each other's lips.

She shyly took my raw sword into her hand and stroked it. "And what would this be?"

Being creative was hard at times like these. The harder my dick was, the less thinking I could do. "That's the staff," I said. "What do you want to do with it?"

She pushed my body down toward the piano bench. I slowly sat down. She backed away from me with a smile and I enjoyed watching the orangey glow from the candles dance on her. Charlize moved like Halle Berry did in that cat suit; her body purred and I was ready to feed her kitty. "I think I'd like to place my treble clef on top of your staff," she said.

"Come here and let me see that treble clef."

She removed her panties then walked toward me on the bench but turned her back to me, bent down, and spread her legs. "Wow!" The word escaped me. Viewing pussy from the back is a beautiful thing. My hand couldn't stay down. I hiked the sheer material up, reached out, and rubbed her with my pointer, middle, and ring fingers. Her juicy, overly excited cunny-hole spat on my fingers and she got wetter and wetter. I taunted her clit so much that she was grinding down on my hand for more. Then it was me that couldn't take much more. "Come here." I pulled her backward toward me and then downward by the waist, and when her tight watery pussy sucked my dick in, my lips found her back and showered her with kisses.

She used her legs to slowly move up and down as my elbows, in cahoots with her rhythm, banged the piano keys. She was amazing and worked that thing on me like there was a director with a clapboard nearby giving instructions. After a while, I reached around to the front of her and squeezed her breasts while she rode me backward with her hair swinging in my face. Holding on to her breasts, kissing her back, and having my dick two miles up in her was good, but I longed for greatness. I spun her around, held her up by her thighs, and walked over to the nearest wall, then I put her back against it and pushed into her fast and hard. With her nipple in my mouth and my dick that she had to be feeling in her chest, Charlize cried out incoherently.

By the time I laid her spread-eagled on the carpet, we were both drenched in sweat and her eyes were seconds away from rolling back. It was going on thirty minutes; I needed to cum before this chick passed out on me. I finished with deep strokes and brought each one out all the way to the head and plunged back in again, giving her the total Tremel experience. I wanted to feel her entire body tremble one more time before the night was over. "Oh, oh, oh, Mel. Oh yeah." Oooooh, did she tremble? It felt like her vaginal walls were made up of vibrators.

"That's right, baby, say my name."

"Mel."

I pulled all the way out and beat her clit up with my piece. "Say my name."

"Tremel."

"Oh yeah," I said. "You want more?"

"Yes."

I pushed the head in and pulled out quickly. "You don't want more."

"Yes, I do." She grabbed at my tool. "C'mon."

I smiled. "Here you go."

Oh, man! I almost blew my own back out trying to hit her spot, but I did . . . over and over again. I must've thumped it about twenty times before my vessel burst. I pulled out and spewed my thick white juice all over her fat brown heaving lower lips. Her panting and soft moans flowed on a melody that was reminiscent of Beethoven's "Ode to Joy."

She blushed. "I guess every good boy *really* does fine."

> "I'll get in contact with Conrad when I'll be in the area again. Maybe we can hook up. I'll be sure to bring Dwayne with me."
> —JULIAN ODOM, *Going Broke*, Bank Statement Six

Sarai

4½

I'm not the first woman who may have looked at another woman and wondered how hard, big, and sensitive her nipples were, and I'm damn sure not the last. And I couldn't be the only woman who had fantasies about licking and slowly sliding a finger into another girl. My word to women: "Lie to yourself, but I believe that ninety percent of all women think about being sexual with another woman. Now either the opportunity never presented itself, you were too concerned about liking it and getting turned out, or all of the societal stigma connected to being attracted to someone of the same sex forced you to shut the thought down. So don't thumb your nose at me, keep it real with yourself."

It's been two weeks since I left Syd's apartment. Walking to my car the next morning and on my drive home, you couldn't tell me that not everyone knew that I spent the entire previous day going down on a woman . . . and liking it.

I feel like a different woman, and I guess I had every right to feel that way because I was. Don't get it twisted . . . I'm not ruling out dick, not by a long shot, I was just curious and I acted on and enjoyed it.

I didn't want to think about Sydney, but certain memories of her would probably be embedded in my memory until I collected my final Social Security check. She plagued my thoughts just like an ugly man with a big and good dick would. Every woman has had an ugly-big-dick-dude story. If you don't . . . here's how it goes: You figure no one else wants this ugly bastard, and think that with just the right amount of attention, you could have his ugly ass eating out of the palm of your hand and paying a few of your bills. But he has a bit of self-esteem and won't completely succumb to *just* your personality, so the day comes when you think that a spoonful of pussy will have this man commit murder for you. Then *bam*, that ugly muthafucka flips the script and has not just a big dick, but a great dick, bomb head, and stamina that fucked your mind the fuck up. You are sprung . . . taking this ugly bastard to church, family reunions, gathering with friends . . . and everyone is looking at you cross-eyed like they want to ask, *Is he blackmailing you or something? Are you in trouble . . . why are you with* him? Before you know what hit you, you're trippin' when his phone rings, wondering where he is all the time, and hoping that other women don't know what secretly lies beneath his repulsive appearance. When things go awry, you actually have to wean yourself off of good dick; you can't stop cold turkey. That shit will send you into a state of shock.

How does this relate to Sydney? She was the beautiful woman playing the part of the ugly-big-dick dude and I felt like the slut who thought I was about to turn her out and now the tables are turned. I didn't expect to get so worked up about Syd . . . now I had to stop myself from trippin'. I was glad that she was still calling me, but I didn't want to talk to her. Since our rendezvous, I've been *purposely* too busy for us to link up again. C'mon, what we did was wild and fun, but I wasn't trying to be a lesbian. Lord knows that at nights, I think of our time together, feel myself up, and moan myself to sleep, but my curiosity was fed. I wasn't trying to walk through the mall holding hands. I wasn't looking for a *girlfriend*.

Whenever I did answer her calls, Syd's voice turned me on at "hello." But I pretended to be talking to someone in the room before I said hello back, so that she wouldn't think of asking to stop by. I wanted to see her again, but I wasn't ready to be getting capriciously giddy over a woman.

"That was quick." I was starving, so when I heard the knock on the door, I sprinted toward it with $12.62, exact change plus a two-dollar tip for my delivery from Mia's Italian Cuisine. "I'm coming!" I yelled as I reached for the knob. When I opened the door, Sydney didn't appear to be a happy camper. It probably had a lot to do with the fact that she had called both my cell and house phones less than ten minutes prior and I didn't pick up.

"So what's really good, Sarai?" she asked.

"Hey." I tried not to act stunned beyond belief. "Come in." She had never been in my apartment, but it was the only thing I could say.

After she stepped in and I closed the door, she asked, "Why didn't you answer my calls?" With her back now to me, I studied the way her behind looked in those dark blue denim boot-cut jeans. When she turned around, her tight-fitting low-cut red shirt called every bit of my attention to her breasts, the ones I had been timidly dreaming about. "Did I do something to offend you?"

"I was busy," I lied.

"Busy?" she asked, and looked around the apartment and saw no activity, not even the television was on. "Busy doing what?"

My hands rushed to my head. "It may not look like it, but I was trying to clean when you were calling." I paused. "I had planned on calling you back." I gestured to the couch. "Have a seat." I was nervous. "Would you like a drink?"

"Oh, I'm actually *welcome* to hang around?" she asked jokingly.

"Don't be like that, Syd." I rolled my eyes playfully. "What can I get you to drink?"

She stepped toward me and I held my breath. "Do you have any wine?" she asked as she walked over to the picture window, peered down, and left her purse on the sill. "Chardonnay would be perfect."

"I have Chardonnay." I went into the kitchen and poured two glasses before joining her on the sofa.

Our glasses kissed and then we drank in silence until she spoke. "Sarai, I think you have what I call lesbian phobia."

"What?" I tried to laugh her comment off. "I don't even know what that is."

Syd said, "In case you're wondering, I'm not looking for anything serious."

"Okay," I said, but felt a little disappointed. Was I being rejected before I had a chance to say that I didn't want that either? "Wait a sec, what are you saying?"

"I'm saying that I liked what we did and how we did it, I'd love to do it again, but if it never happens, I'm cool with being friends if you can deal with that."

"Yeah." A sigh of relief escaped me. "I can deal with that." I knew that I could never be friends with her, and the minute she walked out of my place my plans were to delete her from my cell phone, and if your number wasn't in that, then it just didn't exist to me. I didn't want the temptation of possibly desiring her again.

She sipped her wine. "That means that I won't hear from you again, huh?"

How did she know? "Of course not," I lied.

"Yeah, right." She smiled. "Well, did you at least enjoy—"

"Immensely!" I answered before her question was complete.

"I did too. I think about it often." Syd winked at me.

I swallowed hard and decided to keep it real too. "I actually haven't been able to stop thinking about it." I paused. "I enjoyed it, but it's the whole being-gay-or-bi thing that—"

"You're not gay." She giggled.

"Well, whatever I am . . ." I stuttered. "I mean, no one needs to know about what happened."

"I agree." She was very soothing.

I continued as if she never said a word. "I don't know how you roll, but I don't need everyone in my business."

"Sarai, I said that I agree." She raised her voice a little. "No one has to know anything." Syd moved closer to me on the sofa. "But just so you know, I don't give a damn about what people say or think of me. I told you that I consider myself . . . limitless. I don't allow anything or anyone to tie me down. I just go after whatever it is that I like at the moment." She got right up into my ear and whispered, "And right now, Sarai, I like you."

I was flattered yet a tad offended. "So what, I'm your flavor of the week?" I rested my glass on the coffee table.

"If you were my flavor of the week, then I want you next week too, and the week after that, and the week after that, and so on." She sipped her wine. "You're the one that's been hiding from me." Syd rested her glass on the table and her hand started working its way up my thigh.

"I wasn't hiding," I said.

"That's right." She smiled and got on her knees in front of me. "You can't hide a pussy as juicy as yours from me." She buried her face in my lap and sniffed me through my skirt. "You're already wet, aren't you?"

Before any words could leave my lips, she turned me around so that I was kneeling on the couch looking at the kitchen over the back of it. Syd pushed my skirt up toward my waist, pulled my thong to the side, and sank her warm narrow tongue deep into me. From behind, she licked and sucked on my lips and clit as I buried my mouth into the sofa to muffle my yelps of pleasure and held on to the top of the chair for dear life.

The lustful noises her lips and tongue made on my wet flesh were intoxicating, and the things she made my body feel had to be similar to the results of illegal drugs. I was hallucinating, hearing things, trembling, and speaking incoherently. I was fucked up, high on Syd!

After having her fill of me, Syd turned me over. Now I was sitting with my buttocks scooted way down to the tip of the sofa. She crawled up my body with kisses until she reached my lips. "If you want to know why I'm here, taste this." She teased me with her tongue, sliding it in and out of my mouth so provocatively that when I finally caught it, I sucked her in hard. "You taste how sweet you are?"

"Yeah," I whispered.

She pulled away and said, "I am back for more." Her eyes didn't leave mine; it felt as though they dragged our lips toward each other again, but this time I allowed myself to get lost in her, a woman, just as I did the first time we had ever kissed. Shortly after, I was lying on the couch and she was on top of me. For close to an hour our lips were locked. The delivery boy from Mia's must've been pissed because he pounded on the door for ten minutes before he realized that I wasn't coming up or out for air anytime soon.

Later, we were in my bedroom peeling our clothing off. She asked me to lie down and I obliged her. Her lips slowly found mine and then our tongues toiled again. Then out of the blue—well, really out of her black handbag—Syd resurfaced with a hot-pink double-headed, soft plastic, but firm dildo. When she slipped five inches of that shared pleasure stick into me, I inhaled, but when she climbed on top of me and inserted the other end into her, I exhaled.

We were sharing the same double-edged sword. When I jiggled, wiggled, or moved, she felt it, and when she gyrated, grinded, or thrust, I felt everything. It was an endless circle of pleasure.

Coincidently, my Billie Holiday CD was playing, *"You better go now because I like you much, too much. You have a way with you."* The words to the song took on new meaning. Why? Some serious rumors say that Miss Billie was gay, or bisexual at the least, and something tells me that she wasn't singing this song to some ugly man with a big dick.

She was singing to a woman whom she liked much too much.

"You ought to know now just why I like you very much. The night was gay with you." The night was "gay" with you.

I fell asleep knee-deep in pussy and suddenly was up to my neck in dick. Julian's voice woke me up. I heard him say just as plain as day in my ear, *"I'll get in contact with Conrad when I'll be in the area again. Maybe we can hook up. I'll be sure to bring Dwayne with me."* I woke up in a cold sweat, switched on the lamp on my nightstand, and found my body drenched in perspiration. Syd was gone, but back in my mind were the memories of being fired, meeting Conrad, my entire trip to the Bahamas, coming back, and running into Tremel at Nat's school and him giving me attitude, and my sexual tryst with Dr. Baker. "Holy shit!" I was ashamed of myself, but even more so of him, Dr. Baker.

By this point in the game, I was able to tell when I was remembering something and when I was dreaming. This wasn't a dream . . . this was my superwild life. The one thing I couldn't regret, regardless of how marvelously smutty it was, was sleeping with Julian. Did I say sleeping with? Oh, pardon me; there was no sleeping . . . that man fucked me crazy! Julian Odom had a dick that would make an old woman sell her soul to the devil for younger days. "Whoa!" I smiled at the memory of riding his thickness backward while he clutched my breasts. I couldn't be mad at the thought of him removing his blade from my flesh to bend down and softly lick my juices from between my fold. "Lord have mercy." I smiled and smiled until the thought of him writing me that check came back.

It wasn't so much the thought of him paying me because I needed that money, but it was Conrad pimpin' me without my knowledge that got to me. "Conrad, Conrad, Conrad." Saying his name brought every feature of his face to my mind. It was as though I was looking at a picture of him just inches away . . . and then I nearly pissed my sheets, the man I was remembering as Conrad was the same older man at the end of the bar at Erogenous Zone in the taupe three-button Donna Karan suit, Cartier timepiece, puffin' on a Camacho

Liberty who thought I needed another drink. If he knew me, why didn't he speak to me? Why was he there? And what happened the last time I had seen him?

I was suddenly afraid of what I wasn't remembering. For hours, I tried to trick my mind into giving me something, anything, more, but it was shut down and in fortress mode once more. I needed to know more about what I had done. I couldn't wait on my memory to drip-drop piece by piece anymore. Conrad's sliminess I could handle. And honestly, having sex with Julian was something I might have done drunk or not, broke or not, Bahamas or Japan . . . but Dr. Baker? Now I couldn't believe or conceive in my mind why I consented to sex with him. He was a mentor to me. I knew his family; he was my doctor. I began to tremble and my eyes became brightly lit candles melting . . . my wax dripped until the sun came up.

A little after seven, the sun was completely up, so I called Nat. She wasn't home and her cell phone's voice mail came on after the first ring . . . she was at work. I raced into a pair of jeans, a T-shirt, and flip-flops and made it to Northern Miami Middle faster than Dale Earnhardt Jr. ever could. The children were in the midst of changing classes, so I pushed my way through the maze of book bags and braces and burst through Nat's classroom door like a fart someone thought would come out silently . . . unexpected and embarrassed. "Sarai." She examined me quickly. "What happened?"

I had wasted no time on taking a shower, makeup, hairstyling, or wardrobe coordination, so I'm sure I looked like the next *Ambush Makeover* show victim to the few faithful students that had already gathered in the classroom. "I need to talk to you about something." I was hyperventilating.

"Sure." She grabbed my hand. "Let's talk in the hallway."

"Okay." Before the door pulled shut behind us, I blurted out, "I think I remember my trip to the Bahamas and some other stuff about when I came back."

"You do?" Nat's eyes bugged out.

"Yeah, but"—my palms were sweating—"I hope that at least some of it isn't true, and that's what I need you to tell me."

"Tell me, but you have to hurry, my class is about to start." Nat glanced at her watch. "I have to give a test today."

I took a deep breath. "Did I meet a man name Conrad?"

She answered. "Yes."

"What about Jul—" I stopped myself and then continued: "Julian Odom of Jump Records, did I tell you anything about him?"

"Yes, everything," Nat said without a smile. "And I mean everything."

I said, to clarify, "We had sex!"

"Yep," Nat went on, "sex on the first night and you said that he—"

"Okay, I don't need the play-by-play . . ." I interjected humor. "I was there." It all played out like a movie as I spoke. "I remember meeting Conrad at the bar on my first night. I had lunch with him and his friends, and met Julian that day." I paused. "I can't believe I had sex with him that night."

Nat joked, "Yeah, you're a slut, but you normally make it past forty-eight hours."

"I thought that that bastard was giving me his phone number, but that boy wrote me a check." I shook my head. "And Conrad, with his 'be my ho' speech." I laughed. "I mean, don't get me wrong, from the way he described it, the Elite Establishment sounds like the Super Bowl of escort services, but what in the hell did he take me for?" I paused. "And then Dr. Baker." I was in disbelief. "I can't believe I did that. He's like an uncle to me, a damn role model, and he—"

"Now, that was some funny stuff." Nat laughed. "I still can't get that out of my mind, when you met him at the hotel and you let him play doctor on you."

"Nat, you're doing the play-by-play again, I don't need that." I recalled the night and nearly lost everything I ate for an entire week. "And he came to the hospital to see me." I wanted to cry. "That fat bastard. How could he do that?" I continued: "I need to know what other stupid shit I did. I can't keep finding out things in trickles." I kept my voice below the radar of the children. "Tell me what happened to me because I saw Conrad at a club a few weeks ago."

"What?" Nat's neck nearly snapped. "Where? What did he say?"

"Well, first I must admit to you that I lied about going out with Tremel," I said. "I went out alone to this club on the beach, and that's where I saw him, but I didn't know who he was until this morning when I remembered that stuff. Anyway, he bought me a drink . . ."

"Tell me that you didn't drink it," she said with her eyes bugged out.

"I did." I frowned. "I didn't know who he was," I tried to explain. "I mean nothing happened; he actually didn't even speak to me, he just sent the drink over."

"Sarai, he could've slipped you something," Nat said.

"No." I spoke with certainty. "I saw when the bartender was fixing it. I just didn't know that it was for me; she brought it straight to me."

"Do you remember everything that happened that night?" Nat asked.

I was not about to tell her that I woke up in bed next to a woman. "Yeah, I remember," I lied, but it was a good lie. I didn't want her worrying about me. "You saw me the next morning, remember?"

"Yeah . . ." She thought for a second. "But why didn't he say anything to you if he knew who you were?" Nat sighed. "There is something you need to know." She took a deep breath. "After your vacation you came back and things got worse. You had no money, couldn't get a job, your father was about to get removed from the nursing home, your car was up for repossession, and you were about to be evicted."

"Okay, and . . ." I wanted her to go on.

Nat spoke at a snail's pace. "You eventually started working for Conrad."

I chuckled. "I only did Dr. Baker; I wouldn't consider that working for him."

"No, Dr. Baker is the only one you're remembering," Nat said. "Sarai, there is a lot that you still don't know." The school bell chimed. "I have to tell you before you run into Conrad again. If you see him, get away from him as fast as you can."

"Wait!" I said, shaking my head. "So I was a prostitute; you mean, like a . . . hooker, a whore?"

"Well . . ." She tried to smile. "If this is any consolation, you weren't a streetwalker. Conrad's organization is very high-class from what you told me—like high-class clients, A-list celebrities, business owners, professional men." Three kids ran up late. "Look, I'll tell you everything you need to know." She pulled me into a quick embrace. "You want me to stop by later?"

"No, you don't have to come by, just call." I didn't know who I had become and suddenly I wasn't interested in finding out. However, it was out of my control . . . memories would keep coming . . . and just like the weather . . . I'd have to deal with whatever fell from the sky. "Don't be surprised if I don't answer; suddenly I don't think I want to know."

"C'mon, it's not that bad." Nat smiled. "I'll call early, before nine, because Nick and I are leaving on that cruise in the morning."

"Oh, that's right, tomorrow is the Wednesday that y'all leave." I remembered. "Fourteen days in paradise! So you two don't need a honeymoon!"

"Oh, yes we do." She blushed. "This was a prewedding gift from his company." She pushed my hair back with her hands. "By the way, sista, you look a hot mess." She laughed. "Go bathe." We said our good-byes then she went on to educate.

Scared about what I had remembered and even more frightened by what Nat had informed me of and still had more to tell, I went to the restroom and ran some water on my face. I looked into the mirror and couldn't tell if I was crying or if it was simply the water draining down my face. Since the moment I woke up, it felt like I was crying, so it was probably a little of both. I allowed myself to cry and be pitiful for a moment and then pulled my hair into a more sensible-looking ponytail as I tried to find my way out of Northern Miami Middle.

"What the hell is this, a maze?" I asked myself, frustrated, after going in circles three times trying to get back to the front of the school. It reminded me of my life: nothing new was coming . . . I was just going in circles trying to get back to where I needed to be and no one was around to guide me. I was disheveled and near tears again. Passing a hallway, I saw a man walking toward a door on the other side of the hall. "Excuse me," I called out to him, "can you please tell me which way I need to go to get out of this place?" I was crying . . . one damn emotional wreck.

He turned around and seemed almost disappointed when he looked at me. "Go down that hall behind you." He pointed. "Make a left at the second set of double doors and a right at the trophy case, and then you should see the entranceway." He turned his back and began walking away.

"Well, hello to you too." I was astonished that that was all he thought he had to say to me. "Tremel, don't you feel you owe me an apology?"

"For what?" He stopped.

"For standing me up!" I shrieked. "I called you that night and your, I guess, girlfriend, answered the phone and I heard you tell her to tell me that you were busy, and you never called me back."

He turned around. "I didn't stand you up."

"Umm, let's see." I pretended to think. "In every language it's called being stood up when you're dressed, expecting someone to pick you up . . . because they said that they would . . . and you wait for hours without them calling to cancel and they never show up."

"Well, I had my reasons." He never moved toward me. "I apologize for not returning your call, but there was a reason for that too."

I couldn't believe his unconcern. "Yeah, well, whatever the reasons, that wasn't cool."

"Well, Sarai," he huffed, "cool isn't something that I've been striving to be," Tremel said. "Honesty is much more important and honesty is what I believe in, and . . ." He stared at me peculiarly. "Are you crying?"

"No." How could he have seen that from so far away? "No, I'm not crying," I lied, and prayed the tears would somehow evaporate back into my skin.

He walked over to me. "Are you okay?" Tremel softened and stepped even closer. "I'm sorry if I said something that was hurtful."

"You didn't." I wished my life *was* that simple. I wished the only thing I had to worry about was a guy that I barely knew standing me up and then saying something to hurt my feelings. If that was all, I would be here laughing in his face. Instead, I reflected, again, on the new information I had learned about my past and shook my head from side to side. "No, it's nothing that you said." I wiped my eyes. "I've had a long day . . . already."

He then lifted my head. "What's going on?"

I looked into his eyes and couldn't hold a grudge against him anymore if someone was paying me millions to do so. There was something about him! "I was here to see Nat," I sniffled. "I remembered some things this morning and came here to talk to her about it."

He appeared anxious. "What did you remember?"

"A trip to the Bahamas." There was no way I was going to tell him about Conrad, Julian, and Dr. Baker. "I'm not going to share the details with you, but . . ." I wiped my eyes. "I'm learning things . . . shameful things about myself, and I'm not sure how I'm supposed to be dealing with it all."

"It's okay," he said, and pulled me toward him. In his arms, I felt like a lost shivering puppy that had been carried back to a warm home. "It's all right."

"Am I supposed to govern my life by the things that I am now remembering or am I supposed to start over?" I wasn't asking *him*, I simply just needed to state the question so that I could try to figure out the answer.

"Shh." He quieted me. "We all make mistakes." Tremel's warm hands moved up and down my back and I closed my eyes and felt my body relax. "Live your life by learning from your mistakes."

"Yeah, but after it's all said and done and I remember everything, I am still the same person that did all of those things," I said.

Tremel looked me in the face. "After all is said and done and you remember everything, you will be the person who did those things and lived to tell that she made mistakes and has learned from each one."

I took a deep breath and managed to smile. "Thanks a lot."

"No need to thank me," he said as I pushed away from him and stood on my own. "No thanks needed at all."

"Oh, trust me." I scanned him from his shoes up. "I never thought I would be thanking you for anything after that shit you pulled."

He hit me with a perplexed stare. "Sarai, I apologize, and just as you said that you didn't care to discuss the details of your issues, I'd like to postpone my issues too."

"Postpone?" I asked.

"Yeah," he said. "Let's put both of our pots on the back burner for now."

I flirted, "What if they boil over and make a mess?"

"They won't," he assured me. "But when the time is right, I will bring mine to the table and dish it out." Tremel smiled. "In the meantime, I have a question." He extended his hand in peace. "Can we call a cease-fire?"

"My troops weren't armed, Lieutenant, just a little angry." I blushed as I shook his hand. "Cease-fire in effect. So, will you help me get out of this school now?"

"Sure." As he spoke, I looked up into his handsome face and wondered how I had passed on him in the past. Either something was seriously wrong with him or I was stupid.

We finally made it to the entranceway. "I thought you told me that you weren't working here anymore. What are you doing here? You're not into little girls, are you?"

"That's sick, my last name ain't Kelly and my first initial is T, not R!" He grimaced. "I was talking to my old supervisor about getting my job back, but it doesn't seem likely."

"I thought that you were a trucker now."

"More like a van-er." He let out a big laugh. "I deliver flowers."

"It's a living," I reminded him.

"Yeah, well, I landed this gig mistakenly." He seemed embarrassed.

I tried to lift his spirits. "Well, a wise man once told me that after all is said and done, all that matters is living to tell about the mistakes you made."

He joked, "A wise man, huh?"

"Yep," I said, smiling.

"Was that a wise man like the old ancient Chinese man in the movie *Gremlins* that told the dude not to feed them little rats after midnight?"

"No," I flirted, right as we reached my SUV. "This was a young, very handsome wise man that may, one day or night, take me to the movies and then dinner somewhere around midnight."

"May this young, handsome, wise man call you soon to set that up?"

"Sure." I opened the door to the vehicle, hopped in, and said, "I'll talk to you soon, Wise Man."

> "Memory is a way of holding on to the things you love,
> the things you are, the things you never want to lose."
> —KEVIN ARNOLD

Tremel

WITHDRAWAL SLIP #5
ENDING BALANCE: $42.81

Talking to Sarai at the school earlier today, I felt like a sinner standing before God on Judgment Day and giving Him the finger . . . in other words, I felt extra wrong. Why? Because for two weeks Charlize and I had been going at it sexually twice or sometimes three times a day . . . every day. I liked Charlize, but the first night we messed around, I was caught up in feeling sorry for the way her man had treated her. Ever since then, I had been using her body as a substitute for the woman I really wanted. Okay, put it like this . . . you have a Jaguar, but it's in the shop. Would you mind driving around in a new Lexus for a few weeks until it's ready? Hell no! Well, Charlize is my Lexus, but my heart and mind were still with my Jag, and as soon as she's willing, I was ready to ride her again.

I would normally fall asleep seconds after Charlize climbed off of me, but tonight was different. With her head on my chest, I rubbed her arm and stared up at the ceiling thinking about calling Sarai to make this dinner-and-a-movie thing a reality.

"Mel," Charlize said, breaking the silence.

"Yeah." I could've played that I was asleep if I wasn't still rubbing on her.

She took a deep breath, and anytime a woman takes a deep breath, some serious shit is behind it. "Why do you have sex with me?" Just as I thought . . . some serious shit *was* behind it.

"What do you mean?" I knew what she meant; I just needed time to think of a suitable, nontear-jerking answer.

"Well, we've been sexing up a storm these last two weeks." She sighed. "The first few times I thought, wow, I can get used to having a man around. But now my emotions are involved and I'm thinking, wow, I have a man around."

"I'm not sure if I understand the difference." I was still buying time. "Explain it for me, baby." And calling her baby probably wasn't helping.

"Well, I guess I should just ask you." She took another deep breath. "*Do* I have a man?"

"Huh?" I choked. "Do you have a man?" I repeated the question with slight laughter. "What do you mean?"

She got blunt with it. "Are you my man?"

Whoa! How in the hell do you answer that question when it's posed by a woman you've had sex with at least thirty times within a two-week period, but you've only been doing it to pass the time? "Charlize, I hadn't put any labels on what we have."

A creepy silence painted the room for about ten seconds and then a not-so-happy Charlize giggled. "No labels, huh?"

"Yeah," I continued cautiously. "Why have labels?"

She sat up. "Well, the last I heard, stores won't sell merchandise without labels. They won't even stock those products. If something has no label, it cannot even be returned to the manufacturer because no one knows who sent it." Charlize was hurt; she stared at me. "Things without labels get thrown around and then thrown away." She moved to get out of the bed and I went into "fix it" mode.

"Wait." I grabbed her by the arm but she resisted me. "Wait a minute, Charlize, look at me." She hesitated, but eventually turned to me. "Maybe I don't believe in labels." I pulled her back toward me in bed. "Maybe I'm *into* opening cans without knowing what's inside; that's called being surprised and satisfied with whatever is within." I smiled. "Get off of that label shit." I kissed her on the shoulder.

"Why should I, though . . . ?" She spoke timidly. "Would you *commit* to eating whatever is in a can with no quote unquote label?"

"Yeah," I replied.

"Are you currently eating out of every can or just mine?"

Currently? Ha, ha, ha . . . meaning right now . . . at this very moment . . . 10:27 p.m. "Just yours!" She opened the door for the lie, so I walked in it.

"Good." She smiled. "Mel, my feelings for you are starting to—" *Ringggggggg.* "Damn, the phone would ring now, huh?" She got up to get the phone from her dresser. "Hey, Cherry!" She spoke into the receiver. "I got your message about the picnic. It's *this* Saturday, right?" She paused. "Yeah, I don't see why not." She looked over at me and quickly covered the bottom of the phone with her hand. "Would you mind accompanying me to a picnic on Saturday?"

"Me?" That should've come out as no.

"Yeah, you." Her eyes begged.

I couldn't disappoint. "Yeah, I'll go."

She blushed and spoke to her friend again. "I'll be bringing my new friend."

I whispered, "I'm going to take a shower." I hopped up and got out of her room quickly.

I was wrong with a capital *W*. Charlize was a hell of a woman, and I know that I am a good man, but not the man for her at this time. Right now, I'm no better for her than Fire. Because just like Fire, she could have all the dick she wanted or needed, but eventually she'd want more and that was the part I couldn't give her.

While in the shower, I knew that after two weeks of holding her until morning, she would wonder why I wanted to sleep in my own bed tonight. Thankfully, when I exited the bathroom, she was still on the phone. I managed to slam on some jeans and a polo shirt and grabbed my keys. I stuck my head halfway in her door and said, "I'll be back."

Before she could put her girlfriend on hold, I was closing the front door and all but running to my truck, and without a cell phone, there was no way to reach me. I knew where I wanted to be and managed to find one of the only working pay phones left in Miami.

Sarai answered, "Hello."

"Hey, did I wake you?" I asked.

"No." I could tell that she was all smiles. "How are you?"

"I'm good." I had butterflies, talking to her again. "What about you?"

"Well, I'm okay. Just had a long talk with Nat about some things." She sighed. "But that's on the back burner . . . what's up?"

"You up to going out?" I asked.

"When?"

"Now." I bit my bottom lip. "I know that it's late. You don't have to get all dressed up or nothing." I kept talking. "But if you don't want to go, I can understand because it's last minute." I frowned to myself. "I just thought—"

"Can I get a word in or do you always answer your own questions?" she interrupted.

"Sometimes." I chuckled nervously. "Go ahead."

"I'm not doing anything but sitting here getting depressed watching the news." Then she added, "A friend of mine left about an hour ago."

What? Who in the fuck was at her place? "Cool!" I played it off and took a deep breath. "I'll be there in about twenty minutes."

"Okay, I'll be downstairs at the gate."

"At the gate?" I joked. "Can't wait to see a brotha, huh?"

"No, I don't want you in my apartment," she said, and then offered me her signature giggle. "Yes, I am excited about hanging out with you."

My heart did a cartwheel. "I'm on my way."

She hung up and I rushed into Publix Supermarket and bought a bottle of Ballatore. I couldn't do Veuve Clicquot Ponsardin, her favorite champagne, on my budget. I also got two already-made ham-and-cheese sandwiches at the deli, a box of chocolates, and an assortment of purple flowers that were just $4.97.

I pulled up in front of the security booth of her apartment and there she was in dark blue jeans, a rust halter top with matching colored gettin'-it-from-the-back heeled sandals. I put the truck in park when I reached her, hopped out, and made my way around to her. Damn, she was working those jeans. "I feel like less of a gentleman picking you up on the street."

"Don't." She smiled as she opened her arms, inviting me to a quick hug. "I needed the exercise. My apartment is in the first building, so the walk was nothing."

My fingertips touched her waist and I instantly remembered not to slide down to her ass afterward. I had to work my brain a little extra so that that mistake wasn't made. Her perfume nearly hypnotized me. I had to pull away before my lips made a beeline to hers. "You clean up good, Sarai," I said. "You've come a long way from that hospital ponytail and that paper gown with one booty cheek hanging out."

She blushed. "Tell me you didn't see my butt."

"I didn't," I lied. "But almost, that one time I met you coming out of the bathroom." I laughed. "I don't think they make hospital gowns for asses like yours."

"Stop." She slapped me on my hand. "You're embarrassing me." I reached for the truck and opened the door to reveal the small arrangement of purple flowers on the seat . . . for me it was déjà vu all over again . . . for her it was something brand-new. "Oh my goodness, thank you." She picked them up. "Purple is my favorite color." She nose-dived into the flowers. "Thank you so much, they smell great."

"No." I grabbed her hand. "Thank you for making time for me

this evening." I smiled, still holding her by the hand. "Let me help you in."

We got on the road and made small talk. Mostly about safe topics like the weather, local news stories, music, and other miscellaneous crap.

"So where are we going?" she asked.

"Everywhere, but nowhere." That was my answer to her.

"Huh?"

"You'll see!" And in a few minutes, she did.

I pulled into an empty lot near the Miami International Airport's runway and turned off my lights. "What are you doing?" Sarai must've thought I was up to something.

"We're here," I said.

"Here?" She looked around. "Where?"

"Where everyone is going everywhere, but we're not going anywhere . . . the airport," I said.

"Is this a joke?" She was confused. "Where are we going?"

"I thought we could watch the planes take off and land." It sounded like a good idea until I said it, and then even less when she looked my way.

Sarai sighed. "You're not serious, are you?"

"Actually I am," I assured her. "It's not as boring as it sounds."

She asked, "How could it not be?"

"Well, look at that plane!" I pointed at the American Airlines 757 barreling down the runway away from us and slowly lifting itself into the air. "There are about one hundred and eighty people on board that aircraft." I hoped that I didn't sound too corny, but I did this alone whenever there was too much on my mind. "Maybe it's the writer in me, but I just like to think about where they may be going and why."

"I don't understand." She had the same what-are-you-smokin' look on her face. "Give me an example."

"All right." I glanced up at the plane that was becoming increasingly smaller by the second. "They're going to Los Angeles and on board there is a twenty-three-year-old girl that has an audition for a small part in a big movie. She spent the last of her money on the plane ticket, she don't even have enough for a hotel room. She's going to wash up and change in a handicap stall at LAX. She's studying her lines right now; tomorrow she'll nail it. Actually, she'll do so well that she'll get a bigger part and in five years directors will pass up Angelina Jolie to cast her for the lead role in a summer blockbuster hit."

"Wow!" She stared at me. "That was awesome and interesting. I never thought of a plane as a group of people on their way to something, someone, or somewhere." She thought for a second. "I mean, I did think of it that way, but not *that* way. Ya know?"

"Yeah, I know." I was glad she didn't think I was a freak. I was just a brotha on a budget trying to be creative. "Why don't you try it with this plane coming toward us?"

"But it's landing." She frowned.

"Okay . . ." I said. "But where is it coming from and who's on it?"

"Ummm." Sarai paused and then smiled. "It's coming from . . . Iowa."

"Iowa?" I laughed.

"Yeah, Iowa, and there is a guy on it named Jacob that has never seen the ocean or a girl in a thong in person before. Tomorrow he's gonna take his backwoods country ass to South Beach and get drunk, get in the water, and get laid." Sarai covered her face with her hands. "I am no good at this."

"Yes, you are." I pulled one of her hands away from her eyes. "Backwoods-ass Jacob is thanking you right now for your premonition."

There was another plane approaching the runaway in the distance. "Okay, you do that one," Sarai said.

"All right." I thought for a few seconds. "It's coming from Jamaica. Two girlfriends went on what was supposed to be an innocent vacation, but ended up fooling around with each other." I chuckled. "One is returning to Miami confused and a little angry with the other because she thought they were about to take their 'party' back to her apartment, but the other chick just announced that her boyfriend is coming to pick her up, and homegirl is pissed."

She rolled her eyes teasingly. "You are such a typical man for thinking about two chicks hooking up," Sarai joked. "Is that really every man's fantasy?"

I couldn't lie. "Hell yeah, just about."

"Would you want to be with two girls?" she asked.

"Yeah . . . yeah, I would, but not if she was a serious girlfriend or my wife, though."

"Mmm, interesting." She blushed. "You think you know a man and then you tap into his fantasies."

"Any guy that says no is either lying or straight-up gay." It was the truth, and even a gay dude probably wanted to be with two other gay dudes . . . ugh! "Well, enough about all of that, this next plane is yours." I looked at the way the darkness held her sexiness. "Talk to me."

She sighed and stared at the runway like she was afraid of it. "This plane is on its way to Dover, Delaware." She paused. "There is a woman on it on her way to see her father in a nursing home." Sarai turned her gaze away from the plane. "He used to be a strong and great musician. She is . . . or was, a daddy's girl, but he has Alzheimer's now and every time she takes a flight to see him, she says a prayer and begs God to let this be the time that he'll remember her." She paused, let out a sad half smile, and then looked at the plane again. "On the flight back home she is always in tears because nothing ever changes and he, the stranger he has become, is the only constant fixture in her life." She thought the darkness had her camouflaged, but I watched a suicidal tear jump from her eye and onto her shirt.

"I could be a constant fixture in your life." I grabbed her hand and kissed the back side of it. "I could if you allowed me to."

Sarai looked at me as if I had taken out a chunk of her flesh with my kiss. "What made you think that I was talking about myself?"

I reached over to the right side of her face and traced the path that the tears had cut through on her makeup. "You wouldn't be crying if you weren't the girl on that plane."

"You weren't supposed to see that." She offered me a shy grin. "Now, what are you going to think about a girl that cries on their first date?"

"I think she's gorgeous." I kissed her hand again.

A few minutes later, I popped the cork on the Ballatore, poured some into two plastic cups, and opened the sandwiches and the chocolates. And as we pigged out, we continued talking about the people aboard the planes soaring high above the Miami skyline. However, there were no more tears; only happy people were on the planes.

Two hours later, we were on the elevator slowly rising up toward her apartment. When the doors opened, I heard a man ask, "Hmm, you're out pretty late. Wanna have drinks again?" He couldn't see me and it wasn't until I leaned up from the side and stepped forward that I realized that the brotha was talking to Sarai.

I looked at him and then back at her. She was lost for words. "Craig, this is Tremel." She looked over at me. "Tremel, this is my neighbor, Craig."

My hands stayed in my pocket. I wasn't about to shake this bastard's hand. "What's up!" I rendered a head nod.

"Nothing but the rent, brotha"—Craig changed the tone—"and it's high as hell in this building."

Who in the hell was this cat? And when and where did they have drinks together before? See, Nat was supposed to be on top of this type of shit. Sarai wasn't supposed to be kicking it with no men. What the fuck was *this*? He and I bumped shoulders as he entered and we exited the elevator.

"See you later, Craig," she said politely.

"Okay." Then under his breath and as the doors closed he mumbled, "I hope more sooner than later." Then he yelled out, "Nice meeting you, Tremaine."

I was about to explode, implode, self-destruct . . . something. And as bad as I wanted to ask *Who the hell is he and why and what the fuck are you drinking with him?* it came out as, "I see that you have a fan."

"Who?" She kept walking.

I was jealous. "Greg!" I mispronounced his name on purpose. "Was he the *friend* you had over earlier?"

"It's Craig not Greg," she corrected me, "and no, he's not the friend that was over earlier. He's new in the building and is still in that be-nice-to-your-neighbor mode. I'm sure that in a month's time he'll be banging on the wall to ask me to lower my television," she joked. "All new neighbors start out nice."

I forced myself to laugh and then got back on course with my questioning. "Yeah, but he said something about you two having drinks together before."

"Oh," she recalled. "I went to this bar on the beach a few weeks ago, on the night that someone that shall remain nameless stood me up, and he happened to be there. He bought me a couple of drinks."

"How long has he been living here?" It couldn't be long because I had never seen him.

"He moved in while I was in the hospital."

Damn, he was the one! Someone did move in during that time, but I didn't know if it was a man, woman, or a couple . . . all I knew was that someone was getting fucked all the time in that apartment. I could hear them. "He lives alone?"

"Yep," she replied.

Yeah right, not during the time I lived next door. He's probably scoping her out to be his next victim. Damn, I was hatin' on dude big-time. But I was no better than he was; I was all up in Charlize about four hours ago.

"And for your information, the friend that I had over earlier was Syd," Sarai said.

"Sid, huh?" Now who in the hell was that? "Wow, you have all the guys chasing the cat."

"*S-Y-D!* Syd's a girl and she has her own cat." She laughed. "Are *you* chasing the cat?"

I cleared my throat. "Your cat?"

"My cat!" She blushed.

"I'm not chasing your cat. I think I already caught it and have it on a leash." I held my hand up, holding the imaginary harness.

"Hmm." Sarai stuck her key in the lock and turned the knob. "This was a very interesting evening, Tremel."

"Thank you," I said, hoping that my words weren't too forward. "I know that this wasn't the dinner-and-a-movie date that I promised you, but that will come next time if you'll let me take you out again."

"Again?" She pretended to have to think about it. "Another date, huh?"

"It'll be worth your while." I came up with the airport thing because it was free. Being low on cash makes you creative. "So what do you say?"

"I'm going into my place to have another glass of champagne." She flirted, "And if you have me on a leash, then you have to go wherever I go." She smiled. "What do *you* say?"

My mouth couldn't contain my smile. "I say sure."

As we walked in, she disappeared into the kitchen. "Have a seat on the sofa, I'll be right back." I felt so at home again that I thought nothing of reaching for the stereo remote and clicking it on. Like always, there was a John Coltrane CD as one of the selected six she had on standby and it came on. Soon she resurfaced with a bottle of Veuve Clicquot Ponsardin and two champagne flutes. "Do you know who that is?"

"What? Who?" I didn't know what she was talking about.

"On the stereo?" She continued: "Who's playing?"

"You've got to be kidding me?" I looked at her oddly as she sat down. Did she really think that she was going to stump me . . . the master of music? "John Coltrane, and this track is called 'Lazy Bird.'" I smiled. "Need I go on?" I did anyway. "Coltrane was born in 1926 on September twenty-third in Hamlet, North Carolina."

"Nat told me that you were a music man." She was impressed. "Okay, you know your musicians, but you could be lying about Col-

trane's birth date. I don't get down into all of his personal business."
She giggled. "I just like the way he hypnotizes me with that saxo-
phone." She closed her eyes for a second and inhaled heavily as she
bobbed her head from side to side.

With the two of us together on the sofa, she poured the champagne and for a while we didn't speak, we just listened to what Coltrane expected us to understand. When he played the sax, it was as
if each note was a word . . . he was talking to us and the piano player
was backing him up by agreeing with every utterance . . . each note.
After about the fifth song, Sarai turned the volume down and broke
the rhythm with a comment. "You know, when I saw you earlier, you
never really answered my question."

I was lost. "What question?"

"When I was talking about you standing me up, I said, 'I called
you that night and some chick, who I guess is your girlfriend, answered the phone and I heard you tell her to tell me that you were
busy.'"

"Okay!" Oh, shit. "What is the question? That wasn't a question."

"Who was the woman answering your phone?"

Damn! "Well, that *wasn't* my phone; that's her phone and she is
my roommate, or better yet . . . my landlord."

"Mmm." She sized me up. "So y'all live together."

"I am her tenant." I laughed nervously. "I just moved there, and
I'm moving out soon."

I could tell that she didn't believe me. "Really?"

"Really!" I said with a straight face.

"How soon are you moving out?" She had to know.

"Soon," was all I could say.

Sarai's perfectly pouting lips sipped from her glass and then
parted to ask, "Why are you moving?"

I searched for something to say. "It was just a temporary thing. I
just needed a place for a minute and she had a room for rent." I continued: "She's the sister of a guy I used to work with at the school."

"Well, she didn't hang up the phone right, and it sure sounded like she was more than just your landlord." She continued in a mumble, "Unless you pay her with something other than money."

"Whoa." That was a low blow. "What do you mean?"

"Well"—she wore a cocky smirk—"I'm not nosy, but the phone was still up, so I listened, and it just sounded like you two were in the middle of something steamy."

"Is that so?"

"Oh"—she grimaced—"it's so."

"Now what exactly does 'steamy' sound like?" I asked while resting my glass on the coffee table and then took hers and did the same. "I bet it didn't sound like this." I slid her body toward me on the couch and slowly moved my face closer to hers. For the first time in weeks, I didn't care if she'd ever remember me. I was willing to make new memories. Her trembling lips invited me in, but her eyes stared back saying, *Keep out,* but I knew what was best for her . . . damn what her eyes said. Our lips touched and my hands tightened around her waist.

I had Sarai in my arms again. My lips were on hers. I gently pulled her bottom lip in between mine and softly sucked on it. After a few more sweet innocent pecks, my tongue parted her lips and teeth and went in for the kill. She could put up a fight or accept it, but I was prepared to conquer her either way. Suddenly I felt a reluctant yet insistent suction. She was reeling me in as a fisherman would a barracuda and I stayed attached to her line as if my life depended on it.

Before long, our tongues were flicking at each other like two live wires and Sarai was surprisingly now on my lap, facing me, with her legs bent at my sides. She was breathing heavy and moving at the speed of light. Her hands rushed down to my shirt bottom and pulled it off over my head. Almost as though I had passed some unseen permission tollbooth, my hands dropped down to her ass and squeezed.

Our heads sprang around, up and down and side to side, while our mouths continually went at each other. I untied the strap to her halter top, watched the fabric fall, and revealed her brown breasts. I trailed her neck and chest with harsh kisses in pursuit of her nipples. My hand slid under her left arm and into a dent about an inch wide . . . it was her wound . . . created by Damian. It was the first time I felt it and instantly I wanted to stop. I felt like there was so much else we should be doing, yet what she was doing felt so good, I couldn't stop. So as she kissed my forehead, I flicked my tongue over her dark brown nipple again and again before putting it between my lips and pulling on it. "Yes, that's what I need," I heard Sarai say between her panting.

She somehow reached into my pants and palmed my dick. She moved her hand back and forth. My meat was stiff solid. It felt so good that my concentration on her breasts was gone . . . I just rubbed my mouth on her chest, kissing her every few seconds. "This is what I need, Tremel." She squeezed me roughly. "Make me forget all of this bullshit." She got too rough and tried pulling my dick out of my jeans without taking off my pants. I looked up at her like *what the fuck?* I was shocked by the tears running down her face.

"Sarai?" I was confused. "What's wrong? What's going on?"

"I need you." She continued to pull on my third leg. "Tremel, just do this for me."

"What?" I removed her hands from my pants and tried to make her look at me. "What are you talking about?" She wouldn't open her eyes.

She fell onto my chest and wept. I didn't know what she was talking about. I didn't know what she remembered and what she needed to forget, but she needed me . . . and not necessarily inside of her. I stood up and cradled her in my arms. I sat back down on the sofa, covered her breasts with her shirt, and kissed the side of her face while she cried.

We sat there for close to thirty minutes before she calmed down. "Talk to me, Sarai, what's going on?"

"Well," she sniffled, "I had a dream, or remembered something last night, which was why I was at the school today." She paused. "I wanted to talk to Nat to see if what I had recalled really happened to me." She cried softly. "I did some really awful things and I just need somebody to make me forget about it for a while," Sarai said. "I'm sorry for bringing you into this."

I felt bad for her, but I was pissed off again. "So you just went out with me to forget about things?"

"No." She looked up at me. "No, I went with you because I really wanted to spend time with you, but I won't lie. I invited you in for you to take advantage of me."

"What?" I couldn't be hearing right.

"I wanted you to"—she swallowed hard—"use me, take advantage of me sexually, so that I could feel sorry for myself for something I couldn't control instead of hating myself for the things I allowed to happen." She was dead serious.

I had to ask. "You mean like rape you?"

She looked away. "Not exactly rape, just . . ."

She began to cry and I sprang up and placed her back down on the sofa. "What in the hell do you mean not exactly?" I was a decibel below yelling. "Sarai, I cannot believe that you think that I am the type of guy that would do that to you." I was highly disappointed. "Have I given you that impression?"

She stuttered, "I figured since you had a girlfriend that you were just going to use me anyway, so why not tonight?"

"I do not have a girlfriend." I raised my voice. "And I would never do anything to hurt you." My hands raced up to my head. "It hurts me that you think that I would do something like that." I knelt down in front of her. "Haven't you thought about the reasons why I was the first one at the hospital and the only person there when you first woke up again the next morning?" I asked, but didn't need her answers. "Since the day I first met you at that party, all I wanted to do was make you smile." I touched her face. "I would never allow anyone to, nor would I ever, harm a hair on your head."

She wrapped her arms around my neck. "I'm sorry," she cried. "It just feels like I'm losing it, like I don't know who I am anymore. I am so sorry."

"Come here." I pulled her up to her feet and held her in my arms.

Somehow, our bodies fell back onto the sofa. We lay there until morning and I woke up to the smell of breakfast. Sarai had made French toast, bacon, and eggs, and so that the opened champagne wouldn't be a waste, she made mimosas. We didn't discuss the fiasco of what happened the night before. After breakfast, she walked me to the elevator, and before I pressed the button to take me to the ground, I kissed her on the cheek and simply said, "There is a plane about to land at the airport right now; tell me who's on it."

She responded, "There is a woman on it that knows this guy, he's a nice guy and she likes him a lot." She sighed. "However, she has some unresolved issues at the moment, but she's dealing with them as best she knows how. She hopes that he'll be patient with her." Sarai smiled as she reached in and hit the "G" button for me. "As soon as the plane hits the ground she turns on her phone and hopes that she will hear from him again."

The elevator doors kissed each other and I began my descent.

"Your blood type is A-negative. Your last HIV test was taken last month on the nineteenth; it came back negative. Need I go on?"

—CONRAD JOHNSON, *Going Broke*,
Bank Statement Seven

Sarai
5½

I closed my apartment door and started cleaning up the kitchen when my phone rang. I ran to answer it. "Hello."

"Hey, I'm at the airport to pick you up," Tremel said.

"I can't wait to see you!" I smiled. I was so glad that he didn't think I was a crybaby or a freak after last night's weird-ass freak-out. He had only been gone about fifteen minutes.

"Me too." The caller ID said that he was calling from a pay phone again. He asked, "Which baggage-claim section should I meet you in?"

I answered him with a question. "You don't mind that I have baggage?"

"Who travels without bags?" He continued: "You don't have to lift a thing, just relax, and I will handle your baggage for you. Do you trust me to do that for you?"

"Yes." Something in me exhaled. "Yes, I trust you to do that."

"All right, pretty girl, go get some rest, I'll call you later," he said.

I felt like I needed to say something. "Thanks for—"

"Sarai, don't do that," he said, cutting me off. "*Thanks* is a word meant for strangers."

"So what do I say to you?" I had to know.

He thought awhile. "Say, 'Let's do it again.'"

"Let's do it again real soon," I said, doing one better.

"What about Friday night?" he asked.

"Perfect." I blushed as I spoke. "See you then."

I was such a wimp. I couldn't believe that I broke down in front of Tremel. How could I expect him to have sex with me if I was drowning in tears? I was so lame. After hanging up the phone with Nat earlier, after learning a little more about what I had been doing for money and with whom, I was mentally drained. Syd came over and didn't seem to care that I was crying. She just rested her oversize handbag on the coffee table and didn't even ask what was wrong. All she wanted to do was kiss, feel on me, and beg me to finger and lick her. Was that supposed to be comforting? I was pissed and asked her to leave.

I at least wanted someone to pretend that they cared, but after drinking half a bottle of champagne, I figured someone who didn't care might actually work out even better. And Tremel called and walked right into my plan. Number one, I needed a man to shake me out of this girl-on-girl shit I've been enjoying. Number two, I wanted someone to do me wrong so that I wouldn't feel like a slut anymore, but a victim instead. However, I guess my soul needed him to do exactly what he did . . . care for me.

It was Wednesday morning, so waiting until Friday night to have company again was hell. Tremel called me before he left work that evening around six. I was surprised that he still had so much to say to me after what happened. He made me feel good.

At the end of our conversation, he asked, "So are you free on Saturday?"

I was baffled. "I thought we said Friday."

"I know what we said"—he was smooth—"but I'm asking for a third date."

I was one, or maybe even two, steps past blushing. "Yeah, I'm free on Saturday." I thought and then spoke. "Are you sure you want to commit to Saturday in advance? What if things don't go right on Friday?"

Tremel chuckled. "I have a feeling that things with you could never be not right."

"Hmm." I sighed. "Stop it; you're making me smile too much."

"Oh, I'm sorry." He was being sarcastic. "Where I come from that's a good thing."

"Where I come from"—I paused—"*you're* a good thing." Oh my Lord . . . what was I saying? I had to sound desperate.

"Where I come from you're the best," he said, but quickly followed up with, "All right, Miss Sarai, I think I've taken up three hours of your time, I won't hold you any longer."

"I'm not complaining." My heart spoke up for me.

"That's good to know." He laughed. "Honestly, I need to get out of here. I've been done with my work for a while now."

"All right." I was disappointed. "See you on Friday and then again on Saturday." I smiled.

"Oh shit," he exclaimed. "Damn it, I forgot!"

"What?" I asked him.

He sighed heavily and then continued: "I just remembered that I promised somebody that I would go somewhere with them on Saturday."

My curiosity was piqued. I didn't care where he was going, but I wanted to know who with. "Oh, well, enjoy yourself; we can get together on Friday and then again whenever."

"I am so sorry." He was genuine. "I'm gonna see if I can get out of it, though."

"No, no." I faked understanding. "If you already said that you'd go, don't go breaking any hearts." I had to throw in that last sentence as an entrance to the real question I wanted to ask.

"Don't go breaking hearts?" he retorted.

"Yeah." I hated when men didn't just come out with answers. "Someone is looking forward to spending time with you . . . don't let her down."

"Oh, I see where you're going with this." He laughed. "So you assume that it's a woman."

"Did I say *her*?" I pretended to be stunned. "I'm sorry, I meant to use that her-slash-him combination. You know . . . proper English?"

"No, I don't know proper English," Tremel teased. "For your information, a guy friend asked me to help with something." He paused. "But it shouldn't take all day, so if it's all right with you, maybe we can still get together on Saturday night."

"Saturday night should be cool." I was embarrassed about my assumption.

"Great," he said. "You have a good night."

"You too," I said softly as I hung up. I grabbed my digital camera and snapped a quick photo of myself. The smile on my face was definitely one I needed Nat to see when she returned from her fourteen-day cruise. I lay on the sofa clutching a pillow tightly and thinking about our three-hour conversation. *I'm feeling this brotha*, I told myself. When the phone rang again, I answered it, hoping it would be him. "Hello."

"Hey, baby," Syd said. I hated when she called me baby. It just made me feel like we were in a relationship; it just felt unnatural.

"Hi, Syd." I tried to smile.

She asked, "What are you doing?"

"Nothing really, just on the sofa."

"You horny?"

"What?" I couldn't believe my ears.

She giggled. "You hungry?"

I lied. "No, I just ate." I was starving, but I just didn't want her to come by.

After seeing that her first method failed, she just came right out and asked, "You want some company?"

"Syd, after what happened last night, I just don't know about this." I was honest.

"Last night?" she asked. "What happened?"

"Hmm, let's see . . ." I paused. "I was crying my ass off and you wanted me to finger you," I continued sarcastically. "Do you remember that?"

"Okay, Sarai, you need to decide." She sighed.

"Decide what?"

"Decide what the bloody hell you want!" Syd yelled. "You were the one saying that we'd do what we do with no emotional attachments, right?"

"Syd, you don't have to be emotionally attached to someone to ask them why the fuck they're crying," I vented. "You don't walk into someone's apartment, see them in tears, and ask them to eat your pussy."

"So now you want a girlfriend?" Syd asked.

"No." I was angry. "I just want a damn friend." The phone line was inundated with silence, as we both didn't know what else to say, or maybe there *wasn't* anything else to say. "That's it, then," I said, and hung up before Syd's voice could disturb my peace.

I swear, in less than five minutes, there was a knock on my door. I opened it and saw Syd. "I'm sorry if I came off insensitive." Syd continued: "Truth is, I'm no good with dealing with issues. I work hard to pretend like they never happen." Her voice cracked. "I thought you were like me, I thought you needed to forget. That was *my* way of comforting you." She grabbed my hand. "I'm sorry. Will you forgive me?"

Her words actually meant something to me. "Yes." I smiled. "Come in."

She stepped in, and as I closed the door, she enclosed me in a tight embrace. "Bring those tears back so that I can wipe them away," she whispered.

"I'm afraid they're all gone," I said. "I'm all cried out."

"So you're not gonna cry for me tonight?" She kissed me on my cheek.

"This ain't Hollywood, I can't cry on cue," I joked, and then instructed, "Have a seat."

"Ooh, I'm invited to stay?" She laughed.

"Sure! How about a glass of Merlot?" I asked as I walked over to the kitchen.

"That would be nice, thanks." A few seconds later, she yelled from the living room, "Do you mind if I smoke?"

"Smoke?" I had to spring out of the kitchen. "I didn't know you smoke, I hate cigarette smoke."

"Who's talking about smoking a cigarette?" She held up a joint so thick it resembled a cigar. "I've got that sticky icky, baby."

"What?" I asked. "Weed?"

"Yeah." She waved the joint around teasingly. "Care to join me?"

"Nawh, you go ahead."

I went back into the kitchen to find my wine opener and started thinking back to the last time I recalled myself smoking weed. It had to have been two years ago. Nat, India, and I were at India's apartment. We were supposed to be giving one another perms. Because Damian and I had had an argument before I left home, Nat had a student's parent threaten her with bodily harm the previous day, and India was passed up for a model job, we were all pissed off. After our hair was kinky straight, we went to Overtown in search of ganja.

"I cannot believe that y'all got me out here like a crackhead," Nat said nervously as I drove down yet another street looking for guys standing on a corner. "I changed my mind, I don't know about this. I'm a damn teacher. I don't need to be strung out on anything."

"Nat, you are such an ass," India huffed. "You can't get addicted to weed."

Nat had never smoked before. "Well, what if I overdose?" She was dead serious.

India and I nearly squirted out pee, we were laughing so hard.

"Nat, you'll be the first person to overdose on weed," I said. "We're not talking about cocaine, heroin, crystal meth, or crack; it's a fuckin' herb. Chill out!" I looked ahead and saw six or seven dudes on a street corner. Two of them were sitting on chairs . . . dining-room chairs on the damn corner . . . the rest were standing, three were smoking, and two were drinking. "Y'all wanna ask them?" Suddenly I was too shy.

"You ask," India said.

"No!" Nat yelled. "Couldn't we get it from a better-looking group of guys? These guys look too hoodish."

"Hoodish?" I was getting upset. "Nat, we are in the *hood* looking for *hood*lums to get it from."

"Why can't we go to a better neighborhood?" she suggested. "Like North Miami or on the beach."

"So that we can end up buying from an undercover cop?" India asked. "I don't think so, Nat."

Nat asked, "Okay, so how do we know that these guys aren't cops?"

I laughed. "Because they got their mommas' dining-room and La-Z-Boy chairs out on the damn sidewalk, that's how." I was only ten feet away from the guys now. "What do y'all want me to do? Stop or go?" The guys were already looking to see who was approaching.

"Umm, stop," India said.

I slowed the truck down. "They're on your side," I reminded India, "so ask them."

"What in the hell am I supposed to ask them?" She was trippin'.

"Just say what's up or something!" I coached.

By now, the truck was stopped right in front of them. "Why don't we just ask Damian for some?" India asked.

"Because he pissed me off right before I left home," I informed her. "Plus, he deals more in coke, he barely ever has any weed, and he doesn't keep any of that shit in our apartment. Are you insane?"

One of the guys reached in his pocket while whispering some-thing to another guy. "He's got a gun!" Nat yelled, and my body's natural reaction was to step on the gas. We peeled off, ran two stop signs, and waited for bullets to burst through the windows. We made it a mile away to a park before my heart started to beat again.

"Which one of them pulled out a gun?" I asked, trembling.

"Well, I don't know exactly if it was a gun, but he had his hand in his pocket like he could've had a gun."

"Nat," India said, "you've got to be shittin' me. So you didn't see a gun?"

Nat was serious. "It was all in his attitude, India."

"If you're already this paranoid, I don't know about you smoking, Nat. You're going to have to relax," I schooled her. "Now we've fucked up our chances of asking them if they had any or where we could get some."

"If you two have smoked before, where did you get it?" Nat wanted to know.

"It has just been available the few times I wanted it," I said. "I smoke like twice a year . . . if that."

Nat was scared. "This neighborhood is spooking me out."

"I agree, this neighborhood is a piece of shit, but we're turning around," India instructed. "Let's go back, nobody had a damn gun."

I spun the truck and headed back down the street and toward the corner. "You gonna ask?"

"No," India joked, "they'll be on your side now."

Nat, in the backseat, ducked down as we approached the guys again. I rolled down my window and turned on a big smile. "What's up?"

They all peered at me suspiciously. One of the guys sitting stood up and said, "What's good, ma?"

"Umm." I was lost for words. "We're looking for . . . umm."

"Y'all lost or somethin'?" He tried looking past me at India and then at the back window to see Nat shaking.

"No, we're not lost." I was not about to ask aloud for some weed. "Can you come here for a minute?"

He looked at the other guys as if to get clearance to leave the sidewalk. As he approached, he brought his game with him. "Damn, you cute."

"Thanks." I blushed.

"What's up, man, y'all trollin' the block like y'all the po-po and shit." He leaned in to the truck to scope out who was in it. "What's up, y'all want weed, huh?"

India and I looked at each other and burst out laughing. "Yeah, we just didn't know how to ask."

He laughed. "What y'all need, a couple nickels or a dime?"

"Let me get a dime." Before the letter *e* in the word dime was out, he, with the flick of his wrist, pulled a small bag from his sleeve and dropped it in my lap.

"Damn, that was quick," I said as I fished in my purse for ten dollars. "Here you go."

"Yeah." He pushed it up his sleeves. "So, where are y'all headin'? Looks like y'all need some company."

"We're heading down to Homestead," I lied.

"Aww, damn, all the way down there?" He frowned. "That's too south for me."

I playfully winked. "Maybe next time, then, huh?"

"Yeah." He smiled. "Come through and I'll hook you up."

"All right, thanks," I said as I slowly let the window up.

On the drive back, India cleaned out the few stems and seeds still in the bag. Once we were back at her place, she gutted a Dutch Master, sprinkled in the weed, rolled it up, licked it, dried the wet spots with the lighter, and then lit it. On her first hit, she was already giggling. "See, I don't want to be doing all of that crazy laughing," Nat said. "It looks like she's possessed."

"Nat." I showed her as I put the joint in between my fingertips and then my lips. "Inhale by sucking on it, hold the smoke in for as long as you comfortably can, and then let it come out through your nose." I joked, "If I see you blowing my hard-earned ten dollars out of your mouth, I am going to choke you."

"Okay." She took the joint from me. "What am I going to feel?"

"Good." My head was already flowing. "It feels good."

We circulated the piece about four times before Nat spoke up. "I cannot believe that people live in houses . . . houses? Is that what it's called?" she asked, and then kept talking. "Houses have windows and doors." She laughed. "That is so crazy; a door is something that takes you into a house. Why didn't they give it a different name? Like who decided that a fork would be called a fork instead of being called a door? Who said that we wanted the name for door to be door instead of lamp? Damn, words are deep. I bet the bastard that came up with words is so rich."

India and I once again looked at each other and couldn't help but succumb to laughter. Nat just continued: "You know, life is a circle . . . a cycle. Damn, you ever notice how close those two words sound? Circle and cirle, I meant circle and cycle . . . and they mean the same thing." She laughed. "Life is a cycle, think of it." She truly thought that she was schooling us. "Trees come from the earth. We use the wood from trees to build houses, we live in the houses all our lives, and then when we die we are boxed up in a tree"—she was gesturing—"because a casket is made of wood and then we are put into the earth, which is where the tree's journey begins. Life is a circle of cycles." She went quiet for a while. "Am I feeling it yet?"

"Oh yeah." I giggled. "You're feeling it."

I walked back into the living room with two glasses of wine and Syd already had a thin line of smoke leaving her nostrils. The aroma was enticing, but I settled for my glass of wine instead. "So, tell me why you were crying last night," she said while looking down into her purse for something.

"You want the commercial or the made-for-TV long-story movie version?"

"Give me the commercial." Syd walked over to the window, peered out, and then rested her purse on the windowsill as she had done many times before. "Spill it." She sucked on the blunt.

"I remembered a few more things from my past a few days ago." I took a deep breath. "I had sex with men for money."

"What do you mean?" Syd asked.

"Well, I only remember two of the men," I said, "but my friend Nat has informed me of some of the ones I don't recall yet." Then I remembered. "By the way, how often is Conrad at your job?"

Syd nearly decapitated herself the way her neck spun to look at me. "Huh?"

"You probably don't know his name, but the man who bought me that drink the night I met you in the bar where you work, his name is Conrad. I actually know him and would never want to run into him again. Have you seen him since that night?"

"Oh, him? I don't think he lives around here. Conrad? Is that his name? I heard people calling him C.J." She puffed away. "I haven't seen him since that night."

"Good." I sipped my wine heavily.

"So what were you crying about?" Syd asked again as she sat next to me.

"I just told you."

"Child, please, every woman that isn't a virgin has sold pussy." She passed me the joint. "Why you think men buy us dinner, jewelry, drinks, clothes, and shit? All of that is down payment on the pussy and we all know it." She laughed. "The biggest down payment is the engagement ring. All he is saying is that he wants you to be *one* of the women he fucks for the rest of his life."

"You're crazy." I smiled. "I told you that I'm not smoking." I tried passing it back to her.

"C'mon," she urged me. "You need to loosen up."

"I'm fine."

She eyed me. "Yes, you are, but the shit that I bought is mainly for you since you were the one crying." She bent over and pecked me on my lips. Her lips tasted real good, like they were laced with honey. "Let's get high," Syd said.

With slight hesitation, I inhaled hard and got an instant high. So after four tokes, I was sitting with the angels. I swear it had to be the stuff that Snoop Dogg and them are always talking about because I had never before reached that level. It was a feeling you wished something legal like alcohol could bring, but by the time you get to this point with liquor, you're throwing up and can't even see straight. "Oh, my goodness." I was in awe of the almighty weed. "Damn." I fell back against the sofa.

"Wait a minute." I started getting paranoid, looking around and shit like someone else was in the room. "What in the fuck was that?"

"Was what?" She started looking around to see what I was talking about.

"This." I pointed at the joint. "What we smokin'?"

She grinned. "This is krypt."

"What?" My heart was racing. "What the fuck is krypt?"

"Kryptonite!" She spoke as if she was a marijuana aficionado. "It doesn't get any better than this, baby." She pulled on it again. "This is the most potent weed on the planet."

"Damn, that shit is . . ." I couldn't figure out if it was good or bad. It was good because it got me so high so fast, and then it was bad because it got me too high too damn fast. There was a knock on the door and my eyes nearly jumped out of the window.

"Are you expecting someone?" Syd asked.

Don't ask a high person questions like that. I almost lost it . . . who in the hell could be at my door? What if it was Tremel? I would never want him to see me doing something like this. I would never be able to act normal in front of both him and Syd. There was another knock on the door. "Damn," I mumbled, but made no motion to get up. "What if it's the police?"

"Think!" Syd laughed. "Why in the hell would the police be at your door?"

"Maybe they were in the building and smelled the stuff." I panicked. "Put it out, go flush it or something." I grabbed my purse and drowned myself in perfume. "I'm coming!" I yelled as Syd laughed.

As fearful as I was, I managed not to look through the peephole. I cracked the door, saw Craig standing there with a bottle of wine, and wondered what the hell he was thinking. "Hey, Craig," I said through a space in the door wide enough for him to see one of my eyes.

"Hey." He had a suspicious look on his face. "You okay?"

"Yeah," I answered quickly. "What's up?"

"I was wondering if you have a wine opener that I can use."

"Yeah, gimme a second." I turned away from the door without closing it and Craig pushed it open.

"I'll be damned, you sneaky little something," he said as he hurriedly closed the door behind him. "What y'all smoking?"

"Krypt," Syd said before I could pretend as if we were just chilling.

He moseyed on over to Syd and asked, "May I join the party?"

"Sure." She welcomed him to stay in *my* apartment. She passed him the weed. "You think you can handle this, though?"

"Oh"—Craig looked over at me—"I can handle this and a whole lot more."

Syd pulled out another twisted blunt, set it ablaze, and passed it to me. And as God as my witness, I saw Jesus' face after just one pull. I was smiling and feeling like if I threw a chair through my picture window, I would sprout wings, fly through downtown, and see the world like I never have. The sensation I had was different. You know the cold chills or tingling twitch that you get when the old people say, "Someone is walking over your grave"? It was like that, but it was continuous and enveloped my entire body. It was so good that it was almost paralyzing in a good way. It wasn't that I couldn't move; I just feared that moving would stop the feeling.

Fifteen minutes later, the three of us were lined up on the couch with Syd in the middle, passing the joints back and forth down the line. My heart was telling me to quit, but my mind was enjoying the vacation. The room was absolutely silent but within me there was a party going on, I was hearing music, smelling fragrances, and dancing. A few seconds later, my outside caught up to my insides and I jumped up. "We need some music." I walked over to the stereo and ran my finger over a few CDs. I stopped on Kanye West's *College*

Dropout. Trying to smother the festival within me, I poured a glass of wine and took a few sips, but when the fourth song, "All Falls Down," came on, I just got up and started dancing alone. "I used to love this song."

A minute later, Syd stood up and danced behind me with her hands on my waist. With each gyration of my ass, her hands inched up and up until she was caressing my breasts. When she began nibbling and sucking on my neck, Craig's eyes couldn't get any wider. He scooted to the middle of the sofa so that he had an even better view of us. Somehow, our boogying landed us in front of him. He put out the roach and rested it on the end table. "You girls are bad," he said with a sexy smile. "Very, very bad."

Syd spun me around to face her and we locked lips and tongues. With my ass now in his face, Craig took the opportunity to squeeze my cheeks through my skirt with both of his powerful hands. Syd's arms were around my waist and her kisses traveled down my neck. She was inadvertently backing me up even more into Craig. He lifted my skirt and the feel of his bare flesh on mine stirred the already heated river within me, and a few droplets escaped. He spanked me on my ass softly, but hard enough for me to feel a sting, and then he kissed my cheeks repeatedly while squeezing them.

Syd grabbed my shirt, pulled it over my head, and undid my bra in lightning speed. Her warm moist tongue flicked over my solid nipples and her suction almost made my knees buckle. Seeing how much joy Syd was giving me, Craig, not to be upstaged, tapped the zipper of my skirt and it dropped to the ground. After removing my black lace panties, he rubbed my thighs, continued to peck on my ass, and guided me, with hand movements, to spread my legs wider.

I couldn't believe what was happening. It was as if I was trapped within a shell of myself. I wanted to stop them both, but I couldn't. It was as though my brain and my body were in two separate dimensions. My mind was in reality screaming, "What the fuck are you doing? Stop them . . . now!" However, my body was caught in between Syd and Craig and the only thing I could say was, "Mmm" and "Oh yes."

With his pointer and middle finger, Craig rubbed my pussy lips and massaged my clit. My moans became outrageous and soon Syd caught on that she was not responsible for the pleasure I was experiencing. She stared me in the face and slowly moved her eyes downward to see that my body wasn't involuntarily humping air, but was working Craig's fingers. Disappointment emanated from her as she whispered, "Oh, that's what you want?"

Syd stepped away from me, but I reached out and pulled her toward me. "I want you," I mouthed, and tried to balance the pleasure Craig was giving me while kissing her. I pulled the clothing from her body as if it was on fire. My hands ran wild over her and soon so did my tongue. After about five minutes of uncontrollable lust, Craig stripped naked and had, just as I suspected, dick for days.

Craig sat down on the couch and, surprisingly, Syd pushed me down onto his lap with my back on his chest. She opened my legs so that Craig's legs were between mine. What occurred next was the sexiest thing I had ever seen. She dropped to her knees, grabbed his thick, dark brown hunk of steel, and put it between her lips. She sucked his dick as if she was giving it CPR, and boy, did it have a pulse. After two or three minutes while stroking him with her hand, she turned her attention to me, licking the juices from my pussy and teasing my clit with her tongue. As she snacked on me, Craig pinched my nipples and I gyrated wildly.

Syd pleasured both Craig and me with her mouth for a while before she caught me off guard. She wet me up real good and, while holding Craig's dick still, slapped a condom on it and slid it right into me.

"Oh fuck!" Craig exclaimed as I felt his body shudder beneath me. "Mmm." He pushed into me from behind, so I was riding him backward. Everything was bizarre, but Craig's dick wasn't one to turn down . . . and since it was already in me, I planned to make it worth it. I rose and fell on him in circular motions and got high off of the squishy noises being made. "Fuck that dick, baby," Craig said as he kissed my back. "Yeah, just like that."

Syd reached over and rubbed my clit while Craig pierced me. "Oh, oh my . . ." I had never felt anything so overpowering before and she made it worse by kneeling in front of me again and sucking on my clit while Craig was still in me. "Oh shit!" I screamed numerous times. That continued for a while before Syd removed Craig from me and sucked him wildly before giving him back to me. Craig worked me over by thrusting upward very fast . . . Syd was now sitting on the couch next to us sucking on my breast and rubbing my clit and lips vigorously. I screamed incoherently and so did Craig. The pressure of his cum was so strong that his last thrust propelled me up and off of him.

I fell to the ground defeated and Syd spread her body over mine. As she kissed me, she began to moan. Shortly after, I could hear Craig spanking on her as he had done me. Soon he was fucking her doggy-style and I was underneath sucking on her nipples.

The next morning, Syd and I lay in my bed completely drained. I couldn't believe what we had done or that I wasn't still high. "Why did you let him touch you?" were Syd's first words to me.

"What?" I looked over at her. "He touched both of us." I shrugged my shoulders. "He fucked both of us."

Syd turned to her side to face me. "It started out with me wanting him to watch us kiss and shit," she said. "But before I knew it, you had his hands all up in you, Sarai."

I couldn't believe her. "You practically backed me up into him," I said. "You had my ass in his face. What did you think he'd do?"

She sighed. "I was pissed."

"Oh, really?" I got sarcastic. "So why would you stick his dick in me, then?"

Syd looked away. "Because it seemed like that's what you wanted." She continued: "You were moaning and groaning and he was only fingering you, so I knew you wanted to fuck him."

"Well, you did too, Syd," I reminded her yet again. "Let's not forget that."

"I know what I did," she snapped. "I was high as fuck."

"You? I was gone," I said. "You sure that shit wasn't laced with something?"

"Are you stupid?" she asked as her hands touched my thigh. "I don't fuck around like that."

"You better not," I said, looking up at her. "All right, be for real, though; you didn't enjoy that shit?"

"The sex?" she asked to clarify.

"Yeah."

"Hell yes." She smiled. "Craig is a monster. That shit was wild."

"It was," I said. "I wanted to stop but I couldn't." I thought back to the night before. "Man, never in my life would I have thought that was going to happen." I remembered: "By the way, where did you get that condom from?"

She looked away. "Craig had it with him, I guess. He threw it on the floor while I had my mouth on you."

"Hmm, I guess that horny bastard knew what he came to do," I said.

"Yeah, but that's not going down anymore." Syd's tongue licked my nipple. "We got wild once, that's it," she went on sternly. "I don't want you screwing him again."

I laughed. "What, are we a couple now or something?"

"I don't care about whom you talk to, hang out with, or go out with"—her hands slid between my legs and cupped my lower lips—"but this . . . this is mine."

"Syd, you know I'm not with that girlfriend shit," I reminded her.

She hesitated. "I know, and I'm not either, but I don't want to share your stuff, it's too good," she said. "I thought I had a handle on what I wanted with you, but last night fucked me up, I really want to be with you." Syd kissed me, and for the next hour, our lips, all four sets of them, were inseparable.

As we took a shower, Syd asked, "What are your plans for Saturday?"

"I have plans in the evening." Instantly, and for the first time that day, I thought of Tremel and felt more than terrible about what I had done. "Why?"

"A friend of mine is having a picnic and I want you to come with me."

She couldn't be serious. "Syd"—I rubbed the soap on my wet towel—"I'm not trying to announce to the world that we have a thing."

"Who said anything about announcing something?" She laughed. "It's a picnic, and if you go you'd just be coming along as a friend of mine." She added, "There will even be some single guys there that you, or we, can mingle with. I just don't want to go alone."

Free food and men were my favorite things. "All right, sure, I'll go."

"Oh, you didn't have a choice." She kissed my wet back. "I was taking you kicking and screaming."

"So you're not going to be trying to hold my hand or anything crazy, right?" I asked.

"Sarai, get over yourself," she joked.

"Fuck you, Syd!" I flicked water in her face.

"Oh, by the way." She changed the subject. "How much was that end table worth?"

I chuckled. "Oh yeah. How in the hell would you sit Craig's ass on my table to suck on him." I laughed. "When I heard it crack, I just knew that he was going to fall."

"Sorry," Syd said. "I don't know where to find another one, but I can give you the money to get it." She recalled, "I'll get the cash and bring it by later."

"It's cool, don't worry about it. I can probably put something on it to hide the crack."

"No," she insisted. "How much was it?"

I answered, "I paid like one seventy-five for it at Pier 1."

"Okay, one seventy-five it is," Syd said. "Is there a Rockwell Mutual around here because I'm not trying to pay high-ass ATM fees."

"Yeah, there's one on Thirty-seventh by that Winn-Dixie," I said. "That's the one I always go to."

"Oh, you bank with them too?" she asked.

"Yep."

After our shower, Syd had a bright idea. "Well, since we're both with Rockwell, I can just transfer the money into your account, then. I can do it over the phone instead of going out there if you trust me with your account number."

"All right." I was trying to find something to wear. I jotted the account number down on a piece of paper and gave it to her.

I checked my account hours later and sure enough she had made the deposit . . . cool.

Friday evening came, and after such a wild few days, I was glad to be back to normal and with Tremel. We had an outside table, overlooking the water, at Smith & Wollensky steakhouse. Tremel was the perfect gentleman. He opened doors, pulled out my chair, allowed me to order first, and even ordered a bottle of Kendall Jackson Merlot. Everything about him just felt too good to be with a girl like me, especially after what went down between Craig, Syd, and me. Nice guys shouldn't have to put up with women like me.

As his sirloin and my grilled Atlantic salmon arrived, I studied his handsome brassy brown face the way one would an old portrait. I was looking for something familiar about him and there was something, but I couldn't put my finger on it. We ate, talked, and finished the bottle of wine. His brown eyes turned my way right before he sipped the last of his wine. "What?" He smiled.

"Sorry"—I was embarrassed—"you caught me staring."

"That's cool; I've been doing it too." He winked. "You just haven't caught me yet."

I sighed. "Tremel, I'm no angel."

"I figured that out when I didn't see any wings on your back." He laughed.

"No." I was serious. "I've done some things in my past that I'd like to tell you about if things continue to progress between us."

"Not if, but when," he said.

I was confused. "Excuse me?"

"You said 'if things continue to progress' and I made a correction by saying *when* things progress, not *if*."

I smiled. "Well, I just hope that you won't run to the hills."

"Florida has no hills." He rested his hands on the table and leaned toward me. "I'm not running."

I decided to test him. "What if I said that I was a man?"

Tremel looked at me strangely. "Well, sir, leave your money for half of the bill and have a good night," he said.

"You wouldn't do that," I teased.

He huffed, "Yes the hell I would."

I giggled. "Okay, what if I said . . ." I thought for a second. "What if I said that I was a kleptomaniac?"

"Then I would put my wallet in a bear trap if I ever spent the night," he joked.

"I'm serious, Tremel." I then playfully asked, "What if I used to be a call girl?"

"That would depend on who was *calling*, and if you answered," he said without chuckling or looking away from me.

I threw in one more for the sake of not looking guilty. "What if I were a killer?"

"If there is a reward of over twenty Gs for you, then I'll have to turn you in." He laughed. "I'll write to you, though."

"Snitch," I said playfully, and smacked him on the hand.

He laid money on the table and said, "Let's get out of here, I have something for you."

"Forgiving does not erase the bitter past. A healed memory is not a deleted memory. Instead, forgiving what we cannot forget creates a new way to remember. We change the memory of our past into a hope for our future."

—LEWIS B. SMEDES

Tremel

WITHDRAWAL SLIP #6
ENDING BALANCE: $471.23

We left the restaurant and nestled onto an empty couch at Vocalize. I ordered two glasses of Merlot and went over my piece, a gift to her, in my head. Two minutes before my name was scheduled to be called, I looked over at her in the darkness and asked, "You okay?"

"Yeah." She smiled. "This place is nice, I like it."

"We're up next," I informed her.

"Excuse me. What?" She looked like she had seen a ghost. "Who's next?"

"We are." I laughed. "I'll recite the poem; all you have to do is listen."

She sighed. "I was just about to run out of here."

A minute later, Twalik, in his regular African attire, was doing his thing. "Do you all want the next act?"

"Bring it on," the Vocalize regulars yelled.

"He might step on some toes. I don't know what he has up his sleeves tonight." Twalik laughed. "You sure you want this brotha?"

Once again the crowd shouted, "Bring it on!"

"All right! Ladies and gentlemen, sistas and brothas, kings and queens, I welcome to the Vocalize stage, Mr. Tremel Colten."

I turned to Sarai. "No need to run, no need to hide, just enjoy." I touched her cheek. "I wrote this for you."

Sarai blushed. "Thanks."

I ran to the stage hoping to God that Charlize didn't make Vocalize her Friday-night spot. However, if she did, she'd just have to be pissed with me just as she was on Thursday morning when I came home to shower and get dressed for work after being out with Sarai all night.

"Tremel, where have you been?" She took it upon herself to wait on my bed while I was in the bathroom.

"What?" I asked, annoyed. I didn't have time for this. "What do you mean?"

"You didn't sleep here last night." She folded her arms across her chest as though it would intimidate me.

"I know!" I stared at her with a towel wrapped around my waist. "Can I get dressed, please?"

"You have nothing that I've never seen before." She sulked and finished with a mumbled, "As a matter of fact, I've been seeing a lot of it from you." She stood up. "Though I don't know where in the hell it's been for the past few hours."

"Charlize, don't start that shit." I waved her off. "We talked about this last night."

"Right, and last night you made me believe that I meant something to you, Tremel," she said. "And the moment I get on the phone

you hightail it to God knows where and come back the next morning to take a shower?"

"Charlize, I live here," I said. "I am paying rent here, remember!"

"I know what the fuck you're doing here," she said, and then
asked, "I just want to know what the fuck you're doing with me." A
tear slid down her cheek. "I don't have sex with just anybody. I . . .
I . . ." She paused. "I have feelings for you, so you need to choose me
as your landlord or . . . or"—she couldn't find the right word—" . . .
or something else, but I cannot be both."

"I give you money every week toward my rent," I reminded her. "I
have not missed on paying you yet, have I?"

"So I guess that answers my question," she said, shook her head,
and stormed out of the room. By the time I made it home that night,
she was asleep. Today, when I left for work, she was already gone, and
when I came home, she wasn't there, so we haven't spoken since then
and now here I am onstage about to recite a poem to her unidenti-
fied archrival.

"What's good, Vocalize?" I smiled at the crowd. "It's me, your boy,
Tremel." The crowd went wild. "I'm spittin' a piece tonight that I am
calling 'Remember Me.'" I cleared my throat and out it came:

> *"Open up your memory's rusted shut back door . . .*
> *Because we've met before; and it's you that I adore.*
> *Your face is my mind's most treasured decor.*
> *Even though my name you cannot recall . . .*
> *We've lived ten lives together and I remember them all.*
> *We held hands and walked through the Red Sea with*
>   *Moses.*
> *And on the other side, I gave you half a dozen roses.*
> *Don't I look familiar?*
> *You wept on my shoulders when they crucified Christ on*
>   *Calvary.*

Though two lowly fornicators, he still died for you and me.
Remember me?
We huddle together with our kids on that smelly slave ship.
They sold you to Kentucky and me to VA; boy, did I trip,
But, massa, he taught me to stop missing you with a
*　　bullwhip.*
Our children we never saw again, but in my heart I prayed
They'd remember what we taught them, even when afraid.
You still don't remember me, huh?
Okay, what about Pearl Harbor back in 1942?
You thought I was dead and never coming back to you.
Weeks later, you opened your door, and on your porch, I
*　　stood.*
I survived . . . like only a brotha from the hood ever could.
Maybe this will jog your memory!
We marched for freedom in '63!
We made love the night before MLK was shot.
And were at the meeting when Malcom X got got!
Damn, girl, you still *don't know me?*
Not even all the times that we . . . you know!
All right, what about tonight when I ordered steak and
*　　you got fish?*
And I requested your favorite red wine to go with your
*　　dish?*
Maybe if I touched you there . . . you'll remember my
*　　name.*
And our life will return to you frame by frame by frame.
If you never remember me, we'll just have to do it all once
*　　more.*
Because your face is my mind's most treasured decor."

As the crowd cheered me on, I returned to the sofa to find Sarai in shock. "Are you serious that that was for me?"

"Who else did I eat dinner with tonight?" I chuckled. "Didn't you order fish?"

"Yeah"—she spoke slowly—"but . . . Oh my God, that was so beautiful. No one has ever done something so sweet for me before."

"Yes, someone has." I kissed her hand. "You just don't remember it."

Her arms reached around my neck and pulled me in toward her. "You make me feel so good." Our lips touched, and through a kiss, our souls conversed. She didn't want to let me go and I promised her that I wouldn't go, and I didn't . . . not until the jazz band rendered their last selection and the houselights lit up the club.

In my truck, on the way back to her apartment, she said, "Is there something that you're not telling me about what happened between us when I first met you."

"Not really." I didn't know what to say. "Once you remember, you'll see that we're right back where we left off."

"I couldn't see myself not falling for you." She smiled. "I just can't see not liking you."

"Yeah?" I asked.

"Yeah!" she replied.

We arrived at her complex and I volunteered to walk her to her door. But in the elevator she said, "I'd like for you to come inside." She held up her right hand to swear. "I promise that I won't jump on you this time."

"Oh, the whole jumping-on-me thing wasn't a problem," I joked. "It was the crying part that messed ya boy up."

The elevator doors opened up and just like déjà vu, her buddy Craig was standing there waiting to get on, but this time he had company . . . a blonde with breasts so big that her nipples got on the elevator before we exited.

"Hey, it's you two again," he said. "How's it going, guy?"

"What's up?" I spoke this time, but only because seeing him with another woman at least meant that he wasn't fuckin' with Sarai. "Have a good night." It was almost three in the morning and there was only one thing they could've just got through doing.

Sarai seemed bothered by him now. "He is such a damn whore," she whispered as soon as we reached her door.

"He was your friend just a few days ago," I joked. "The best neighbor a girl could have."

"Please." She rolled her eyes. "That is the third woman I've seen him with this week, and that's probably only the ones I've seen," she grumbled. "He's starting to get on my last nerve."

We entered the apartment but it had a different smell. It reeked of day-old smoke. "Whoa." The expression left my lips involuntarily.

She quickly reviewed the room to see what I was talking about. "Whoa what?"

"The smell." I had to keep it real. "Was someone smoking?"

"Yeah, I'm sorry." She reached for the air freshener. "My friend Syd was in here, she smokes from time to time." She sprayed for a while as she walked from room to room. "May I offer you a drink?"

"No," I said.

"A snack?" she asked.

"No," I replied once more. "Come sit with me."

She dimmed the lights as she had done nights before. "How about we not sit on the sofa but on the love seat," she suggested. "It's closer to the window and we can look out at the city lights."

We sat on the love seat with no music or wine egging us on and just held each other. "I'm thinking about going to see my dad and then going to Atlanta to find out what's up with my brother next week." She went on: "The two letters that I've written to him came back 'return to sender.' I'm really starting to get worried about him."

I offered comforting words. "I'm sure he's fine." But of course he wasn't . . . his ashes were at Nat's house. "Give it another week or two." Nat and I were supposed to tell her immediately after Nat's cruise.

"When you have a twin it's different," she said. "I feel a void that I've never felt before." She went on: "They say that when a woman is pregnant and is miscarrying that she knows the minute it happens. It's like a disconnection occurs and she doesn't feel pregnant anymore right at the time things change. Well, that's how it is with him and me; I just don't feel like a twin anymore."

"Sarai, I am sure that Savion will—"

"I didn't say his name." She looked at me funny. "How did you know his name?"

"Stop freaking out." I tried to stay calm. "You told me his name when you were in the hospital and I remembered it because that's the name of that tap-dancing guy from *Bring the Noise*, Savion Glover."

"Oh, okay." She laughed. "But yeah, I'm thinking of going to see my dad next week. I need to book a flight to Dover and then fly from Dover to ATL."

"Maybe you going to see your dad is a good idea, but if you don't know where in Atlanta your brother is, then I don't think that you should go." I couldn't have her go to Atlanta all alone to learn that her brother had committed suicide. "Give me a few weeks and I'll go with you." I tried buying time.

"You'd do that?" she asked.

"Yeah," I said. "I wouldn't want you going there alone; apparently he has moved, so you might have to go through a lot to get to him."

"Savion was never good with money," she confessed. "So what if he's homeless or something?"

"I think he would've reached out to you for help before he started living on the streets."

"But what if he did and I was in the hospital and he couldn't reach me," she said. "See, that's another thing . . . I was in the hospital and he never called or came to see me."

I had to think fast. "Nat checked your messages every day. I'm sure she would've helped him in whatever way she could." I hated to let her down. "He didn't call, so she couldn't tell him about what had happened to you," I said. "I'll go to Atlanta with you. Just give me a couple of weeks to be able to get a ticket."

I kissed her on the forehead but my lips slowly moved down to hers. Our tongues crossed the borders and became refugees in each other's mouth. My hands wrapped themselves around her and began caressing her back, but as soon as they did, she backed away.

"Oh Lord." She smiled at me. "I really like you."

"Okay." I smiled back.

Sarai continued: "I like you so much that I cannot keep kissing you, not right now."

"What do you mean?" I asked.

"I don't want anything to happen for us to move too fast." She paused. "Tremel, I want to take my time with you," she said. "I've jumped the gun many times before, but I don't want a false start this time. I want things to progress as they should, and not only do I want to finish the race, I want to win the race."

"I feel you, and I more than respect you for that." I kissed her hand.

"Thanks." She stood up. "I have something else in mind." She smiled. "Wanna play Scrabble?"

"Why wouldn't I?" I teased her. "Bring it on." For the next two hours, we were in double- and triple-word-score heaven.

A few minutes before six we embraced by the picture window and watched the sun come up over the Miami skyline. She walked me to the elevator. "See you tonight," were Sarai's last words.

I got home and expected drama, but it seemed like Charlize was playing the tit-for-tat game. There was a note on my bed, apparently left the night before. It read, *Mel, I'm going out tonight and will not be sleeping home. Please water the plants in the morning and remember to bring the garbage can in from the street. If you still care to join me, meet me at the picnic at MacArthur Park shortly after noon. Your landlord, Charlize.*

Great, so she wouldn't even know that I was out all night, and because I was going out again tonight, I needed to fake the funk by smoothing things out with her so that I'd at least have a roof over my head a little while longer. I watered her plants, brought the can in, and never had to be reminded of that since I moved in, but whatever, and then lay down to get a few hours' sleep.

At noon I got up, showered, and headed toward MacArthur Park. There was a woman selling flowers a few blocks away, so I bought some and was off to butter up my landlord. A guy can never go wrong with roses . . . right?

"... I can have two thousand dollars in your pocket by tomorrow night."
—CONRAD, *Going Broke,* Bank Statement Eight

Sarai

6½

'm leaving the complex right now." I looked at the clock on the dashboard; it was a quarter to twelve. I didn't want to be stuck at this picnic all day, so I called Syd earlier and told her that I would drive my truck and meet her there. She asked me to call when I was leaving. "I'll see you shortly."

This would be the first time I was out in public with Syd and I hoped that she knew that there wasn't going to be any hanky-panky dyke shit going down. I was in this for some rib tips and potato salad.

Around 12:15, I arrived at the park and found pavilion seven, like Syd instructed. I parked, grabbed the two bottles of red wine, my gift to whoever's picnic this was, threw on my sunglasses, and marched over to the orange-and-blue-decorated picnic area. It was the perfect South Florida day, about eighty-three degrees with a much appreciated sea breeze pushing its way through everything. My pink-and-yellow summer dress was doing the damn thing, and in my pink-heeled sandals, I knew that I was working it.

I spotted Syd in a white, almost see-through number sitting at a picnic table talking to another woman. "Good afternoon, ladies," I said on my approach.

"Hey, girl." Syd looked up at me. "How were my directions?"

"Great, almost as good as Magellan," I said as I held up the two bottles of wine. "Who do I give these to?"

"Well"—the woman spoke—"you can start by leaving one right here on this table." She wasn't joking; she reached for a bottle.

Syd took the other bottle and looked around until she spotted a gentleman. "Doug, will you take this to Tamara, please?" Doug grabbed the bottle and walked away. I took a seat on the side of the table where the woman was, across from Syd, who now appeared to be sending or receiving a text message.

"Cherry, do I have to introduce myself to your friend or will your rude ass get around to it at some point today?"

"Oh." Syd's attention shifted. "I am so sorry." She looked at me. "Sarai, this is Charlize, an old college friend." She looked around the pavilion. "We all actually graduated from Florida Memorial in '99." She looked back over at me with a sexy smile. "Charlize, this is Sarai, a new friend of mine."

I extended my hand to her. Charlize was absolutely stunning. She was one of those women who look like their makeup is professionally done all the time, yet their beauty is so natural that it seems like they're not wearing any makeup at all.

"Charlize, it's nice to meet you." I smiled. "I love that name. Charlize Theron is one of my favorite actresses."

"Thank you." She politely gave my hand one last shake. "Your name is unique too, it's pretty." She turned to Syd. "Cherry, I've never heard you mention her."

Still messing around with her phone, Syd replied, "We met about a month ago at EZ."

"Wait a sec." I had to ask. "Who's Cherry?"

Charlize looked at me strangely. "Her," she said, pointing at Syd.

Syd rolled her eyes. "That's my nickname."

"Well, it's the only name I know you by," Charlize joked. "What does your birth certificate say?"

"Sydney." Syd rolled her eyes. "And you know that."

Charlize put her right hand up. "I swear that I knew you for at least five years before I knew your name was not Cherry."

I found the whole thing strange. "You never even told me that you had a nickname," I said to Syd.

Syd stood up and peered over at me. "My college days are over. My Cherry days are now at rest too." Charlize and I made small talk as Syd ventured off to find a wine opener and some cups. I scanned the crowd. There had to be fifty people there now. Many were seated at the various tables playing dominoes or spades. A few were working the two grills and some even played volleyball. It was a nice gathering.

"Here we go, ladies." Syd returned with the opened bottle of wine and four cups. "Charlize, where is your friend?"

"I don't know." She looked at her phone. "He hasn't called. I think he's coming, but I'm not sure."

"Well, call him." Syd seemed disappointed. "I really want to meet this mystery man."

Charlize blushed. "Truth is, I didn't sleep home last night, so he might be pissed at me."

"What?" Syd was astonished. "Why would you do that?"

"Because he pulled that shit a few nights ago." Charlize got hyped and let us in on her business. "The other night when you called, Cherry, we had just finished up from a real, and I mean real, good 'session,' if you know what I mean." She winked at me. "We were all hugged up in bed, the phone rang, and while I'm talking to you, he goes and takes a shower and leaves." She added a dramatic ending: "I didn't see that Negro again until the next morning!"

"What?" Syd asked. "Where in the hell did he say he was?"

"He didn't say where he was." She looked at us both. "But the sad part about it was that I don't think that he did anything wrong." She was starting to sound like a Jerry Springer case. "I actually think he may have been overwhelmed by some things I was saying and he probably just needed time to think."

I had to ask. "So when y'all talked, what did he say?"

"That's the thing, we've been avoiding one another," she said. "I think that we're both afraid of saying the wrong thing."

"And then your ass slept out last night?" Syd asked. "That's fuel to the fire."

"Yeah." She grinned shyly. "But it was just to make him think."

"Think? He's going to beat your ass!" Syd said. "Did you at least get you some last night?"

"Child, please." Charlize rolled her eyes halfway. "I was at the Seminole Hard Rock Hotel in Lauderdale . . . all by myself."

"How pathetic," Syd said, just what I was thinking.

I laughed and then asked, "So why don't you two just talk things out?"

"He's an absolute sweetheart, so we probably will tonight," she said. "He might even still show up here today."

"Well, if he does, that'll say a lot," I said. "And you better tell him the truth about where you were last night before he thinks that he has something to worry about." I smiled. "Don't play games like that."

A few minutes later, Tamara, the hostess, quieted everyone. She thanked us all for showing up, and then she carried on with college talk about the Lions and royal blue and orange forever. The only words she said that meant something to me were, "Let's eat."

I couldn't get to the buffet line before a few burly brothas and some skinny sistas. They nearly ran me over. I saw ribs, chicken, pork chops, macaroni and cheese, potato salad, collard greens, pigeon peas and rice, corn bread . . . food went on for miles, but the line was moving at two miles per hour. It took me over fifteen minutes just to get my food and grab a Coke from the oversize cooler.

As I returned to our table, I saw a man sitting there alone. Both Syd and Charlize were approaching from different directions. It was as though the three of us were in a race to get to him first. From about thirty feet away I thought, Damn, he looks like Tremel from the side. I dismissed the thought by thinking, Whoa, this man really has an effect on me, got me thinking about him, seeing things and all . . . I can't wait to see him. As I continued to make my way to the table, I blinked several times to shake the thought of seeing things. "He really looks like Tremel," I said out loud to myself, and in two steps, I was smiling. It was Tremel. How did he find me?

Charlize reached the table first, and being the gentleman he was, Tremel stood up. However, when he pulled roses from behind his back, he was going too far with the Southern-hospitality thing. C'mon, roses for a stranger? Damn, what was he about to give *me*? Charlize blushed, her hand covered her lips, and as she trembled, his hands made their way around her waist. She rested the flowers on the ugly orange plastic tablecloth and enfolded her arms seductively around his neck. He rubbed her back and pulled her close, closer, and then closest, so that their lips touched. I wanted to stop walking, but I couldn't . . . I had to get to them. As a matter of fact, my legs were going so fast that I ran right into the table and onto the floor. I saw chicken, rib tips, and potato salad go up . . . and then come right back down on me.

Hearing the crash, Charlize rounded the table. "Oh, my goodness," she said as she knelt at my side. "Are you okay?" She reached for my hand, but instead I supported myself on the table's bench and stood up. And after I watched the chicken and ribs drop from my dress to the floor and reviewed the stains on my new outfit, the only thing more pitiful was the look on Tremel's face.

"Sarai, what happened?" Syd asked while resting her plate down.

"Nothing, I'm fine." I was still staring at Tremel.

"Sit down," Charlize coached. "Did you hit your head?"

"I am fine," I said, and grabbed a handful of napkins to wipe the orangey mixture of potato salad and barbecue gunk from my hands and dress.

She got the point, went back over to Tremel, and grabbed his hand. "I'm so glad that you could make it." He was frozen stiff. "I'm sorry about not coming home last night." She kissed the side of his face. "We have a lot to talk about."

"Look, Syd"—I already had enough—"I'm gonna get out of here."

"No, no, don't go," she begged.

"I'm not staying here like this." I pointed to my dress.

"No, listen." Syd had a plan. "I went shopping yesterday and still have bags of new clothes in the car; we're the same size, so you can just change."

"No." I turned away from the sickening couple. "I didn't plan on staying too long anyway," I lied. "I have some stuff to do."

"Aw!" Syd continued loudly. "Well, before you go, at least meet Charlize's man that we've heard so much about."

"Oh right, right." Charlize was chipper and all giddy. "Baby, this is Cherry." She pointed at Syd. "We went to FMC together and were roommates during our junior and senior years." She giggled. "And this is her friend . . ." She looked embarrassed. "I am so bad with names."

"Sarai," Syd helped her. "This is my friend Sarai."

"Yeah, Sarai," Charlize said. "I just met her here today and already managed to talk her ear off about you." She blushed. "Anyway, Sarai and Cherry or Syd or whatever you want to be called these days, this is my boyfriend, Tremel."

"Pleasure to meet you, Tremel." Syd shook his hand.

I couldn't take my eyes off of him. "Nice seeing you." He then held his hand out to me, but I reached and grabbed my shades from the table instead. "Sorry, I still have barbecue sauce on me. I wouldn't want to get it on you." I cleared my throat. "I've made a mess here, so I'm gonna go."

"I'll walk you to your truck," Syd said.

"No." I turned her down. "I'm good. Enjoy your food and friends. I'll call you later."

Tremel never said a word while in my presence. I wondered if he was thinking about the same thing that I was thinking about . . . the poem he recited for me. What a crock of shit that all was. Everything he said was a lie. Everything he did was false. Everything I thought he was . . . belonged to Charlize. I walked away from the table right in time because my tears said to hell with it . . . here we come.

I reached my truck and couldn't get away from the park fast enough. I pulled onto the street like a madwoman. Something on the surface was telling me not to trip . . . the man was merely a friend. No big deal, I could and would recover. However, something deeper within me was making me cry. I felt like Tremel and I had a connection, more than a bond . . . more along the lines of a soul tie. It's a feeling that happens the moment you meet the person you should spend the rest of your life with. From the moment I saw him at the hospital, my soul wanted to love him.

In the garage of my apartment complex, I pulled in side by side with another vehicle, a red truck, which was also parking. Craig hopped out and tried to make out who was driving my truck. He smiled. "Hey, you!"

I waved but said, "Fuck you," behind the glass, knowing he couldn't hear me.

He walked over and motioned for me to roll down the window. "You need help bringing anything up?" he asked.

"No," I said, trying not to look directly at him so that he wouldn't see my red eyes. "I don't have anything."

"All right, I'll hold the elevator for you." He walked away.

I wiped my eyes, and sure enough, he was holding the elevator. I ran to catch it because I'm sure the older lady also aboard wanted to get going. I slammed myself into a corner and pretended to be searching for a number in my cell phone. As soon as the lady got off on the fifth floor, Craig turned to me. "What are you doing later?"

"Nothing," I answered rudely.

"What?" he asked. "Your boyfriend's not coming over tonight?"

I looked over at him, and no matter how handsome his face and how great his body, I was repulsed by him. "I don't have a boyfriend, and to be quite honest with you, if I never see another man in my life, it'll be just all right with me."

"You don't mean that." He walked up on me and whispered, "That shit the other night has kept me up every night and I know that it's done the same to you." He lowered his lips to mine, and when he spoke, I could feel the warmth of his breath. "I can't sleep knowing that you're that close and I'm not inside of you." His lips touched mine and I quickly pushed him away.

"Craig, please! The other night was the result of whatever the hell we were all smoking." I continued as the elevator doors opened: "Besides, I'm sure there is some blond bimbo in your apartment willing to fulfill your every fantasy."

As we both exited, Craig laughed. "Oh, that's what it is?" he asked.

"What, what is?" I turned to him with major attitude.

He stuck the key in his lock. "That blond *bimbo* was my brother's wife. She had left her cell phone up here, he was down in the garage in the car, and I was walking her back down." He opened his door and walked in. "Don't judge a book by its cover." He closed his door as if he had just made a point.

"Fuck you," I whispered, and kept walking. "Don't judge a book by its cover?" I repeated. Okay, yeah, well, maybe if the book didn't fuck my friend and me on the same night, in the same room, and probably with the same condom, I might not judge the book. But hell, if I were judging myself harshly for my actions that night, then why wouldn't I judge the damn book? Fuck the book!

I reached my door and met an official notice on it. "Damn." I had forgotten about paying the rent. I had more than enough money in the bank to do it with, but I had gotten so caught up in the other facets of my troubled life that I had once again forgotten to do what was most important. Three months' rent, late fees, plus some other charges now factored in, I owed $6,819.

"Damn." I snatched the note from the door; not everyone needed to know my business.

I checked my voice mail and the nursing home had left a message. I called them back to learn that they had to change Daddy's medication and they needed a signature for his paperwork. In the midst of giving the nurse my address to send the documents to me, I paused. "You know what . . . I'll be there tomorrow night or the latest Monday morning."

I hung up, and within two hours, I had booked a flight and packed a suitcase. I would be leaving first thing in the morning. I shed a couple more tears for the good thing I thought I had and then buried it with two grilled-cheese sandwiches, a dozen fish sticks, and a cup of chocolate ice cream. I put in my DVD of the first season of the *Chappelle Show* and didn't answer any incoming calls on my cell or house phone.

I didn't want to hear any apologies, explanations, or sob stories; I was ready to pretend that I never even knew a man by the name of Tremel. And I didn't care to see Syd, Cherry, or whatever her name was again either; I was ready to start anew. And the following evening, when looking into my father's eyes, I saw, for the first time, what I believed love looked like and how it's supposed to feel.

"The wheel of change moves on, and those who were down go up and those who were up go down."
—Jawaharlal Nehru

Tremel

WITHDRAWAL SLIP #7
ENDING BALANCE: $369.16

You know the numb feeling you get when the dentist shoots your mouth up with Novocain? Well, someone must've shot me up in my brain before the picnic because that's the same feeling that came over my entire body when I saw Sarai, two feet away from me, covered in potato salad and barbecue sauce. I didn't say a word. Truthfully . . . I couldn't say anything while she was there and I didn't for nearly ten minutes after she had gone.

I wished that she would've called me out, though. I secretly wanted Sarai to get ghetto and tell Charlize about us. At least then I would have had to come clean to them both, and if I didn't have a place to stay, I would've left with Sarai, and even if I had to sell my right arm, I would've gotten back in her good graces. However, when she didn't say anything, neither did I, and that was the biggest wrong I could've ever done to the both of us.

I stumbled down to the picnic bench in defeat as Charlize and

Cherry talked around me. My brain flatlined and I became dead to myself. I kept reciting the poem I had put together for her just twenty-four hours prior. I had talked about loving her over lifetimes, and then managed to fuck up the one life we really had together the very next day. I vaguely remembered Charlize asking me if I wanted something to eat. I shook my head up and down just to get her away from me for a moment.

"Aren't you Tremel, that singer?" Cherry asked.

"Sorta," I mumbled.

"Sorta?" She giggled. "The song, 'Forgotten,' that was you, right?"

"Yeah." I knew that Sarai was somewhere crying and I didn't understand why I was still at a picnic table instead of with her, holding her, or even chasing after her. "Yeah, 'Forgotten,' that *was* me."

"That song is amazing." She licked her lips slowly. "I loved it."

I didn't want to hear what this woman had to say, but I fought to be polite. "Thank you."

"No, thank *you,* Tremel." She scanned the area and then followed up with, "You ever made love to your song?"

"What?" I turned to look at her.

"Have you ever had sex while listening to 'Forgotten'?"

"No." I told the bold-faced lie. "Why?"

"Because I have." She blushed but there was nothing innocent about it. "To be completely honest with you, I've even masturbated to the sound of your voice; those lyrics and that beat are amazing."

"Wow!" I couldn't believe this woman. "Who are you again?"

She was flattered that I asked. "I'm Cherry, Charlize's friend, or Syd, Sarai's girl," she whispered. "But I could be something totally different to you."

"No, thanks." I stood up. "Tell Charlize that I had to bounce."

"So soon?" she asked.

"Not soon enough, actually." I turned my back to her.

Cherry hurled words at me from behind that I could swear were, "Off to mend a broken heart, huh?"

"What?" I turned and glared down at her.

"I said"—she smiled—"off you go. I'll tell her that you had to go, hon."

"Thanks." I walked away.

Guilt was riding me as if I was a bucking bronco. I kept trying to throw it off, but I couldn't shake it. I stopped at nearly every pay phone en route to Sarai's apartment but she never picked up. The new security guard wouldn't let me in the gate and I had given the pass card and key to Nat for her to use while she was staying with Sarai. I stayed down the street on the outside of the complex for several hours until they changed shifts in the security booth, but even the new girl guard wasn't going for it.

I parked across from the complex in case Sarai was leaving or coming in from somewhere, but as the sun started to go down, I cranked up and left before some paranoid woman reported a stalker or a suspicious truck parked across the street. I called her several more times before making it back to Charlize . . . but got no answer.

"What happened?" Charlize rushed to the door as I entered. "Is everything all right? Cherry said that you had an emergency."

"What?" I looked at her. "No, I didn't. That girl is fuckin' crazy," I said. "I told her to tell you that I had to go, but I didn't say that it was an emergency."

"So what happened?" she asked. "Where did you have to go?"

I took a deep breath. "Charlize, there are some things that we need to talk about."

A worried veil covered her face. "What?" She walked over to the dining-room table and sat down. "Talk to me."

"Well"—I cleared my throat and continued to stand—"before I moved in with you, I was in a relationship." I took a deep breath. "It was a serious relationship, actually the most serious one I've ever had, to be quite honest with you."

"Okay?" Charlize had her hands together as if she was praying. "Go on."

"I loved her and would do anything for her. I would go anyplace with her, and she knew it, but . . ." I paused. "She was shot."

"Oh, my goodness," Charlize exclaimed as her hands covered her mouth. "I am so sorry, Tremel. I didn't know any—"

I interrupted her. "I'm not done. She's okay, but she was in a coma for almost a month, and when she woke up she didn't recognize me, she didn't even remember knowing me." I finally sat down in the chair in front of her and she grabbed my hand. "Her memory went back to before the time that she met me. She actually still thought she was with the dude who shot her . . ." I paused. "It's a confusing and very long story that I can't get all the way into." I sighed as she tightened her grasp on my hand. "We used to live together before everything went down, so the doctor suggested that I move out for a while until her memory starts to return and I can reintroduce myself to her."

Charlize let go of my hand. "She remembers you now, huh?" Tears dripped from her eyes. "So you're leaving me? You're moving out?"

I reached out to her but she pulled away. "Hear me out, Charlize."

"No." She shook her head. "I don't need to hear anything else."

"Charlize, just let me—"

She cut me off to ask, "Are you in love with her?"

"Charlize, please let me talk!" I said.

"No, Tremel." She was angry. "You owe me an answer. Are you still in love with her?"

"Yes"—I touched her hand—"and I've been seeing her—"

"Noooo!" Charlize cried. "I don't want to hear any more." She jumped out of the chair. "Why didn't you just tell me this from the time you moved in?" she asked. "Why have you been lying up in my bed, Tremel?"

I answered, "Because I wanted to, Charlize."

"What about what I wanted, Mel?" she cried. "What about my feelings? Why would you toy with me like this? You should've told me this the day you moved in because that's the day that I . . . fell for you."

"Charlize, I tried but—"

"But shit, Tremel." She interrupted my sentence. "But shit! You can pack your shit and be out of here tomorrow."

"What?" Why did I think that she would understand any of this? "I paid you for this month already." I was pissed. "You can't just put me out."

"Isn't that what you want?" she yelled. "You can go move back in with your girlfriend now."

"I can't," I said. "She still doesn't remember us being in a relationship."

"I don't give a damn, Mel. You've been seeing her and probably sleeping with her, that's enough for her to go on," she said.

"I haven't had sex with anyone but you since I met you," I informed her. "And that's the truth."

"Well, that's refreshing," she joked. "Get your shit and you get out of here. I will give you your money back for this month." She let out a sinister chuckle. "Shit, I'll give you your money back for last month too if you leave tonight."

"Charlize, I'm not leaving!" I said. "You turned the shit into something that it wasn't supposed to be." I continued: "I moved in here to be your roommate, not your fuck buddy."

"What the fuck?" She charged at me. "So I just wanted a fuck buddy, that's what you think?"

I grabbed her. "I'm sorry; I didn't mean it like that."

"Then what in the hell do you mean?" She was still crying. "Please tell me what in the hell I should be thinking and feeling right now."

"Charlize." I stared at her and couldn't believe that I wasn't trying to make this beautiful, educated, successful black woman my own. "Charlize, I care about you," I admitted. "I'm crazy about you. I've had nothing but good times with you. You are an awesome friend, a smart woman, a great cook, a fine and very sexy dime piece, and you bring me to my knees in bed." I sighed. "But my heart, the part of me that I know you want and I want to give to you, I don't even have it . . . it's in her hands." She leaned against me and cried as I held her in my arms.

I slept in her bed again that night, but I was there as a friend . . . nothing happened.

The next day, Sunday, I returned to Sarai's apartment building. This time I only stayed for about an hour. Her cell phone was sending me straight to the voice mail, and her voice mail was full, probably on purpose. Once when she was mad at me she confessed to calling herself ten times, letting it go to voice mail, humming for a second or two, and hanging up. Therefore, whenever I called, I couldn't leave a message and she could continue to be mad at me. So I couldn't help but think that she had probably done that again, but this time . . . she had good reason to.

By Wednesday, I was acting on pure insanity. I walked up to the gate of the apartment complex, locked my hands around the bars, and looked in pitifully as if I was a caged animal at the zoo. As I searched the parking lot for her truck, I spotted a maroon Chrysler 300 with a "For Sale" sign on it. I scribbled down the owner's name and number and rounded the corner to the pay phone that had recently become my friend. "Hi, may I speak to Jake?"

"This is he."

"What's up, Jake? I wrote your number down about the Chrysler you have for sale." I went on: "I was wondering if I could take a closer look at it."

"Sure." Jake was excited. "When do you want to come over?"

"Well, I'm actually around the corner from the complex." I hoped that this would work. "Is that where you are?"

"Yeah," he said. "I can meet you down there in about ten minutes if you like."

"Cool." I tried to sound official. "How much are you asking for it?"

"Well . . ." Jake paused. "I just want someone to take over the payments. I got in over my head with that son of a bitch. The payments are five ninety-five."

"That's doable," I lied. "I tell you what, I don't want to take up too much of your time, I just want to look at it today. I'm interested in it for my wife." I sighed. "Maybe I can just look at it today and then bring her with me another day this week and then you can come down and talk to us."

"Okay, that'll work," Jake said. "What's your name?"

"Mel." I cringed as I offered him my real name.

"All right, Mel. I'm in six-eleven. Give the guard my apartment number and just have them call me up when you're downstairs and I'll let you in. Take a look at it and let me know what you think, or call back and we can talk, man."

"All right, cool." I ended the conversation.

When I approached the security gate, the new security guard asked, "May I help you?"

"Yeah, I'm here to see my friend Jake in apartment six-eleven," I said. "His number is . . ." I then rattled off the phone number I'd rehearsed.

He searched for the number in the computer and then called it. "I have a gentleman here by the name of . . ."

"Mel," I said.

" . . . by the name of Mel to see you." He listened to Jake. "All right, thanks." He turned to me. "Go ahead." The iron gates opened and I cruised on in.

Security at the apartment was always changing. I'll bet that in two weeks the tough brotha at the gate will be crying at the unemployment office; nobody ever lasts longer than a month. Just in case Jake could see me from his apartment's window, I parked behind the Chrysler and walked around it slowly several times. I peered into the windows and nodded in approval a few times before I hopped back into my truck and drove into the garage area where Sarai's parking spot was; her truck wasn't there. However, minutes later, I still found myself knocking on her door like a maniac.

I heard a lot of mechanical noise on the other side of the door. "Sarai!" I yelled. "Open the door; I need to talk to you." The noise continued, so I knocked louder. "Sarai . . ." I was frustrated. "Sarai!" I yelled again, and out of anger, I turned the knob and was surprised to find it unlocked. I opened the door and what I saw was more than astonishing. An elderly man was shampooing the carpet, but all of the furniture, pictures, throw rugs . . . everything was gone. I looked on the outside of the door to assure myself that I had the right apartment.

"*¿Qué?*" The old Spanish man stopped the machine and removed earplugs from his ear. "*¿Qué?*"

"Umm . . ." I tried to keep it real simple. "Where is the girl that lives here?"

"*Yo no entiendo.*" He hunched his shoulders. "*Estoy limpiando la alfombra para el nuevo arrendatario.*"

"What?" I stared at him. "Sarai . . . *el niña*, the girl *en es un apartamento*?"

"*¿Qué?*"

"Damn it, man." I threw my hands up and apologized in advance for what I was about to do. "Sorry for this." I started walking toward him.

"*Ah no, ah, dios mio.*" He looked down at the rug. "*Por favor, señor, no pisa la alfombra.*"

"Sorry, man." I ran across the carpet to her bedroom; nothing was there. Her bathroom, closet, kitchen . . . the entire place was empty. "What the fuck?"

When I made it back to the living room, the man was livid and pointing at the door. "*Salga ahora!*"

"I'm sorry, man." I tried to calm him. "Sorry."

"No, sorry," he yelled. "*Salga ahora.*"

I left, and as I closed the door, I saw Craig going into his apartment. "Um, excuse me."

He looked over. "Yeah?"

"Do you know what's going on with Sarai's apartment?" I asked, hoping that he'd know something, but not too much, about her.

"Yeah, she moved out." He grinned. "What, she didn't tell you?"

She'd never mentioned moving. "When was this?" I was in shock.

He thought a bit. "Started on Monday and finished earlier today."

"Damn," I said louder than I was supposed to. "Do you know where she moved to?"

"Nope," he said sarcastically, "I sure don't."

"Look, man." I was angry. "If you know something, I would appreciate you telling me."

He glared at me as if I should be intimidated by him being a few inches taller. "Didn't I just tell you that I didn't?"

I shook my head and walked away. "No wonder she can't stand your big country ass."

"Oh yeah?" He opened the door to his place. "Was that before or after she sucked my big country dick?" Before I could turn to him, he slammed the door.

"Pussy-ass coward!" I yelled at him through his door. "Bring your ass back out here."

"*Llamaré a la policía,*" the old Spanish man yelled as he peeked out of Sarai's door. "*Llamaré a la policía.*" I didn't need a translator to know what *policia* meant. I got my ass as far away from the building as I possibly could. Nat was gone for another week and some . . . so I knew no one would know where Sarai was. Suddenly I felt like I had really lost her this time.

I cursed myself out ten times on the drive home. I called myself a million names and wanted to spit in my own face for not correcting all of this bullshit the minute it went down. I couldn't make any sense out of where Sarai was and why. As soon as I got home, I grabbed the phone and called Nat's house. Maybe she would check her messages from the cruise ship. "Nat, hey . . . this is Mel." I sighed. "If you're checking your messages, chances are that you've heard Sarai's side of the story. Please don't write me off, I have a lot of explaining to do, and things aren't quite what they may appear to be." I paused. "Anyway, I went to Sarai's place today and her shit is gone. I need to know where she is, please call me."

I quickly called Sarai's cell phone again; no answer. Still sweaty from the workday, I lay back in bed, clicked on the television, and told myself that by the end of the night, I would be explaining myself to Sarai.

"Hey, roommate!" Charlize said sarcastically as she walked into my room with a large McDonald's bag. "Want some?"

I smiled. "What you got?"

"Twenty-piece nuggets." She frowned. "I didn't feel like cooking tonight."

"You?" I was shocked. "Martha Stewart?"

"Yes." She sat on the bed. "I'm drained."

"Oh yeah?" I asked. "Long day at work?"

"Yeah," she replied, "but that wasn't even the strenuous part." She took the box of nuggets out of the bag and rested it on the bed. "Cherry came in for a massage today. She was my last client and that damn girl"—she giggled—"that girl can talk."

I agreed. "Cherry has issues." I never told her about Cherry coming on to me. "What was she talking about?"

"Oh, my goodness," Charlize joked. "What wasn't she talking about?" She opened the box and whatever "mystery meat" those chicken nuggets were made out of smelled like chicken to me. "Her job, her car, her house, her love life . . ."

"Whoa, scary Cherry has a man?" I asked.

"A man?" Charlize asked. "Let's try a woman!"

"What's up with these sistas, man?" I was amazed. "She's gay?" I grabbed a nugget.

"Mel, you are so dense," she said. "That girl at the picnic was her woman."

"What girl?" I stopped chewing.

"Sarai," she replied.

I coughed quickly. "Who?"

"Sarai, the one who left with the stuff all over her dress." Charlize went on: "Before you got there on Saturday, Cherry was telling me about their sex life." She stuffed a nugget in her mouth. "Strap-on dildos, licking each other, et cetera . . ." She seemed disgusted but continued anyway. "I nearly vomited on her. I don't want to hear about that."

"She's not gay," I stated, still stunned with food in my mouth.

"You're right, she's not gay, she's bisexual at the least, she has been since college, that girl is a freak." She went on: "I literally had to stop her from giving me too much information."

"I think she was telling you that to fuck with you." I laughed it off. "Maybe she secretly wants *you*."

"She already tried," Charlize said. "She knows that that ain't going down here. I am strictly dickly."

"I'll believe anything about Cherry or Syd or whatever her name is," I said. "But Sarai didn't strike me as that type of person."

"Well, she is," Charlize assured me. "Because before she arrived, Cherry forced me to listen to some of the voice mails that Sarai had left her, and it was her voice." She sipped her Coke. "They're a couple of freaks. Cherry told me that they screwed two guys together, her boss, and Sarai's next-door neighbor, *together*."

My internal audio blacked out. Charlize's mouth was still moving, but I couldn't handle anything more she had to say. All I could hear in my mind was Craig's comment: *Was that before or after she sucked my big country dick?* This had to be a mistake. She couldn't stand that guy. *Was that before or after she sucked my big country dick?* Was that why she hated him now?

Charlize was unaware of the disaster she had created within me, so she went on: "Cherry said that they're moving in together." Charlize jumped up from the bed. "Well, I gotta go make some phone calls."

Moving in together? I asked myself. *I'll be damned!*

I was paralyzed by anger and rightly so, because if I could move, I would probably kill someone or something. My eyes were fixated on the ceiling, my heart felt like it was struggling to beat, and my fingertips were ice-cold. I tried counting to ten, but on my sixteenth attempt, I realized that it wasn't working. I couldn't believe that this girl had played me . . . again. Was I that much of a jackass that she would do this to me again before she even realized that she had already put me through this? Or maybe I just needed to realize that that was the type of person she was and move on with my life.

An hour later, I found myself in the shower, not washing or scrubbing, but just standing under the showerhead as though the water knew how to find the dirt and sweat between my ass, balls, and underarms. If I was going to get clean, it wasn't going to be because I put forth any effort.

I thought about the poem I'd recited to her and I considered myself a loser for writing it. How could I have put so much passion into such a ridiculous woman? I knew that I shouldn't have trusted her again. "Damn." Sarai was playing Little Miss Innocent with me while fucking this freak whore Syd, her neighbor, *and* Syd's boss, whoever he was.

Yet all the while, she remained the perfect woman to me. What great acting! "Encore! Bravo!" I began clapping my hands for her right there in the shower. "Fuck Halle Berry, Sarai. Because you . . . you, my friend, deserve the award . . . you are a class fuckin' act." I continued: "I guess some things never change . . . only this time you aren't selling the pussy, it's being shelled out for free. Come one, come all, come fuck the greatest pussy in town."

I was standing under the water with my hands pressed against the wall when I heard Charlize knock on the door. "Mel?"

"Yeah."

"You're in the shower?" she asked.

I figured that was obvious. "Why?"

"I need the shampoo you borrowed last week," she yelled through the door.

"The door isn't locked," I yelled back. "Come in, I'll pass it to you." I grabbed the Herbal Essence from the windowsill and heard her open the door. "By the way, the next time I want shampoo, please don't try me with this fruity shit." I tried to sound normal. "Old-fashioned Head & Shoulders is fine by me."

"Shut up," she joked. "Where is it?"

I commanded, "Gimme your hand." She stuck her right hand behind the shower curtain and I, with the shampoo bottle, walked to meet it, but at the last second, my plans changed. My mind changed about Charlize when my soul confirmed to me that Sarai had indeed hurt me again. I hadn't been Mr. Innocent either, so why stop now? "Gimme your hand!" I beckoned to Charlize and I rested my semi-limp dick in her palm.

"Mel?" she shrieked, and quickly pulled her hand away. I caught her by the wrist and brought her hand back into me, this time taking it to my mouth. I kissed her pointer finger and then trailed the length of it with my tongue, after which I inserted it into my mouth and sucked on it as if I was sucking on her lower button of flesh. "Mel, stop," she cried weakly, and tried to pull away, but I fought to keep her.

I kissed, licked, and sucked every finger on her hand. I felt her squirm, heard her moan, and smelled her wetness infusing the air. With the blue shower curtain still between us, I tried to pretend that she was Sarai. However, it didn't work. I realized that she was the type of woman I wanted Sarai to be . . . but that was like asking Satan for an ice cube, that wasn't happening . . . at least not until hell froze over. In some crazy fucked-up way, Charlize was a better version of who I thought I wanted, which was Sarai.

After feasting on her fingers, I lowered her hand back into the original position and inserted my now-hardened flesh into it. She was reluctant, so I closed her wet fingers around it and let go of her hand; I wasn't going to force her. I pulled back a little and watched her tighten her hold, and when I thrust forward, she didn't let go. I rested my palms against the back wall of the shower and plowed into Charlize's hand repeatedly. Her grip was just right, but I wanted more. I pulled back the shower curtain and found Charlize from her chest down to her knees wrapped in a purple towel and her face draped in tears. "What are you trying to do to me?" she asked.

"What?" I stepped out of the shower. "What did I do?"

"I can't do this with you, Tremel," she said. "You might think that I'm this strong woman that can put up with anything"—she paused—"but I can't. I cannot."

"What do you mean?" I asked.

"You're in love with another woman," Charlize said. "I can't just do this with you and walk away like it's all good," she cried. "I invested emotions into you before, and when you told me about your girlfriend, I respected that and tried recalling everything I felt for you," she reminded me. "It's only been a few days, but I'm doing just fine," she said. "You don't have to pacify me with your dick."

"I'm not trying to pacify you." I touched her face. "I'm putting you first."

"No, you are not taking me back there." With her eyes closed, she swung her head from side to side. "I cannot go back into a lie with you."

"Listen to me." I grabbed both of her hands and her towel dropped. "It's not a lie, Charlize."

"Yes, it is." She pulled away. "You said that she has your heart."

"Not anymore," I whispered. "Not anymore, Charlize. I want to be with you."

"No." She refused to hear me. "Don't do this."

"I need you, Charlize."

She opened her eyes. "Do you know what you're saying, Mel?"

"Yes." I meant every word. "I want to be with you."

My smile turned into a pucker that went in search of her lips. When our tongues tangoed, I felt her body gradually relax. I dropped the toilet-seat cover and slowly sat down on it, pulling her inch by inch along with me. Facing me, she gently guided her body down onto my lap and I didn't have to support my dick . . . it was on the runway, ready to accept her incoming air traffic.

The head of my carburetor shivered as it came in contact with her saturated and overheated engine. She smoothly doubled down on me and my hands caressed her breasts. I squeezed them and brought them halfway up to meet me as I tongued her nipples. She revolved her pussy in circles and I pushed deep into her. "Is this all you really want from me?" Charlize asked softly in my ear.

"Yes." I closed my eyes and groaned. "Give me that sweet pus—" Before the double *s*'s were out of my mouth, she shot up off me and bolted through the door. It happened so fast that I was still thrusting . . . but my dick was in the air.

"What the fuck?" I ran after her and found her facedown on her bed, weeping. "What happened?"

Her voice was muffled from talking into the bedspread. "Do you even know what you said?" She didn't bother looking over at me.

"No." I approached her from behind and rubbed her back. "What did I say?"

"I asked you if that was all you wanted from me and you said yes." She sniffled. "I told you before that I am not your fuck buddy, Tremel."

"I didn't mean it like that, baby." I was being sincere. "It was just feeling so good, I would've said yes to anything at that time." I continued rubbing her back. "I'm sorry if you took it that way."

"Maybe you and I doing it again just isn't such a good idea," she said, still talking into the sheets.

"You're right," I said, but looking at her thick brown body sprawled out on her stomach, my dick came alive and I climbed on top of her. "It's not a good idea, it's a great idea." Because her legs were already opened, I guided myself into her fold before she could speak or move. "Are you telling me that we shouldn't do *this* anymore?" I asked while kissing her ear.

"Ooooh, Mel," she moaned.

"You don't want me?" I asked, and could feel the tip of my sword tapping her G-spot. "You don't want this?"

"Yes," she answered, "but I want all of you."

"I'm ready to give it to you, baby." I kissed her neck and plunged into her faster.

"Not just sex—"

I interrupted her. "I'm ready to give you whatever you want from me, Charlize."

She braced herself on her elbows and backed it up on me in a rhythm that made my toes curl. Soon she was on all fours and I was holding her around the waist. I barreled into her repeatedly; I pulled out to the very tip and filled her up again. Her tightness was working me, and even the blood vessels in my soul wanted to burst. The last time I heaved out and plummeted back into her inner walls felt like wet silk. Her body bucked and pranced wildly and she howled like a wolf. She sucked me in, but I couldn't pull out . . . our bodily fluids collided, and when I eased out of her, I watched our sweet sugar drain out of her still-contracting honey pot.

"No more just fuck buddies." I turned her over, kissed her on the lips, and said, "I want you in my life." Who knew that by the end of the night I would be explaining myself . . . to Charlize.

Sarai
7½

It was Wednesday afternoon and I was in a rental car heading back
to Baltimore from Dover to catch my six o'clock flight. I had spent
three days in Dover with my father. He wasn't as feisty as he normally was, so the visit was pleasant. He allowed me to talk to him,
read to him, and watch TV with him. It was almost like the old days,
except he didn't say too much. Before I left him, I broke down in
tears. "How about you move to Miami with me?"

"Girl, please." The Alzheimer's spoke: "I don't know nobody in
no Miami."

"Daddy, you know me," I cried. "I want you to be with me. I feel
like I don't have anybody, I'm so alone down there." I grabbed his
hand. "I can't get in touch with Savion, and we have no other family.
I need you with me, Daddy."

"Stop crying." Daddy felt sorry for me. "I'll help you find your
dad. You want me to call the nurse?"

"No." I smiled. "No, I know exactly where he is." I wrapped my arms around him and squeezed him tightly. "I'll call you tomorrow, okay?"

"Okay," he said. "I'm going to watch *Price Is Right*." We had already watched it, yet he had asked what time it was coming on twice since it went off.

I kissed him on the cheek. "I love you."

"You a friendly l'il girl, you know that?" He smiled. "I love you, too."

I had made up in my mind that in a few months I was moving him to Miami, kicking and screaming, because I couldn't see moving back to Dover. I needed him closer to me. "'Bye, Daddy," I said from the doorway.

He waved at me from within. "'Bye, Sarai."

Seeing Daddy again coupled with the silence on the airplane forced me to realize that I had no one in Miami besides Nat, and with her being out of town, I was a hot mess in the friendship category. When I lost Damian and my job, I lost the friends that had come along with them. Speaking of friends, my mind quickly raced to Syd. I needed to put whatever we were doing to an end . . . and I meant a complete *stop*. If she needed me to say it in French . . . *arrête*. Spanish . . . *parada*. Russian . . . остановка. Dutch . . . *Het einde*. Basically, in any language, Syd and I had to S-T-O-P!

As the plane descended, I glanced out of the window and could see the glimmering Miami lights. I wondered if Tremel had taken Charlize to the airport to watch planes arrive and depart as he had done with me. He was probably down there now, parked along the tarmac's gates, with yet another chick who thought that he was so sweet for doing something so romantic and creative. "Who's on that plane?" I heard him ask her.

The bitch . . . whoever she is, not half as cute as me, says, "There is a girl aboard, a nasty girl. She's having an off-and-on sexual affair with another woman, and she fucked her next-door neighbor. She's confused, she has nothing going for herself, she doesn't even have

SARAI

203

a job . . . and she's not looking for one. She's a sad excuse for anything. She forgot to pay her rent again before she left town. This girl is a loser and I have no clue why she's even coming back to Miami because we could all benefit from the oxygen that she's wasting just being alive."

I wish I had gone with my gut feeling about Tremel from the time that I called him and heard him and that woman going at it. I had done this to myself . . . I had played myself and couldn't really be mad at anyone but me.

The airplane's tires struck the tarmac at the same time as the tears were hitting my cheeks. I sat on the plane until absolutely everyone who wasn't staff was gone. I was in no rush to get back to my life because it included no one and nothing. I slowly grabbed my carry-on from overhead and made my way through the maze of an airport and to the parking garage, which was equally baffling. I clicked on my phone, and as if she had been watching me, Syd was already ringing my line. "Damn it." I looked at the caller ID. "Hello," I answered.

"Oh my God," Syd said in a panicked tone. "Where have you been?"

"I'm fine, thank you for asking," I said sarcastically.

"Fuck that, I can hear that you're fine," she scolded me. "Where have you been? I have been calling you since Saturday right after the picnic, Sarai . . . it's fucking Wednesday night and this is the first time that you've picked up." She went on: "I have been trying to come see you and I can't get in. What the fuck, Sarai?"

"Syd, calm the hell down," I said. "I am just getting back in town. I went to Dover to see my dad."

"Is he okay?" she asked sincerely.

"He's the same as always." I sighed. "I just picked up and left. Sorry that I didn't call . . . I have a lot of shit going on."

"Yeah, Sarai, we all do, but a simple phone call could work wonders." She went on: "I was so worried about you. I started to—"

My truck came into view and I froze. "Holy shit." All four of my tires were flat. "Holy fuckin' shit!" I yelled.

"What?" Syd asked. "What happened?"

"My tires are flat." I ran over to my truck, pulling my bag behind me. "Muthafuck!" I said loud enough to startle the elderly couple on the other end of the parking facility.

"They're all flat?" Syd wanted to know.

"Fuck!" I exclaimed, and then answered, "Yeah, they're all fuckin' flat." I saw a small slit in one of them. "Somebody did this shit; they're slit."

"Who the fuck would do that?" Syd asked. "Where are you?"

"I told you . . ." I was pissed. "I'm at the airport. I'm just coming back."

She asked, "Miami International?"

"Yeah," I said.

Syd demanded information. "Where are you parked?"

"In the Dolphin parking garage," I said.

"Okay! Get in the truck and lock the doors, I'm on my way." She sounded concerned. "I'm on Biscayne Boulevard; I'm like five minutes from you."

"Okay." I did as she said and sat in the truck. When she reached the parking area, she called again and I guided her to where I was. Soon I saw her car headed toward me. "I see you," I said into the phone. I opened my door and waved my arms.

She parked in front of my truck and walked over to me. "You okay?" She hugged me.

"Yeah." I was angry. "Who would do some shit like this?"

She looked at the tires. "This is some jealous-ex-girlfriend-type shit." She slapped my ass jokingly. "You cheating on me?"

"Shut up." I was pissed. "We need to call the police."

"Yeah," she said. "I saw security at the gate. I told him and he's on the way up on a golf cart."

Minutes later, the security guard came with his flashlight and a clipboard . . . I was not impressed. He couldn't do anything for me and I politely asked him to call the airport police . . . the big dogs with guns. They came and asked a bunch of questions, took some information from me, and gave me a card with a case number on it. Within thirty minutes, Syd and I were standing alone again.

"What the hell was that?" I was confused. "I thought they would take fingerprints, take pictures, and all of that."

Syd laughed. "This is not a homicide investigation."

"Someone slashed my fuckin' tires," I said. "This is a big damn deal to me."

"Sorry, baby." She walked over to me and kissed me softly on the lips. "Let me make it better." Her lips touched mine again and again until they were pressed up against me and our tongues met. Sydney was like a drug. Why couldn't I say no to her? My spirit could feel something within her that was dark, but when she touched me, I always wanted more.

It was a few minutes past midnight. "Are you gonna take me home?" I asked.

"No." She smiled. "I'm taking you to a better place."

We drove out of the garage and onto the expressway. I nodded off for a few minutes and opened my eyes in front of the Biscayne Bay Marriott. "What are we doing *here*?"

"This is where I'm staying." Syd pulled up to the valet. "I checked in this morning."

"Why?" I asked while grabbing my bag out of the backseat.

She blushed. "Every once in a while a girl has to treat herself."

As soon as the door to room 1412 closed, Syd was on top of me. We were naked in seconds, licking in minutes, and she couldn't get that black strap-on dick up in me soon enough. We were under the sheets and Syd was on top of me when I thought I heard the door unlock. I looked over at it but everything appeared normal. Syd started pounding me as if it was our last time together.

I started to scream, and in the midst of me trembling, Syd stopped moving and her expression changed. "Thanks for fuckin' with my life." She sprayed my face with spit, jumped off of me, and then out of the bed.

"What?" I wiped the sticky saliva from my face in utter confusion. "What the fuck are you doing?" Then out of the corner of my eye, I saw three men walking into the room. I grabbed the sheets and covered my body. "What the fuck is this, Syd?" I sat up and pulled the sheet up over my breasts.

The third man held the door open and in walked Conrad Johnson in a beige suit smoking a cigar. "Well, good evening, Miss Emery!" He closed the door and the third man removed his coat as if he was working for James Brown. Conrad then continued to speak. "It is such a pleasure to make your acquaintance once more." He approached the king-size bed and my now shaking body. "Are you enjoying your stay thus far?" He extended his right hand to me, but I refused it. "That's cool, I wouldn't shake my hand either because I'm a slimy cat and that shit might rub off on you." The men all chuckled.

He sucked on his cigar. "Cherry, go put your clothes on, baby . . . you've been a great help. I'm going to take care of you as promised." Cherry eyeballed me as she gathered her things and then vanished into the bathroom.

"Sarai Emery." Conrad smiled. "We meet again."

I studied him and his friends. "What is this all about, Conrad?"

"Y'all hear that? She remembers me." He looked back at the men and laughed. "You remember me, great. That saves me from the bullshit storytelling segment of the evening." He sat on the bed. "Do you know any of them?" He pointed at the men.

One by one, I stared them down. "No," I stuttered, "I don't know them."

"Well, I've been patiently waiting for you to remember the mess you made of my establishment by snitching." He blew smoke in my face. "But I've grown weary of waiting, so ready or not, here I come." He smiled. "I'm here to take back what you owe me."

"What are you talking about?" I asked as tears marched down my cheeks like soldiers. "Are you all going to rape me?"

He ripped the sheets from my hands and exposed my naked body. "Sarai, as much as I want to fuck you right now, there is something that turns me on ten times more than pussy . . . and that's money."

He touched my thighs. "And currently the money I want is in your bank account." Conrad pulled out a Rockwell Mutual receipt; it was for a deposit of $175, Syd's deposit to pay for my table . . . the receipt also included my account number and my ending balance. "I want my money," Conrad said.

"What money?" I cried. "I don't know what you're talking about."

"Bring me that box," he asked one of the men. "Look inside," he instructed me, and I did just that. In the box was hundreds of DVDs.

"What do those have to do with me?" I seriously didn't know. "What are they?"

"These . . . are your choices," he said. "I will put these DVDs on the streets for five dollars a pop to get my forty-five Gs if I have to." He tossed a DVD to one of the men, who then put it into the player on the dresser. "Now you decide," Conrad said. "Are you going to give me my money or do you want me to make it selling these?"

The man touched play just as Syd was coming out of the bathroom. On the television screen popped up me the night I met Syd at the bar. She was talking to me, flirting with me, and I was all smiles. Then it cut to Conrad and me sitting in the backseat of a limousine. "What is this?" I asked, but quickly figured it out when I saw I was wearing the same outfit I was wearing when I met Syd, but I had no memory of it. On the television, I moved to sitting on Conrad's lap. He started kissing me, and in the next scene, I was completely naked and performing oral sex on him. Soon I was riding him and he was spanking me.

"You bitch," I screamed at Syd. "You drugged me?"

She smiled. "That goes to show you not to drink everything a stranger gives to you."

"What have I done to you, Syd?" I asked. "Why would you do this to me?"

"For the record, my name is Cherry, and as soon as you get your memory back, then you'll know exactly why I did this." She rolled her eyes. "I thought we were cool, Sarai, and you went and fucked with my life . . . so how does it feel?"

"What are you talking about?" I felt helpless. "What is any of this about?"

Cherry spoke up. "You sent me to this very same hotel room, room fourteen-twelve, a few months ago." She got closer to me. "You set me up! You sent that bitch up here and I went to jail that night. I sat in there for a month." She gloated. "But who's sorry now, bitch?"

"I don't know what the fuck you're talking about!" I yelled.

"Okay. Shut the fuck up," Conrad yelled at both of us. "Both of y'all shut the hell up," he said again. "I'm trying to watch a movie here."

The room fell silent as I watched, on the screen, Conrad putting me in various positions and having his way with me. It was vile and disgusting. However, it didn't stop just there. There was a compilation of about ten scenes . . . Cherry had videotaped every time she and I had sex . . . even in my own apartment. Her purse was rigged with a camera; she caught everything on tape by strategically placing it on my dresser in the bedroom or windowsill in the living room, including our night with Craig. Conrad had the scenes fine-tuned and edited into a two-hour-long DVD he politely referred to as *Sarai Fuck Fest*. "So . . ." He turned to me again. "The choice is yours. You can give me the forty Gs or I can earn it with these," he said while holding up the DVD with a picture of me sucking Craig's dick on the cover.

I rocked my body back and forth. "I'll give you the money," I cried.

He then turned to the men. "Somehow I thought that she would choose to do that." He looked back at me. "All right; now, in the morning, I'm going to take you to Rockwell to withdraw the money. Is that going to be a problem?"

"No," I said weakly.

"I'm going in with you." He pointed at the man in the middle, who then unbuttoned his coat to reveal the handle of a gun atop his belt. "You don't plan on doing anything stupid while we're in there, do you?"

"No," I mumbled while looking at the gun.

"You were going broke before, but when I'm done with you this time, you'll be dead broke." Conrad laughed. "Now, before I go, there is still a little problem." He glared down at me. "I don't have time to explain to your forgetful ass just how you swindled my clients' wives out of their money. The long and short of it is that I need forty-five Gs from you. It'll make up the revenue I lost due to your little blackmail scheme, but you only have forty-two thousand two hundred and ninety-six dollars in the bank." He bent down to my ear. "You wouldn't happen to have another twenty-seven hundred available, would you?"

I shook my head. "No . . ."

"I thought you would say that." He smiled. "Don't worry; I've already made arrangements for you to get it." He pointed to the three men. "I've sold your mouth, pussy, and your asshole if they so desire, to them for nine hundred dollars each, to make up for what you were missing in the bank." He stuck the cigar in his mouth and turned away from me. "All right, gentlemen . . . go easy on her. I need that bitch to be able to walk into the bank in the morning." Conrad grabbed Cherry's hand and exited the room.

"Guys," I begged, "please don't do this . . . I can pay you each two grand apiece." I pointed at my purse. "I can write you all checks right now."

One of the men was already on the bed taking his shirt off. "C'mon, a little bit of dick never hurt nobody . . . all we want is blow jobs."

"Yeah." One man walked out of his pants and toward me. "Open up and say ahhh." He held his dick out to me.

"C'mon . . ." I cried. "Don't do this to me . . . please."

He grabbed me by my hair and slapped me in the mouth with his dick a few times. "Open your mouth; we're not here to play games with you," he said. "You're going to suck every muthafucka in here . . . this is what you get for trying to be a badass."

• • •

He was right; in the midst of my tears, I sucked all three of them. I started out battling the first guy, but by the time the second entered my mouth, I had no fight left. As they finished, they each left the room. After the third guy came, he had the audacity to make a phone call. "Yo, Rock, you asleep?" he asked. "Come down to fourteen-twelve and get you some of this." He was smiling. "A bitch, what you think?" He went on: "Huh? Yeah, Conrad wanted us to keep her in line, so we did," he said. "C'mon, Rock, 'cause I'm tired as shit. When you're done you'll have to stay and watch this bitch, though."

The guy must've been in the next room, because before Dick Number Three closed his cell phone, the man he referred to by the name of Rock was knocking on the door. I couldn't believe that he had just invited his homeboy to have a piece of me, as if I was bread in a basket.

Rock entered the room looking like he had been asleep for hours. He was slender and stood a little over six feet, with light brown skin, brown eyes, and a body that said that he did a little more than hang out with Conrad's entourage all day. On an ordinary day, I wouldn't be able to tear my eyes away from such an attractive man, but the truth was that this wasn't an ordinary day . . . he was here to violate me.

The expression on his face was unreadable. His eyes were fixated on me, his prey, as if he couldn't wait to get his hands on me and his appendage up in me. He slapped palms with the other guy like this was a relay race . . . it was now his turn and I was the baton that they were handing off.

Rock locked the door after Guy Number Three left, and without saying a word to me, he turned off the lights and walked over to the bed. In no time, I felt him rustling the covers and lying next to me. As the darkness settled into the room and my eyes adjusted, I lifted the covers to find that he was still fully clothed. "What, I have to undress you too?" I asked fragilely.

"No," he said, and began wrestling with his pants under the sheets until he kicked them off and onto the floor.

I was ready to be done with him and the whole ordeal sooner rather than later, so I began touching his penis. I stroked and teased it for about fifteen minutes and it had little reaction to what I was doing. I moved to pull the covers over my head and make my way down south. "You don't have to do that." Rock grabbed me by the hand and whispered as he pushed me back toward the bed.

I was tired. My head fell to his chest accidentally, but my hand continued to try to bring him joy . . . to no avail. My hand dropped to his side as my eyes closed. I think that's when I started dreaming because I faintly remember feeling Rock turning to his side and speak directly into my ear. "I didn't know that they were doing that to you, I would've stopped them," Rock said as he rubbed my back. Moments later he softly said, "I won't hurt you."

That morning Rock stayed with me, as instructed by Conrad. Though he didn't degrade me as the others did, I was still just as afraid of him. And I couldn't believe that I had the audacity to wake up with my head on his chest and my arm draped around his waist. He had to watch me shower, eat, and get dressed to make sure I wasn't up to anything.

I was sitting on the bed and he was at the desk, but I kept looking at him out of the side of my eyes. I guessed he noticed it. "Nobody's going to hurt you," he said as we waited for Conrad and the others to come to the room.

"I can't be hurt any worse than I am already," I said without looking at him. "They didn't fuck me, but right now I can't tell the difference."

"Are you going to the police?" Rock asked.

I looked over at him as if he was crazy. "No." Why would I say yes to him?

"Look, about what happened before I got here . . ." He paused. "I'm really sorry . . ."

"Sorry for what?" I was pissed. "If your dick could've gotten hard, you would've wanted me to do you too!"

"You think so?" he asked.

"I know so." I was pissed.

He stood up. "So it couldn't be that I actually felt sorry for you?" He walked closer to me.

"You came in here for me to suck your dick," I said, looking up at him. "And if there was some Viagra around, maybe you would've been man enough to get it up and have it done."

"Fuck you," he said without flinching, and turned his back to me. "Damn it." He returned to the desk.

I sighed. "Sorry, but as you can imagine, I am pretty fuckin' upset." I started playing with his intelligence, or at least I thought I was. "Why don't you let me go?" I stood up. "Let me walk out of here, you're obviously the best guy of the group."

Rock turned to me. "I can't do that."

"Why, what's stopping you?" I asked. "Just say that I overpowered you or I just bolted for the door and got away."

"I wish I could." He raised his shirt, unveiling a gun neatly tucked into his pants. "No one will ever believe that you overpowered me." He seemed annoyed with me. "Just sit and chill. All he wants is the money, I promise you that."

"I am a human being," I reminded him. "I am someone's daughter, someone's sister, and the mother of a child," I lied. "Imagine the look on my daughter's face when they pull me from the Miami River or some shit that you could've stopped from happening."

"You don't have a kid." He laughed.

"Yes, I do." I tried convincing him.

"Save it, Sarai." He shut me up. "I am not just some random guy that they asked to watch you . . ." He stared at me. "I know more about you than you'll ever believe."

Minutes later, Conrad, Cherry, and the rest of the crew were present. Conrad and I went into the bank while the others waited in the limo. I requested a cashier's check and asked them to make it payable to Conrad Johnson. The check was for my entire existing balance, not a penny less. Afterward, we traveled to a branch of Conrad's bank, where he cashed the check and returned to the car with the nearly four hundred hundred-dollar bills in a large envelope.

Because Conrad had the money, I was now useless to him and afraid for my life. He instructed the driver where to go from a phone in the back. I was crying my eyes out. I just assumed that I would be beaten and thrown into a lake or a highway to be run over by an eighteen-wheeler. I was hysterical and Syd found my state amusing. The car stopped and Conrad's voice filled the air. "Sarai, let's come to an understanding." He continued: "You pretend none of this ever happened and I will never bother you again."

"Okay." I looked out of the window and was surprised to see that we were just a block away from my apartment complex. "I promise, I won't say a word." I was eager.

Conrad went on: "If a word of this leaks to anyone, those DVDs will be distributed across the country and all over the Internet." He talked as if it was nothing for him to do this. "I don't need the money; I'll put that shit out there for free just to fuck with you."

"I promise I won't tell a soul," I said.

He opened the back door of the limousine. "Get out." I struggled to make my way past Rock and all of the other men, but as I stepped onto the pavement, Conrad grabbed my hand. "I must admit, that pussy of yours is a real winner. I see why you made me so much money." He chuckled. "You're always welcome to come back and work for me." He paused. "I just had to show you who the hell is in charge . . . I run this." Conrad winked and let go of me. "If you suck the devil's dick, then he's gonna fuck you." He placed my suitcase on the ground. "Try to enjoy the rest of your day," he said sarcastically, and then slammed the door shut.

I watched that limousine disappear and take a piece of my life with it. I stumbled back to my apartment complex, and though something was wrong with my magnetic key card, the guard recognized me and allowed me in. It was a little after six in the evening and all I wanted to do was get in my bed and cry.

On the elevator, I nearly fell down as it jerked to move . . . I didn't have the strength to stand. Walking to my apartment was another chore . . . but I made it. The locks looked shinier than ever. I inserted my key and wiggled it . . . nothing happened. I tried my key repeatedly until it broke off inside the lock. "Shit." With my back against the door, my body slid down until I was on the floor. I knew what was going on . . . my lock wasn't broken . . . my lease was. I was homeless.

I buried my head in my hands and cried and cried until I heard voices . . . they were coming to me all at once and from every direction . . . but it was all in my head. Soon the voices were joined by faces, places, and things . . . I knew what was happening, it had happened a few times before. I was remembering things and this time it wasn't stopping. I was quickly remembering all of the men, sex for money, Daddy, losing my job . . . Cherry . . . conversations with my brother, Nat and India . . . Conrad . . . Dr. Baker. I could recall my dates with Tremel, making love to Tremel, meeting his family, his uncle Norman. I remembered loving Tremel and then losing him because of my lies. I remembered *everything*!

Things were coming to me out of sequence, but the longer I kept my eyes closed, the more they lined themselves up and fell into order. I had my memory back. And out of nowhere came what was supposed to be the final chapter of my life:

"I wish you were there when it was snowing." Tremel pulled me closer. "It's beautiful up there. You'll love it."

I cuddled up next to him and thought of being with him and closer to Daddy as well. "I love it already." I rubbed his chest. "Thank you."

"For what?" he asked in the darkness.

I answered, "For coming back." Suddenly I heard a noise come from the living-room area. "What was that?" I asked him.

He chuckled. "It's probably just the crab. It may have crawled out of the garbage and hit the floor."

Then there was another sound, as if something had fallen down in the kitchen. "Whoa." I was scared.

We both sat up and Tremel now seemed very concerned. "Did you lock the door behind you?" He sat up.

"I think so." I tried to remember, but it was too late. The bedroom door swung open, the lights came on, and in stepped Dwayne Cart/ Damian Carter.

"Damn, how the tables have turned," Damian said. His face was evil and full of rage. "I come home and you're in bed with someone else." He laughed.

"What the fuck?" I threw my bathrobe over Tremel then reached into my dresser drawer and grabbed my ugly and bulky green housedress.

Tremel, in my robe, was pissed. He passed me on the way to Damian. "How did you get in here?"

Damian frowned at Tremel. "The same way that you did, mother-fucker."

I didn't want problems, so I got between the two of them and pushed Damian out into the hallway. "Damian, what are you doing here?" I was scared out of my mind, but happy that Tremel had picked this night to come back. "What do you want?"

He said, "I'm here to finish what you started."

"What in the hell are you talking about?" I asked as I backed him up into the living room. Whatever was going to happen, I didn't want it to take place in my bedroom.

"You fucked up everything that I planned." He didn't flinch, falter, or back down. "Me fuckin' with India was part of a plan," he said. "She had exactly what I wanted—money. Her shit was supposed to be the way I started my own company. But you and your jealous ass had to find out and go ballistic. Then you sent her up to my hotel room. That was wrong, that was dumb. I almost killed that bitch that night. I put her in the hospital, and I've been in jail for almost four months. I got fired from my damn job at the firm. I've lost everything."

While Damian spoke, I saw Tremel grow angry. I watched his hands form fists and knew that that wasn't the answer. I spoke up before he did anything. I believed that I was the right one to handle the situation. "I'm sorry, Damian." I wasn't sure if I meant that. "I didn't mean to cause all of that to happen to you." I tried to calm him. "What can I do to help you?"

He reached into his jacket and pulled out a nine-millimeter. "You can start by getting this nigga the fuck out of my house."

"I'm not leaving." Tremel wasn't intimidated. He stood bravely beside me and grabbed my hand. "And if I do, she's coming with me."

This was a whole new ball game. "Please put the gun down," I begged. "I'll do whatever you say. Anything you ask me to do, I'll do it. Just put the gun away, Damian."

"What now, pretty boy?" He aimed it at Tremel. "What the fuck are you gonna do now?" Damian's eyes were watery and his pupils were dilated as if he was on something. "There is something that you can do for me." I had never seen him this way. His clothing was wrinkled and dirty, and he smelled as if he had been rolling around in vomit. "You can suck my dick again, right here in front of your man."

"You're out of your fuckin' mind." Tremel let go of my hand and leaped toward Damian. He pushed him onto the sofa, where they wrestled around a bit. I saw only hands and feet; I couldn't see the gun.

"Stop!" I screamed. "Please, stop." My fear was that Tremel wouldn't walk away. I yelled, "Stop it!" as it happened. I heard the trigger click and then the gun went off. Tremel's body stopped moving, then so did Damian's. I was confused; I couldn't move. My hands rushed to my mouth. I couldn't even scream when I saw a sign of life. Both Damian and Tremel stood to their feet. They were fine.

As crazy as everything was around me, I found the strength to smile as Tremel walked over to me. I was happy that he was all right. "Sarai." Tremel looked at me. "Sarai," he called out to me again. As badly as I wanted to answer him, I couldn't.

"Oh my God!" he screamed, but my eyes couldn't focus on him. I couldn't focus on anything. My sight just got dimmer and dimmer until I couldn't see, then I felt my legs fold under me. "Sarai," he called repeatedly. He thought I was close to him, but in reality, I was already miles away. He yelled at Damian, "Look what you did! Look what you did!"

He asked Damian to call 911, but Damian yelled something back and I heard the door slam. Tremel left me only for a moment to run and get the phone. He hit three buttons, then I heard him telling someone my name, address, and the entire story of what happened.

"I love you, Sarai," he cried. "Please don't leave me like this." I felt his tears hitting my face, and if I could cry, I would've. If I could do anything, I would've. He ran his warm hand down the side of my cold face. "I love you. Please don't go, Sarai. You can't leave me like this." He rocked my upper body back and forth. "Please stay with me. Let me sing for you." He tried to stop crying. "I had forgotten how to live, forgotten how to give. I forgot how to trust, and how to lust. But through you, I learned to care. Please forgive me if this seems rare. Now that I've found you, my life seems brand-new. So, you'll never be . . . forgotten." It was the chorus to the song he wrote for me.

"Where are you damn guys?" he screamed, growing impatient that there was still no sign of the police. "We can't wait on them," he wept. He cradled my lifeless body and walked me through my apartment; he struggled to open the front door. "Don't you leave me," he yelled at me as I heard the elevator doors open.

"I shouldn't have come here tonight." He blamed himself. "Just hold on, Sarai." His voice was starting to sound farther and farther away. "Don't you leave me."

I didn't know how to tell him, but I was leaving. As we made it to the ground floor, I heard sirens. Tremel burst out of the elevator doors with me folded up in his arms screaming for help. Help was waiting, but I was already gone.

Everyone had been lying to me; I hadn't been shot in a bank robbery. I opened my eyes screaming at the top of my lungs. The wave of memories took me through the full range of emotions a hundred times over and the only way I could express them all at once was to shout. I was still sitting on the ground in front of my apartment door, hysterical. I heard about five doors open and felt eyes on me, but I couldn't stop. "Sarai." Craig ran out of his apartment and shook me. "What's wrong?"

Holding me close to him and rubbing my back, he managed to calm me. Some of my other neighbors were also now gathered around me as if I was the girl from *The Exorcist*. I was breathing heavy and sweating. I was shaking and my eyes were bulged out. Craig cradled me and walked me into his place. "What's going on, Sarai?" he asked as he closed the door and rested me on his sofa.

"He shot me," I said. "Damian shot me."

"What?" He examined me with his eyes. "You're fine, no one shot you."

"No." I tried to tell him. "Not right now, it happened months ago, before you even moved here . . ." It took me about twenty minutes to tell Craig the whole story of me being shot and in a coma and then left without a memory up until a few moments ago. He brought me a blanket and a cup of hot tea.

Sitting on his couch made me reflect on my own sofa. "I was evicted, huh?" I asked calmly.

"Yeah." He looked away, embarrassed. "I tried calling you when they started moving your shit out."

"What?" I was new to the eviction scene. "They moved my stuff?"

"Yeah, they put all of your stuff, clothes and all, out by the Dumpsters."

For the longest time I thought that when people were evicted, the landlord would just change the locks but would allow you, under management's supervision, to come back and get your belongings within a reasonable time period. "My shit is in the trash?"

"Well, it was as close to it as it could get." He smiled. "I rented a moving truck and put it in storage for you."

"Oh, my goodness." I was surprised at Craig's superhuman qualities. Here I was thinking he was just a fuck monster. "Thank you, Craig."

"No problem." He smiled. "I'll give you the key to the storage space tomorrow. You can stay here for as long as you need to."

"You won't have to deal with me long," I said. "I'll start looking for a place tomorrow." Yeah, right . . . I'll be on Nat's doorstep as soon as she's back in town.

"Go get in my bed, I'm heading out." He glanced at his watch. "I'm supposed to meet my homeboy on the beach."

"Okay, thanks again," I said. "I will gladly pay for the storage as soon as I can."

"Don't worry about that now." He waved it off. "We'll work something out later, get some rest."

As soon as Craig left, I crawled into his bed and got excited about all the things I had remembered, and recalled them all one by one like toys to play with. Tremel was on my mind. What a man he was for not forcing himself on me, allowing me to remember him on my own. I wanted to call him up and tell him that his girl, his woman . . . his lover . . . was back. I wanted him by my side. I rooted around in my purse for my phone and then it hit me . . . the Tremel I was remembering was the same Tremel I had seen at the picnic with another woman . . . a woman that he was living with. Suddenly I wished I hadn't remembered everything. It hurt so bad to get Tremel back . . . and to lose him again all in one single thought.

I balled myself into the fetal position and closed my eyes. I couldn't shake the thoughts of Tremel, so I tried to escape them by falling asleep. However, that just meant that I'd dream about him, and that I did. Tremel pulled me close to him and kissed me. As his tongue swirled around in my mouth, I sucked on him gently, but then, when his hand crept into my panties, the feeling was too real, so real that I was awakened by it. Craig's tongue was in my mouth. "What are you doing?" I was startled at finding my pants pulled down.

Two of his fingers slipped into my vagina. "Stop!" I yelled, and noticed that he was naked. "Craig, what are you doing?"

"You don't want me to stop," he said, and continued fingering me. "We had so much fun before."

Pinned down by one hand and with him lying on the other, I tried pushing him off of me by raising my body, but couldn't. I felt his steel-firm erection on my thigh. "Craig, don't do this,". I begged.

Craig kept on kissing me. "Don't you want the key to the storage?" he asked.

"I can pay you." I tried pushing him off again but still couldn't. "I'll give you the money for it."

"I don't want money, I want this pussy." Craig pushed his fingers farther into me. "Why are you making this so difficult? I've had you before." He lined his dick up to enter me.

God couldn't have forsaken someone as much as He had forsaken me in the last thirty-six hours of my life. This couldn't be happening to me. I looked into Craig's eyes, and from somewhere within me came strength and it all gathered in my right leg. As he moved his dick around to get it into me, my right knee taught him a lesson his dick and balls would never forget.

"Get off of me!" I yelled as he rolled to his side in agony. I jumped out of the bed, pulled up my pants, grabbed my purse and tattered suitcase, and bolted from his apartment and down the fire escape. Adrenaline is a power thing! Never in my life did I think I could make it down eleven flights of stairs and live to tell about it. Not only that, I ran like a track star down the street until I reached a dim streetlight. I stopped and searched my purse for the $200 that I had taken out at an ATM at the airport in Baltimore. "Thank God." I smiled as if it was a million dollars' worth of diamonds. I walked to a gas station and called a cab. It was 5 a.m. when the Haitian driver dropped me off at the airport. I wobbled my way to my incapacitated truck, got into the driver's seat, and felt like I was safer there than anywhere I had been all week.

I got hungry that afternoon and ventured into the airport's food court. The Chinese restaurant had free samples of orange chicken and that shit had me at hello. I ordered some pork fried rice and orange chicken and stayed seated in the food court until around 8 p.m. When the various security guards and police started looking at me as though I was some sort of terrorist, I ordered three slices of pizza and a large orange soda to go from another spot and headed back to my truck. I ate two slices and fell asleep in the backseat listening to 103 the Beat.

I had cold pizza for breakfast and used an airport restroom to wash up and change. I even did my makeup. There is no saying that if you're living in your car you can't be cute. I hung out at the Starbucks all day . . . ordering something cheap every couple of hours while thumbing through a magazine. I returned to the truck after nine with dinner, Burger King, locked the doors, and grubbed.

I couldn't believe that I was living in my truck and couldn't even go anywhere remotely cool because of the tires. I was down to $140 and Nat wasn't due back for another three or four days. Therefore, this was the way it was going to have to be until then. I hopped in the backseat, covered my upper body with a shirt, and closed my eyes.

Bam! Bam! Bam! "Miami PD, please open the door, ma'am." I woke up with what looked like a twenty-thousand-watt flashlight shining in my face. "Miami PD, open the door."

I struggled to sit up and nervously opened the door. I couldn't see the officer's face. "What is the problem, sir?" I asked.

"Ma'am, we've been told that you have been sleeping in this truck for the past two nights. Is that true?"

I shielded my eyes from his almighty light. "Well, this is my truck, and I am sleeping in it tonight because I missed my flight." I was scared. "Someone flattened my tires earlier today, and I just don't know what to do."

"Step out of the vehicle, ma'am."

"Why?" I gave up . . . I was sobbing. "What did I do?" I covered my face with my hands and wished that he would just shoot me . . . at least I could get a hospital stay . . . or better yet, you didn't need insurance at the morgue . . . I was fed up. "What did I do?"

"You didn't do anything." His light went off. "I can't let you sleep out here. Sarai, I'm taking you home with me." He held his badge out to me. "I'm Officer Keenan Tanner." I looked at the badge and then my eyes traveled up his long brown arms until I was staring at the face of the limp-dick man I met in the hotel room named Rock.

I was stunned. "What?"

"I need you to come with me," he said.

"You're not a cop." I tried to close the door but he grabbed me.

"Yes, I am, Sarai, and I am putting a lot on the line just being here." He grabbed my belongings. "I told you that I would never hurt you." He pulled me toward him. "Please come with me."

> "Regret for the things we did can be tempered by time; it is regret for the things we did not do that is inconsolable."
>
> —S. SMITH

Tremel

WITHDRAWAL SLIP #8
ENDING BALANCE: $102.54

After a long day at work, I was looking forward to seeing Charlize, but I returned to an empty house. It always felt bigger and colder when she wasn't there, and I always felt like a candle waiting on a match without her. It had only been about three days since I decided that I wanted to try out having a relationship with her, but I longed for her to strike a match and light my fuse when I was in from work.

As much as I wanted to be close to her, talk to her, and touch her, there was still somewhat of an emptiness within me that I couldn't understand. There was a spot on the window of my heart that her Windex couldn't wipe away. Was I craving her so much just to stop wanting Sarai? I told myself that I couldn't be. Sarai had made her bed again and decided to lie in it with a fuckin' woman and various men, and I wanted no part of it. I told Mr. Jimenez about my situation and his advice to me was basically the Spanish version of "you can't turn a whore into a housewife."

I needed to be knee-deep in between Charlize's thighs to shake the feeling of Sarai, which was clinging to me like spandex. I sat on the sofa and watched the door like it was a movie. The sound track I hoped to hear was a key being inserted into the lock. I waited for about ten minutes, but the movie never started.

I took a shower with the door wide open hoping to hear Charlize say, "Mel, I'm here," but all I heard was the tip-tip-tapping of the warm water striking my skin. I dried off, put on my clothes, and went back to the couch . . . nothing. When I reached over toward the phone to call her, I noticed a light flashing on the answering machine. I pressed the black button next to the flashing light and listened to the automated voice calling off the date and the time earlier this morning, minutes after I left for work. The living room was filled by Charlize's voice. "Hello!"

"Hey, girl!" Cherry said, and followed up with, "Is he gone, can you talk?"

Charlize sounded like she was moving around a lot. "Hold on, though, this answering machine is trippin'." Her words were followed by a series of beeps, clicks, and then finally silence. "Can you hear me?"

"Yeah," Cherry replied.

"What's going on?" Charlize asked.

Cherry followed up with a question of her own. "Is he there?"

"No, he just left," Charlize informed her, and by now I was sitting on the edge of the sofa hungry for the information that she couldn't get if I were around. "What's up?"

"Everything went down a couple of days ago," Cherry said. "We got the money."

"Seriously?" There was happiness in Charlize's voice. "It's about time. How much?"

"About forty grand," Cherry said. "He gave me ten, and I'll give you your four like I promised for helping me out." Cherry went on: "I hope that's still cool with you?"

"Hell, yeah, I'm going shopping." Charlize laughed. "That's not bad for a few months' worth of doing nothing, plus he's been paying rent and helping out with other things anyway, so that's an added bonus."

"Cool, but Conrad wants you to get him out of the house before he catches on," Cherry said.

"Oh, tell Uncle Conrad to hold his horses," Charlize said. "This has actually been kinda fun."

"Fun?" Cherry squawked. "I couldn't bring myself to tell him that you actually enjoyed fuckin' Tremel. It was supposed to be a part of the plan, not recreation."

"Well, that's what I had to do to get him away from Sarai so that you could get to her, right? Plus I ended up finding out all of that shit for y'all. None of this could've gone down without me." Charlize continued: "And I know that you're not complaining because you were indulging in a little sex yourself."

"Yeah, but it was all business for me. It's called payback," Cherry said. "And boy, was that shit sweet."

"So how did it all go down?" Charlize was anxious to know.

"While she was in Dover with her dad, I called the front office of her apartment complex pretending to be her. I went off on the lady." She giggled. "I even threatened her, so needless to say that sped up the eviction process. They put all of her shit out the next day."

"That's wrong," Charlize said, but still laughed. "You're a vengeful bitch; I would hate to be on your bad side."

"Oh, that's not all," Cherry was proud to say. "I flattened her tires. It had nothing to do with the plan, I was just pissed, but it ended up working out in the end! I picked her up from the airport, took her back to the hotel in the same room she fucked me over in, and Conrad showed her the video of them doing it after I had put that shit in her drink. That bitch was gone; she really doesn't remember any of that." She laughed. "Then he showed her us doing it when I had the camera in my purse, and then again when we were high with that dude from next door." She went on. "It was wild."

"So how did she react?" Charlize asked.

Cherry had no remorse. "Of course she was crying and carrying on, but Conrad's boys took it to her ass . . ."

"What do you mean? Did they hurt her?" Charlize seemed genuinely concerned.

"She got what she was looking for," Cherry exclaimed. "Ha! Ha! Ha!"

"You're not talking about rape, are you?" Charlize asked. "I sure hope not, I didn't sign up for anything like that."

"Relax." Cherry hesitated. "I know you're not getting soft for that bitch."

"I'm just asking, Cherry," Charlize said. "Because that would be a bit much if—"

"Well, I'm not saying what happened, then," Cherry interrupted. "All you need to know is that we have the money and your uncle wants Tremel out of the house."

Charlize reminded her, "This is my house."

Cherry replied, "Well, he told me not to give you the money until that bastard is gone."

"See, that's not right," Charlize said. "All of this shit happened by chance anyway. It wasn't until a few days after he moved in and I was talking to you about him that you put two and two together and came up with this plan then ran to my uncle with it," she whined. "I need a roommate to help with the damn mortgage," she huffed. "Uncle Conrad ain't gonna help me every damn month! And that four grand is good as gone as soon as I hit Macy's."

"Well," Cherry said unsympathetically, "you can always come back to work for the Elite Establishment." She continued: "I'm working the Southeastern Physicians' Conference tonight, that's an easy fifteen hundred a pop." Cherry seasoned Charlize's pot. "I know that you miss the money. Why don't you come down there with me? You can hook up with one guy, and *boom*, you got your mortgage."

"I know." Charlize paused. "But you know if Uncle Conrad ever found out that I was an Elite girl, he'd die." She sighed. "Plus, that kind of money makes me feel dirty."

"What's the difference in what you've been doing with Tremel?"

Cherry asked. "The only difference is that Conrad was paying you to fuck him instead of him paying Conrad to fuck you." She was hyped. "It's the same damn thing."

"Well, if I go, what am I supposed to tell Mel?"

"What?" Cherry was frustrated. "Charlize, why are you acting like he's your boyfriend for real? The shit was all a part of the plan, the game is over . . . you don't have to tell him shit, just put his ass out before he finds out something."

"How am I supposed to just kick him out?" she asked.

"Make up something," Cherry advised.

"Something like what?"

"I don't know what, Charlize, just say anything." She pondered. "Make up a story, just get him out. We have what we want and that was the purpose of us doing this."

"Yeah, but . . ." Charlize seemed confused. "I think he's a little attached to me."

"What the fuck?" Cherry yelled. "He's not a kid, he'll get over it." She paused. "Plus, it sounds like you're the one who's a little attached. I cannot have this whole thing crumbling because you caught feelings."

"Cherry, who died and made you fuckin' king?" Charlize was upset. "As far as I am concerned, you and I are one and the same, I don't take orders from you," she huffed. "Have Uncle Conrad call me, but you're not about to tell me what in the hell to do, I don't answer to you."

"Oh, I can have him call you," Cherry continued in an evil tone. "But before he calls, I'll be sure to let him know that you, his very own college-educated, family-oriented, can-do-no-wrong niece was working for the Establishment under an alias," she said. "And was fucked by some of the men he considers his best friends, and even by a few that are now his enemies . . . all for the love of money." Cherry sounded exultant. "I have the video from Cancún to prove it." She paused. "You have forty-eight hours to rid that house of Tremel Colten or I press play, not only for your uncle, but for your entire family to see." Cherry hung up.

I was frozen, but somehow managed to stand. I pressed the button and listened to the entire recording again. Charlize was Conrad's niece? Our whole friendship, relationship, and what I thought was a bond had a $4,000 price tag on it? I fell back onto the sofa and put my head in my hands. "Damn."

Not only were they screwing me over, they had turned me against Sarai and had pitted her against me . . . all for money. It was all a well-orchestrated plot to weaken us because they knew that together we'd never let anything happen to each other, and I fell for it . . . she fell for it. I sat there angry and in shock for at least an hour. My plan was to play the recording as soon as Charlize walked in, tell her to kiss my ass, and then pack my shit and leave. However, when she walked in smelling like lavender, I fell mute like I was under a spell.

"Hi, baby!" She put down her bags and walked over to where I was sitting. "I missed you." She kissed me on the cheek, sat down, and draped her legs over mine. "How was your day?" I couldn't believe that this was the same woman, *my Judas,* who had sold me to the enemy. I stared at her in bewilderment. "You okay?" she asked.

I decided to wait on her and see what her next move or words would be. "Yeah, I'm fine." I cleared my throat. "How about you?"

"Well"—she sighed—"today has been a difficult day for me. A day I certainly wasn't expecting." Charlize looked away, like there was something she wanted to confess. "I have to talk to you about something."

Nothing in my thoughts told me that she was going to reveal everything to me, apologize, and beg for my forgiveness. I didn't have a plan for that. If she confessed, it would say a lot, but that wouldn't keep me around. It would just say that she possibly did have a heart, and might even give a shit about me. "What do you need to talk about?" I asked.

"It's something serious," Charlize said without looking my way.

"Okay." I grimaced, knowing what she was about to reveal. "Lay it on me."

"Well . . ." Charlize sighed. "I just found out that my fourteen-year-old cousin has been living on the streets and possibly prostitut-ing herself."

"What?" I was appalled, but not for the reason she thought.

"Yeah." She sighed again. "Apparently she left home and has been out there for two months." A tear escaped her. "Her mom is a crack addict and has been for as long as I can remember. I don't give a damn about what's legal, I'm not calling the police and have them take her away to live with strangers when I am right here and able to provide for her." She wiped her eyes. "I want her to come and live here with me."

I listened attentively, watched her cry, and thought, Bring on the fuckin' Academy Award. I couldn't believe this bitch . . . she was lying . . . she was plotting to put me out. I played along. "That's a great idea, she can live here with us, and you will be the perfect ex-ample for her."

"Yeah," she continued, "but I don't have enough room here."

"There is more than enough room. We can put a twin bed in your music room," I said. "It's not that big but—"

"No." She shook her head. "It's too small to convert into a bed-room for a teenager."

"You're right," I agreed. "Okay, she can have my room." I faked a smile. "I hardly ever use it these days anyway." I went on: "I'll just move my things into your room," I reluctantly teased. "That's what you've been wanting anyway."

"Yeah, but I don't want to give her the wrong impression about a man and a woman sleeping together without being married. That's all she's ever been around. It's time that someone sacrifices them-selves to be an example for her." She conveniently added, "We're not married, and it just won't be the right example."

"What?" I continued with a question to encourage her to just come out with it. "So what are you saying, Charlize?"

"I'm not sure, Mel." She dropped her head. "I'm so confused. I want the both of you here. I'll feel terrible leaving her out there to have you here and it'll be even harder giving you up to bring her here."

"So we both can't be here with you?" I asked. "Is that what you're saying to me?"

"It's just that . . . blood is thicker than water." She made herself cry some more. "But at the same time a person cannot live without water."

"So I'm your water, huh?" I stood up and looked down at her pitiful performance. "More like water under the bridge?" I had to bite my tongue not to say something about what I'd heard. I was scared, not for myself, but for Sarai. I didn't want to let on that I knew something and then have Conrad and his friends or Cherry get to her before I could. "You don't have to worry about me; I'll start packing right now and you can have your house back."

"No, Mel, wait . . ." Charlize seemed shocked. "What are you doing?"

"I'm moving out," I informed her.

"You don't have to do it at this very second." She didn't know what she wanted, but she wasn't about to tell the truth; that much was clear. "It's not like that's what I want you to do."

I was hurt. "You're not making any sense, Charlize." I wanted her to be truthful. "You say you want her to move in, right?"

"Yes," Charlize said. "But at the same time I don't really want you to go."

"I'm not going to stay and get in the way of your family business. You want to be an example, so do that . . . be the Virgin Mary for your niece."

"You're not in the way," she said. "Why would you say that?"

"We're not married, so we're living in sin and you want to be a beacon of fuckin' hope for her, right?" I was still biting my tongue. "You have to do what you have to do, right?"

"She's my cousin and I can't see her go down that path," she lied, "but I wasn't telling you to leave right now."

"Well," I said, "I can't stay and get further involved with you."

"Baby, it's not like that." She sprang up and her arms made their way around me. "I want you here more than anything."

She cried and her body trembled. "I wish I could explain it to you."

"Explain what?" I asked.

"Nothing." She clammed up. "Nothing, just hold me."

"No, explain what, Charlize?" I asked again. "Is there something that you're not telling me?"

Everything in her eyes said that she wanted to be truthful, but her mouth told a different story. "No," she stuttered, "I just want you to make love to me." She reached into my pants and then into my boxers and stroked me before planting her lips firmly on mine. "Let me feel you in me, Mel."

I pulled away from her and then yanked her hands from my pants. "I don't think so, Charlize."

"What?" She looked at me in awe.

"Get off of my dick," I said.

"What?" she asked. "You don't want me touching you now? What in the hell is up with that, Mel?"

"No," I yelled, "what in the hell is up with you?"

"What do you mean?" she asked. "My cousin moving here doesn't mean that things have to change between us. I still want to be with you."

"No, you don't." I laughed and widened the gap between us. "You're lying to me. What, you think I can't see right through this carefully constructed story of yours?" I asked. "I know that you want me out and the last thing I'm going to do is stay where I'm no longer wanted."

"You're wrong, Mel," she said.

"I'm wrong?" I asked. "If I'm wrong then how come this is the first time you've mentioned this damn fourteen-year-old cousin?" I stepped away from her. "How come you suddenly care about her now if her mother has been a crackhead since she was born?" My eyes were fixated on her as I backed away. "How come you suddenly got religion now, Charlize?" When she couldn't say anything, I said it for her. "I thought so."

I made my way to my room and started throwing the little bit that belonged to me into the one suitcase I owned and the other things in the various plastic bags I was saving under my bed for a rainy day . . . and boy, was it storming out.

Charlize ran into my room begging me to hear her out, but she still wasn't telling me what I wanted to hear. She went as far as saying that her cousin was once molested by an uncle and that was the reason she didn't think that things would work out with the three of us being under one roof. She tried unpacking my bags, holding on to me, even telling me that she loved me. The lies continued for hours and hours. Around midnight, I started walking my things out to my truck and met her still sitting on the bed when I returned for the final box.

Silence held the room still. "Is there anything else that you have to say?" I asked, giving her one last chance.

Her eyes were puffy. "Tremel, how am I supposed to find you?"

"Don't," I said, "not until you find the truth, then you can bring it with you, but by then, I won't be able to stand you, so just don't look for me." She was crying like a baby and it took everything within me not to comfort her. I wanted to tell her what I knew, but I couldn't put Sarai in any more danger than she might already be in. I had to go look for her, even if she didn't want to be found. I had to see to it that she was all right.

"Good-bye, Charlize." I grabbed the box and exited the room, the house, and her life. Now she could pass "Go" and collect her $4,000.

"Look to your health; and if you have it, praise God, and value it next to a good conscience; for health is the second blessing that we mortals are capable of; a blessing that money cannot buy."
—Izaak Walton

Sarai
8½

When I got into the car parked behind mine in the airport's garage, Keenan was already waiting for me in the backseat. The driver was a big man. I didn't get to study him too much. As I entered the car, Keenan asked, "Do you mind being blindfolded?"

"What for?" I asked. "How do I know that you're really a cop?"

The big dude pulled out his badge and awkwardly reached around to shake my hand. "Ma'am, I'm Officer Ronald Dallas and we're here to help you."

"Okay, you both have badges," I huffed. "They sell them on the Internet for five bucks."

"Listen . . ." Officer Dallas went on: "You can refuse our assistance. We aren't forcing you to come with us."

"He's right." Keenan pointed at the still-opened car door on my side. "You can leave if you want." He chuckled angrily. "We went through a lot just to pull this off. Us not helping you would be ten times easier . . . trust me."

Ronald looked over his right shoulder again. "So what is it gonna be?" he asked sternly.

I didn't know what to think. I just quickly asked God to protect me from all hurt, harm, and danger, then slowly closed the door. "I'll go." I spoke in a whisper and fell back against the seat.

"Cool, but I have to blindfold you," Keenan said, and did so without me answering.

During the forty- or fifty-minute ride, no one said a word. When the covering was removed from my eyes, we were in a three-car garage.

"What is this?" I asked as I exited the car.

Keenan walked up to a steel door, punched some numbers into a keypad, and fumbled with his keys. "This is where I am staying for right now," he informed me. "Once again, you don't have to stay here if you don't want to, but there is one rule—you can't leave without someone taking you." He pointed at Officer Dallas, who was now standing behind me. "If you don't want to stay, Ron will be the one to drive you out. I'll have some new tires on your truck by tomorrow afternoon."

He opened the door to the building and turned on the lights. It was a house, a very nice house, and we were entering through the kitchen. Ron entered and disappeared down a dark hall while Keenan and I stood by the door.

I was still having doubts. "How do I know that you are who you say you are?"

He took my right hand in his. "Allow me to reintroduce myself. I am Officer Keenan Tanner, and I want to keep you safe." He spoke calmly. "I'm working undercover with a team of agents to bring down Conrad Johnson, not only for the operation of a prostitution ring, but under various drug-trafficking charges, and even murder."

"Murder?" I was stunned. "Who?"

"I can't go into any details. I shouldn't even have you here, but after what they did to you, I haven't been able to sleep." He closed the door behind him. "All I kept wondering about was if you were okay."

He showed me around the house. It was one of the only houses in Miami that I ever saw with hardwood floors, wooden beams, and a wood skeleton beam roof. It was big, yet cozy. He pointed out three bedrooms, two bathrooms, a large living room, and a den, but there were a few doors he walked by without opening. As we entered the third bedroom he said, "This one is all yours." He disappeared into the closet for a few seconds and returned with towels. "These are clean," he said, resting them on the bed.

"Thank you, Officer Tanner."

"No formalities needed here." He smiled. "I'll answer to Keenan."

I blushed. "Well, thank you, Keenan."

"It's not only a pleasure, Sarai"—he paused—"it's my duty." Keenan walked toward me and spoke in a whisper. "And because it is my duty, I assure you that the three guys that"—he struggled for the right word—"the guys that *dishonored* you will also be brought to justice."

My eyes watered. "Thank you, but I'm not pressing charges. I just want to forget the whole thing. I don't want to be wrapped up in court proceedings, and testifying, and all of that. I gave them the money, that's all they wanted, so they're through with me . . . I'm scared of what else they could do to me."

"No, you have—"

"No, no, no," I said, and before another tear had the audacity to stain my face, he pulled me into his chest and rubbed my back.

"Don't you worry about a thing," Keenan said. "I got you." He held pitiful little me in his arms and must've lent me his strength, because for the first time in days, I felt like I had some power within my bones. I wrapped my arms around him and wept.

"Shh, it's going to be all right." Keenan held me close, but something about his touch was so innocent. "I know about your apartment situation," he said. "You can stay here as long as you like. You are in good hands here."

After sniffling for a while, I asked, "Why should I feel safe *here,* though? I mean, Conrad was done with me and you've just brought me into something even worse . . . all this drugs-and-murder stuff I had nothing to do with and no knowledge of."

"No one knows that you're here," he assured me as he let go of my body.

"Yeah, but now I'm here with you, an undercover cop. If your cover has been blown and someone is out to get *you,* they'll be getting *me* too." I looked around the room and didn't see any windows. "What kind of house is this anyway?"

"This is where I have to stay when I'm working undercover." He leaned against the door frame. "And I think that you'll have to agree that it beats sleeping in a truck with four flat tires."

"Of course," I agreed. "A blind man could see that."

His hand crept up to my face and cupped my chin. "A blind man could even see your smile." He stared at me. "There was no way I was leaving you out there."

"Keenan." I quickly remembered how rude I was to him that morning at the hotel. "I apologize for the things I said to you the other day." I paused briefly. "The Viagra comments."

"No apologies needed." His hands left my face, but his brown eyes were seemingly locked on my lips. "I didn't take any of that stuff to heart." He chuckled and lowered his voice. "Besides, I was the man they modeled Viagra after." I couldn't say a word and I don't think he wanted me to. "Take a shower, get some rest, and I'll see you tomorrow." He walked out of the room, leaving me with my mouth open.

After my shower, there was no surprise that Keenan was still on my mind. And as I lay down, I was still thinking about him. I thought about going to whatever room he was in and pretending to have some type of panic attack just to feel safer in his arms, but that would just be wrong . . . and desperate. I left my door cracked open a few inches and tried to lie in cute poses to captivate him if he happened to walk by, but he never did.

● ● ●

With no window or a night-light, I managed to get about two hours of sleep. I watched the *Today* show in my room, took a shower, changed, and headed to the kitchen in hopes of finding Keenan or something to eat. I looked into a few cabinets, and was rustling through the refrigerator, when I heard someone call my name. "Sarai?"

I jumped. Stunned, I slammed the door and found myself staring back at an attractive, tall, and very pregnant white woman a few feet away. "Hello." I was nervous.

She took a step closer to me. "Hi, I'm Rebecca, Keenan's wife." She extended her right hand. "He had to leave for a while, so he asked me to keep you company until Ron is up."

Oh, my Lord . . . Keenan had a wife . . . a pregnant wife . . . a white wife! I looked at her hand for a few seconds before reaching for it. "Hi," I stuttered. "You scared me." I smiled.

"I'm sorry." She smiled back. "I thought you saw me sitting on the couch."

"You were on the couch?" Of course I didn't see her. I was too busy looking for her husband.

"Yeah, I was sitting there catching up on some reading." She giggled and pulled a few long blond streaks out of her face. "Would you like for me to fix you some breakfast?"

"No." I was still in shock. "I'll put something together." I decided to be polite. "May I fix *you* something?"

"Oh no, Keenan and I had breakfast together before he left," she said.

Over the next thirty minutes, as I made myself an omelet, toast, and bacon, Rebecca sat at the counter and talked and talked and talked. I just kept smiling and saying, "Wow!" and "Okay" and "Good for you!" and "Oh my God."

While I was eating, I learned that she was seven months pregnant. She and Keenan had met three years ago while he was vacationing in Texas. They got married a year ago in Houston and he moved her to Miami immediately after. They were both eagerly anticipating the birth of Keenan Justin Tanner Jr., their first child.

Through all of her talking, I couldn't help but say these words to Keenan in my mind. *Oh, so this is why your dick couldn't get up? It had nothing to do with respect for me. You don't like black women! You had your pregnant, blond, white, trophy wife waiting for you at home.*

"Keenan told me that you were concerned about your safety here." She looked around. "I just want you to know that he would never put me"—she rubbed her stomach—"and Junior in harm's way, so you are in very good hands here." She whispered, "This house is huge, there are a lot of officers here. They all live in different sections, but it's all connected through that hallway." She pointed.

"Yeah, but this place is creepy, hardly no windows," I said. "I'd be better off where I was."

"Sarai," she whispered, "I know that I'm not supposed to discuss this with you, but what you witnessed was horrific. They were bound to look for you. You can't think that they were going to let you walk away."

I was confused. "But they did let me walk away."

She went on as if I hadn't said anything. "Seeing Colombian drug dealers assassinate an entire family is no laughing matter." She looked serious. "Until they bring them down, my advice to you is to stay here."

She was right, seeing Colombian drug dealers assassinate an entire family was no laughing matter . . . but who had seen that? Not me! Right as I was about to inform her, the burly guy from the car the night before appeared. "Hey, Becky." He touched her on the waist and kissed her on the cheek. "How is baby boy?"

"Hi, Ron." She smiled. "You should ask how I am doing because baby boy is kicking my butt," she said, and once Ron had passed her, she gave me a please-let's-change-the-subject look.

"I got it from here," Ron said. "Officer Dunham is waiting in the garage to take you back to civilization," he joked. "Are you coming back tonight?"

"Nawh." Rebecca turned to Ron. "I have to pee too much now, and the bathroom is too far away. I can only do this about once a week." She grabbed her purse and her book. "Nice meeting you, Sarai."

"Nice to meet you too, Rebecca." I gave her a quick hug. "Good luck with the baby."

She giggled. "Thanks." Within seconds, she was gone . . . leaving me alone with Ron.

"Good afternoon, Miss Sarai," he said to me.

"Hi." I tried smiling.

"How did you sleep?" Ron asked.

"Good," I replied. "A little sunshine through a window would've been better, though," I joked.

Big Ron wasn't a talker. We sat in silence for a while. He made himself a cup of coffee and then did some work on the computer. I just stared up at the ceiling and counted the wooden beams that supported it. I must've counted them thirty times before I dropped to sleep right there on the sofa.

When I woke up it was after three. It felt like the day was seventy-two hours long and would never be done. With Ron still on the computer and not saying more than two words an hour to me, I retired to my room and clicked on the TV. I turned to VH1 and cracked my side laughing at three *I Love the Nineties* shows.

Around nine there was a knock on my door. "You want something to eat?"

Wow . . . room service? I muted *The Five Heartbeats* movie and yelled, "Yeah, that'll be nice." I opened the door and saw Keenan standing there with a paper plate weighed down by four huge slices of pizza and a two-liter of Pepsi. "Hi." I smiled and took the items. "Thank you." With my foot, I softly kicked the door to close it . . . in his face . . . but he stopped it with his hand.

"How was your day?" he asked.

"Full of surprises," I said sarcastically and repeated myself, but this time purposely prolonging each word. "Full . . . of . . . surprises."

"Oh yeah?" he asked. "Was Ron nice to you?"

"Oh, Ron was great; he's not a talker, but he was polite," I replied. "Speaking of nice and polite . . . Rebecca, your wife, was darling. She even offered to cook me breakfast."

"Yeah, she's a sweetheart." He smiled. "I didn't want you to wake up and be alone, so since she had spent the night, I just asked her to keep you company until Ron got up."

"Thanks." I rolled my eyes at the wall with my back toward him. "You sure know how to make a girl feel welcome."

"You mind if I sit in here with you for a while?" he asked. "I did bring enough pizza and soda for the both of us."

"Becky's not here tonight?" I wanted to come off rude, but still sounded nice.

"Nawh," he said. "She only comes every once in a while to bring me more clothes and take my dirty laundry and all of that. This gig is almost up, though . . . another week or so and I'll be back home."

"How sweet!" I was being sarcastic. I was mad at Keenan, not because he was married or had chosen someone outside of his race to wed. I was mad because I was lonely and wanted someone. Last night, I just assumed that Keenan would become that someone to me. I was done with being second on anyone's list; I don't care how desperate I was.

Had Tremel just been patient enough to wait for my mind to melt, I would be in his arms right now. It was hard to remember him being the perfect man for me and lose him to another woman already. I needed Tremel; I wanted Keenan . . . truthfully . . . I *wanted* anyone to care for me, but it looked like I just needed to grow up and learn to be happy with me.

"You never answered my question about sitting with you for a while," Keenan said. "I'm hungry too."

I looked over at him. "Sure."

He came in and joined me on the bed. I took the TV off of mute. "Oh, damn, I love this movie," he said with the biggest, brightest smile.

For the next two hours, like two capricious teenagers, we ate pizza and drank soda in bed with our backs up against the wall watching the movie. We laughed, sang, and ended up sitting closer than I expected . . . no, damn that, his arm was around me and my head was on his shoulder. Once the credits rolled, we both knew that we had some explaining to do.

"What time are my office hours?" He quoted the character Big Red, from the movie. He asked me again, "What time are my office hours?"

"Nine to five." I pretended to be the scared-shitless guy that was being dangled over the balcony when I answered. "Please don't kill me, Big Red."

"Kill you? That's the last thing I want to do." Keenan pulled me even closer to him. "My office is always open for you, Sarai." I looked up at him and he moved down toward me. We inched closer and closer and it seemed inevitable that our lips would touch. "You can have the key to my office and make your own hours."

"But . . ." I wanted to taste his juicy lips more than anything. "But you're married, Keenan." I forced myself to back away.

"I know." He dropped his head in disappointment. "I'm sorry."

"Why didn't you tell me that last night?" I asked.

He posed a question to me. "Would you have wanted to know last night?"

I had to tell the truth. "No," I whispered.

"Well, I didn't tell you for the same reason that you didn't want to know," he said. "And I brought you here to this house when everything within told me not to."

"Huh?" He had lost me. "What do you mean?"

He spoke from the heart. "There is something about you that I want beyond any logical reason, Sarai." He went on: "There is something I haven't been telling you."

"I'm all ears." I truly was.

"Well . . ." Keenan sighed. "Because you were local, and due to your ties with Conrad, you were under suspicion of money laundering, so we had you under surveillance." He went on: "We staked you out for about a week and then noticed that you had nothing to do with what we suspected." He paused. "I was almost sorry that you were innocent because I loved watching you."

"Okay." My eyebrows were raised. "I'm a little freaked out."

"Don't be." He chuckled. "When I walked into that hotel room and saw you, I couldn't believe my eyes; you are beautiful. I nearly blew my cover the next day to be sure that nothing happened to you." He kissed my hand. "The truth is . . . you don't have to be here. I lied to my boss, my wife, and my partner about your involvement with some Colombian dealers just to have you close to me."

There was about fifteen seconds of silence before I spoke. "Keenan, honestly, from what I just heard . . . you are a borderline stalker." I paused and then giggled. "If you weren't so irresistibly handsome, I would be running out of this house right now."

"You don't have to stay," he said right before our lips touched. Keenan pulled my bottom lip into his mouth and sucked on it like he was a bee and I had nectar seeping out of me. He searched out my tongue and played a wicked game of touch me, tease me with it. Before long, gravity pulled my back toward the bed and Keenan was hovering over me.

Our clothing came off slowly . . . item by item, as though he was giving me time to rethink what was about to happen. I was topless while looking at his fully naked body. And boy, was he right . . . Viagra needed to put his erection on their Web site next to the words *This Could Be You!*

My thoughts were the same. I needed Tremel, I wanted Keenan . . . truthfully . . . I *wanted* anyone to care for me, but it looked like I just needed to grow up and learn to be happy with just me. Was it right to ruin another woman's life for five, ten, or fifteen minutes of pushing and pulling? When was I going to take a stand for what was right? It didn't matter that Keenan was fine, sweet, or had an elephant's trunk between his legs. What mattered was how I would feel in twenty minutes. "Wait a minute," I said to him.

He stopped taking down my pants. "What's wrong?"

"Me," I said. "I'm wrong. I've done this all before."

"What?" he asked. "Done what before?"

"This whole married-man thing." I sighed. "I can't do this." I shook my head. For the first time in my "'sex" life, I was standing up for what was right. "Your wife is pregnant with your son, your firstborn child . . . don't do this to her, don't do this to you." Keenan looked absolutely floored and embarrassed. Realizing that nothing else needed to be said, he lay down next to me and fell asleep.

Early the next morning, as Keenan remained in my bed, I took a shower, packed the suitcase that I had been dragging around for days, and walked into Ron's room. I shook his body vigorously. "I want to leave," I said loudly. "I need you to take me to my truck."

He looked at the clock; it was 5:43. *"Now?"*

"Yeah," I said. "I know it's early, but—"

"Damn," he mumbled. "Wait in the living room, I'll be there. I have to get someone to ride with me."

I walked back to the room where Keenan was and watched him sleep for a few minutes. I kissed him on the cheek as a final good-bye, and within an hour, Ron parked the car and the man in the backseat with me removed the blindfold from my eyes. I was in front of my truck, which was parked in front of a Firestone in North Miami, and my baby had new tires on.

"We pimped your ride," Ron joked as he handed me the keys to my ride but also another key.

"What's this?"

"Keenan told me to give it to you. He came to my room right before we left, while you were in the living room," he said. "It's the key to your storage, where your things are from your apartment."

"How did he—"

"Don't ask," Ron interrupted. "Your truck has a full tank of gas and there is five hundred dollars in your glove compartment. It's not much, but it should get you to somewhere or someone that can help you." He hit the button to unlock the doors. "Be safe."

"Thanks," I said, and opened the door. "Tell Keenan that I appreciate everything that he did and sorry that I couldn't stay."

I got into my truck, cranked her up, and as I reached over to the glove compartment, Ron pulled away and became just a memory.

Along with the envelope of money, surprisingly, in the glove compartment was something that I should've been looking for over the last few days . . . the keys to Nat's house . . . I had forgotten that I even had them.

I pulled out of the parking space and onto the road. Finally, I had somewhere to go and I flipped back and forth between 103 the Beat and 99Jamz until I arrived in front of Nat's three-bedroom house. The grass looked freshly cut and watered. I remembered the alarm code because it just so happened to be my birth year.

I looked around. "I'm gonna be here for a while." I couldn't believe that fate was so cruel as to have Nat and me living under one roof again, but I loved her . . . her neatness and systematic way of doing everything I hated . . . but I loved that damn girl. All of the curtains were drawn . . . I opened them. "Let a little sun in here."

Nat's living room always reminded me of something you might see on the cover of a home-decor magazine. Everything was placed perfectly next to something else. The color scheme was just right. The thin blanket she used to cover herself with on the sofa was meticulously draped over the arm of the love seat . . . just like in the magazines. It wasn't just thrown there . . . that crazy girl had probably spent ten minutes to obtain that look. The throw pillows were rustled in just the right places, everything was polished, and you couldn't tell that the fake flowers weren't real. I was about to wreak havoc on all of her neatness.

I went into the kitchen to fix something to eat. When my mission was accomplished, I took my grits, eggs, bacon, and toast to the dining-room table, turned on the TV, and got my grub on. I started thinking about the things that were now on my to-do list: 1) Find a job; 2) Sell the truck and find a cheap apartment, or 2a) Keep the truck and stay with Nat until I had enough money to move; 3) Get a damn life!; 4) Whatever . . . just get a job.

After I was done eating, I washed the dirty dishes and sat on the love seat messing up Nat's magazine look. I flipped through the channels and was bored after every local station had the same story of some more Cubans drifting in. I sucked my teeth and paraphrased that line from the movie *Friday*. "It's Friday, I don't have a job, no man, and I ain't got shit to do. I might as well make me a drink." Yes, it was only eight in the morning, but a mimosa is *so* not hard-core.

I poured the orange juice in a glass but couldn't find champagne anywhere. I knew that Nat had to have some because she bought the shit by the case. I looked everywhere there was to look in the kitchen and came back out to the living room to look there as well.

I opened the cabinet of the end table and saw a box; it was tall enough to have champagne in it, so I pulled it out. So that I wouldn't open something personal of hers, I looked at the label to see if it was from a winery. To my surprise, it was from a funeral home in Atlanta. "This chick plans ahead for everything." I was talking to myself about Nat. "This crazy-ass girl is . . ."

A second glance showed me that the box was addressed to my former address and in care of Tremel Colten. "What in the hell is this?" Every curious gene in my body was piqued. I pulled back the panels and a silver urn and an envelope were revealed. I picked up the envelope and saw that it was addressed to me. The letter was from Savion. Savion, my brother, is in Atlanta! Why would Nat have my letter from him and why would she be keeping it in such a god-awful box?

I looked back and forth from the urn to the envelope and quickly figured out what was up. I nearly passed out. I was shaking so badly that I nearly ripped the letter to pieces just trying to open it.

Sarai,

By the time you read this letter, one of two things will have happened: 1) I would've already called you and asked you to discard this without reading it because I couldn't go through with it, or 2) I will be gone on to a place far more beautiful or worse than this place we call home. I'll come back and let you know if heaven or hell really exists, but let's just say that if I don't come back, that means that I like it . . . so don't worry about me.

I am sure that it'll be a while before you can see what I did as the ultimate act of selflessness, but try understanding that sooner

*rather than later. It would mean the world to me. I couldn't have
you spend your last bit of money or take away from Daddy to take
care of me . . . that would've been selfish. Ending my life this way
was the last resort. I tried other things, including stopping my
medication a month ago. I thought that that would finish me, but
all that has done is make my life more miserable. I have watched
my personality, emotions, mentality, and body die of AIDS and it
has stifled my will to live another day. Please respect my decision to
shed this shell and accept my wings.*

*As twins, we have experienced almost everything together,
but this . . . my twin soul, I must do alone. Please don't let my
departure limit your life. Instead, live as though my heart beats
within you because our souls are still one. Say good-bye to Daddy
for me and I will say hello to Mama for you. I love you! —Savion
Emery*

I swear to you that I didn't read the letter. I simply opened it and
the words just jumped from the paper into my head. It was as though
he was reading the letter to me because there was no way I could've
read it myself without dying. Still trembling and now crying, I carefully raised the urn from the box. I stared at it, cradled it against my
heart, and let out a scream that the angels in heaven had to hear.

When I managed to give my lungs a rest and open my eyes, standing less than a foot away from me was an angel . . . Tremel Colten. At
first, I thought that it was all in my head . . . until he took me into his
arms . . . it was really him.

"You remember me now, don't you?" he asked.

"Yes," I cried. "I remember you." I don't know where he had come
from, but the important thing was that he was there when I needed
him the most.

"Baby, I am so sorry," he said. "I am so sorry." He kissed my forehead. "We're going to get through this."

> "If you want to feel rich, just count the things you have
> that money can't buy."
> —PROVERB

Tremel

WITHDRAWAL SLIP #9
ENDING BALANCE: DOES IT REALLY MATTER?

They say that a mother can recognize her baby's cry in a room full of howling babies, even if she is blindfolded. Well, I wasn't blindfolded, but my eyes were closed . . . I was asleep when I recognized my baby crying. I didn't care if she was laughing, crying, choking, or screaming . . . I had been looking for and hoping to see Sarai for two days.

When I left Charlize's house that night, my unspoken mission was to find Sarai. Around one in the morning, I went back to her apartment complex and just flat-out lied to the security guard. What came out of my mouth was the most unbelievable lie I had ever spoken. I told him that I hadn't heard from my heroin-addicted cousin in two days and suspected that he might have overdosed. I told him that I had two pounds of weed stashed in his closet and needed to take it out if something had really happened so that I could call the police. I also slipped him fifty bucks, and the next thing I knew . . . the gates opened up for me.

I knew that Sarai wouldn't be there. I was looking for her neighbor Craig. I knocked on his door vigorously for about a minute nonstop. "Who is it?" he asked.

Staying away from the peephole, I answered, "Pizza Hut!"

"Pizza?" He sounded agitated as he opened the door, rubbing his eyes. "It's one o'-damn-clock. I didn't order pizza."

"I know," I said. "But I need to talk to you."

"Aw, shit." He finally looked me in the face. "What do *you* want?"

"I need to know where she is," I said. "I know that you know."

"I don't know shit." Craig got smart. "And if she wanted you to know—"

"Look, Sarai is in a lot of trouble, man," I interrupted him. "And honestly, I am probably the last person she wants to see, but I need to make sure that she's all right."

He sighed. "She came back a few nights ago. I found her over there in the hall crying and screaming." He leaned against the door frame. "She was talking some nonsense about remembering everything and being shot by some boyfriend or somebody."

"She got her memory back?" I asked excitedly.

"I guess. I didn't know she had lost it in the first place." Craig didn't seem to care one way or the other. "Anyway, I brought her in here and gave her something to eat, she took a shower, fell asleep." He paused. "The next morning when I got up . . . she was gone."

"Damn." I shook my head. "She didn't mention anyone or anyplace where she might go?"

"Nawh," he said. "Like I said, when I got up, she was already gone."

"Thanks." I passed him a card from the flower shop. "If she happens to come by again, please call me."

"Okay." He looked down at the card and then up at me. "Will do."

On the way out of the complex, I wanted to ignore the security guard, but I didn't. He was all smiles. "So, what's good?" he asked.

"That fool is up in there." I smiled. "His cell phone is broken and his car is in the shop, that's why I haven't heard from him."

"All right." He leaned farther out of the booth window. "Yo, I'm trying to be down, man. Let a brotha move some of that green for you," he said.

I couldn't believe that he was buying my bullshit. "I'll talk to you when I come back through tomorrow."

"A'ight," he said. "Check you later."

I drove to a twenty-four-hour Wal-Mart and parked toward the back of the lot. At almost two in the morning, women were still coming out with carriages full of shit. I turned off the truck and tried to collect my thoughts. I pondered all of the situations that Sarai could be in and closed my eyes to concentrate on which ones made the most sense. When I stopped concentrating, it was ten in the morning and the sun was burning my face. I woke up to a full parking lot, and again, woman after woman was loading her car down with eighty percent of the things they wanted, five percent of the shit they needed, and fifteen percent of stuff that just so happened to be on sale and they might be able to use on a rainy day.

The more I sat there, the heavier the thought of going to the police to file a missing person's report weighed on me. However, I'm sure they'd want to know how I would know if she's missing if we weren't living together and I hadn't seen her in a week in the first place. Plus, they'd say, "She's not missing, she's just evicted. She's in between places right now . . . it happens." In order to be taken seriously, I would probably have to bring up Conrad, the Elite Establishment, and the fact that Sarai used to be a "call girl." I might have to add that I feared for her safety because of her extorting money from the wives of cheating men in exchange for pictures. Who was I kidding? We all knew that the police didn't search for missing black people . . . and Sarai's dealing didn't make the matter any better. If anything, they would probably look for her just to arrest her.

In between flower deliveries, I searched for her. Though I knew that she was far too proud to set foot in one, I questioned people at various shelters about seeing her. No one remembered such a girl. That evening, I was wrestling with the keys to my truck as I returned from McDonald's with a Big Mac in hand when I noticed a strange set of keys. I fought hard to remember what they belonged to. Mrs. White's house? Charlize? Locker at old job? Parents' house? The answer, four times in a row, was no.

Then I recalled the day that I ran into Sarai at Northern Miami Middle School. After she left, I visited Nat, who gave me keys to her house and her alarm code, stating that her neighbor's house was broken into a week prior while they were out of town. She asked me to stop by a few times while she was on her cruise just to make sure that everything was all right.

I entered the dark house and found nothing out of place, except me. I walked from room to room; everything was picturesque. At first, I said that I would just sleep in my truck in front of her house, then I said . . . I'd just lie down for a minute on the couch, but instead lay on a bed in one of the secondary rooms. Before long, I was under the sheets and I woke up right in time to take a shower and get dressed for work.

At work, I made a few calls to local hospitals to see if Sarai had been admitted. She hadn't been. Though I still didn't know where she was, I was glad that she wasn't lying in a hospital bed. I didn't know where else to turn. Damn the consequences. The next day, I was going to file a missing person's report and I was willing to say anything to get her picture on the local news.

Back at Nat's house, I pulled my truck into the garage, then went to cut the grass with Nat's lawn mower. I did it because I felt guilty about sleeping on her clean sheets, eating her food, using her water, and watching her television.

With so much on my mind and an abundance of words in my heart, I started writing. When I was done, I read over the poem and got chills. Sometimes I write things and can't believe they are my words, and sometimes I don't even remember writing them at all. It's as if a spirit takes over and does it for me . . . and when I read it, I am just as amazed as everyone else.

I lay down with the expectation of not being able to fall right to sleep, but surprisingly I did with ease. It seemed like just minutes later when I was awakened by a loud shriek coming from the living room. I sat up in bed and knew right away that it wasn't a robber or Nat returning a day early from her trip. I recognized my baby crying and there was nothing but a door keeping us apart.

I ran to the living room, rounded the couch, and found her on the ground clutching the urn that housed her brother's ashes, weeping. Though she resembled a broken little girl, she was the most beautiful woman I had ever seen. The tears just made her glow, and right there in the midst of her turmoil, I found a reason to smile. Suddenly nothing she had ever done to hurt me mattered, and I would do anything an inch short of dying to gain her forgiveness and make her mine again.

She looked up at me with sorrowful eyes and I intended to offer her words of condolence, but what came out was, "You remember me now, don't you?"

"Yes," she cried. "I remember you."

"Baby, I am so sorry." I bent down and wrapped my arms around her. "I am so sorry." I kissed her forehead. "We're going to get through this."

"What did he do?" she asked, but answered herself. "Did he shoot himself?"

"Yeah," I replied softly.

"Oh my God!" She sobbed into my chest. "When did this happen?"

"We don't have to talk about this right now." I tried to comfort her.

"No," she demanded. "No, I have to know."

I sighed. "It happened the same night that you were shot."

"So, we . . . we were supposed to die together?" She held on to me tightly and repeated, "We were supposed to die together."

"No." I rubbed her back. "No, you weren't, you were supposed to be right here." I kissed her on the cheek again. "You were supposed to be right here for me and with me." I touched the urn pitifully. "He had to go, but he had to do it alone."

"Why didn't you guys tell me?" she cried.

"The doctors didn't think that it was a good idea for you to know until you regained your full memory or at least until you seemed strong enough to handle something like that, so Nat and I discussed telling you when she returned from her trip." I rubbed her back. "We were going to tell you, we were just looking out for you."

I told her everything she wanted to know about what had happened to Savion. We sat in mourning for another hour, and when she cried, I just held on to her. I had missed her and any reason to hold her I had to take advantage of.

"There was no way I would've cremated him, even though that's what he wanted . . . I couldn't see myself giving the orders to do something like that," she said.

I started speaking. "I'm sorry—"

"No, don't apologize," Sarai said. "Thanks for honoring his wishes. I was just saying that I probably would've gone against what he wanted and then I would've hated myself for it in the future, so thank you."

"No need to thank me." Not that her brother wasn't important, but I wanted to change the subject, more for her sake than mine. "So, what are you doing here?"

"That's the question I should be asking you. This is *my* best friend's house." She smiled. "What are you doing here?"

"Nat asked me to check the house whenever I could because someone had broken into the house next door a few weeks ago." I continued: "But with nowhere to go over the last few nights, I just crashed here."

"Nowhere to go?" she asked. "What about your girlfriend's house?"

"She's not my girlfriend. The doctors advised that I shouldn't stay at the apartment with you in your condition, so because I knew her brother, I moved in with her the day that you were released from the hospital." I looked over at her as she listened. "It's a long story and I know what you saw at the picnic. I know what it looked like . . . and it was like that for a few weeks, but only because Conrad and Julian came at me with the truth about how I got that recording contract and then things got out of control because I was pissed off at you."

"*You* were pissed?" She chuckled. "Not more than me."

"Well, none of that is important right now . . . but I will let you know that I know all about you and Syd and what went on with you two and that's also not important right now.

"Sarai, apparently, Charlize is Conrad's niece, and once Cherry found out who I was, she and Conrad came up with this elaborate scheme. They knew that if I was with you, there was no way they could get to you, so they played us against one another so that they could get that money from you." I rubbed her back. "I know about some of the things that happened to you, and I've been looking for you for two days. I had planned to go to the police today." I looked at her in awe. "I am so glad that you're all right. I am so sorry if I hurt you and I am so glad to have you back in my life."

"No, Tremel." She looked away. "I need to tell you everything." Tears ran down her cheeks once more. "I want you to know everything that I have done, and then you can make up your mind about wanting me back in your life."

Sarai's mouth opened like a mini-floodgate, and when it closed, I knew the truth about everything. She went back to the night she met Julian in Nassau; he was her first client. I had already known about all the men in between. However, later, trying to help me out, she contacted Julian about getting my demo heard. She met him at a hotel and, on her knees, halfway through a sex act, realized that she wasn't helping me at all.

She told me about her relationship with Syd and how it all started the night that I stood her up. Sarai told me more than any man would care to know about the woman he loved. And when it came to her telling me about Conrad and Craig . . . I was disgusted. However, when she informed me about being forced to perform oral sex on the three men at the hotel, my anger liquefied and poured down my face.

"Mel, I'm okay," she said as she wiped my watered-down fury and pushed my chin up. "Look at me."

"Wait." I couldn't look at her. "Gimme a minute."

"No, look at me," she demanded. "Look at me, Mel."

I raised my head and prayed that my testosterone levels would rise. "What?"

"I am okay, baby." She smiled. "After all that I've gone through, I am finally free of all of the ties that weighed me down. Unfortunately, all of those things were results of the bad decisions I made from day one, when I first met Conrad. As bad as some of the things I did were, and as nasty as some of the things done to me still are . . . they had to be done." She sighed. "I don't want to press charges; trust me, they will all be brought down . . . I just want to live my life." She spoke in a serious tone. "So what if I am dead broke, homeless, and out of work? I have learned the biggest lesson that there is and I have the best reward a girl could have." She went on: "I have you! Everything that happened had to happen just so that I could be here right now, like you said; I was supposed to be right here in your arms. I have you!"

I kissed her hand and remembered the first time I had told her that I loved her. The words to the poem came back to me like a train to a popular station. I pulled up and they flooded me. "I love your hips, I love your thighs. I love your lips and the way you roll your eyes. I love not just what you say but the way you say what you say. I love being with you, love coming home to you every day. I love when you're strong, but I love it when you're weak. I love when you're happy, but even when you're bleak. I love the big things, but also the simple things that we do. For you I'd do anything, Sarai, because I am madly in love with you."

"Aw, Mel." Just like the first time, she was in awe. "I love you too."

We held on to each other for a while, as if to make up for the months that we were apart. "So, did you *love* her?" Sarai asked, breaking the silence.

"She was very likable, but I didn't love her," I said. "I told her that I couldn't give her my heart because someone else already had it."

"You did not tell her that." She brushed my words off.

"I swear I did, and I meant it." I raised my right hand. "I can't love anyone else until I'm done loving you."

Sarai cuddled up to me. "When will that be?"

"Hmm, let's see." I pretended to think. "Until death, and even then check for a heartbeat because somewhere deep inside it will still be beating for you."

"Oh my God, how sweet!" she cooed, and slowly moved toward my lips with hers until they touched. I pulled her in to me and sucked on her lips. She was warm, soft, and tasted sweet. I didn't care where they had been, whom they had been on, or what she had said with them.

I called in and told Mr. Jimenez that I was sick and Sarai and I spent the rest of the day talking about everything. Neither of us wanted to leave a stone unturned in regard to what took place while we were estranged. I was totally honest about things that happened between Charlize and me, and I had to believe that she wasn't hiding anything from me. Not keeping track of the time, the sun was setting before either one of us even took a bathroom break.

"I want to read you something that I wrote last night," I said while holding her hand and walking her to the room I had taken over.

"What is it about?" she asked.

"Just sit down." I pointed at the bed. "You'll figure it out." I grabbed my notebook and flipped back a page to where it all started.

"*Kiss me; I don't care where your lips have been,*
I can't cast a stone because I, too, am covered in sin.
Feel me, squeeze me, stroke me, caress me, and such.
Don't wash your hands, girl, I need your raw touch.
I don't give a damn what your fingers did clutch.
Call me; erase those other numbers from your phone.
I promise you, no more nights spent all alone.
Because your toe bone's connected to my foot bone.
And as long as there is still blood within my vein,
And possibly, until I need to walk with a cane . . .
I will never allow you to slip to the back of my mind.
And if you never remember me, I still won't leave you
    behind.
Hold me, even if you just let go of another.
You had some brother while I had some other. . .
Girl, pull me, push me, tease me, but please me too.
Taste me! Oh, baby, bite off more than you can chew.
I don't give a damn what others have chosen to do.
Want me, more than anything else in your life.
You are the cure for my misery and strife.
And I promise that someday I will make you my wife.
As long as there is still blood within my vein,
And possibly, until I need to walk with a cane. . .
I will love you from the bottom and the top of my heart.
Sarai, let's let nothing but death keep us apart."

My words left me feeling renewed, and now Sarai looked even more desirable. Her sexy dark brown eyes gazed up at me with trepidation "So it doesn't bother you that I've been—" She looked away nervously. "It doesn't matter to you where I've been and what I've done?" she asked.

"No baby," I whispered as I took her hand in mine, pulling her up from the bed. "Didn't you just hear what I said? I don't care where your hands have been." I guided her palm to my chest. "You're touching *me* now." I bent my head and kissed her fingertips gently.

"You are so good," she paused . . . "you are *too* good to me Mel." Tears leaked from her eyes as she moved closer to me. "I am so sorry for all that I've put you through."

"Show me." The words came out of my mouth without me truly thinking them through.

"Huh?" she asked probably thinking more logically than I had been. She went through hell and high water over the last few days but somehow my desire for her selfishly superseded that. "What did you say?" She wanted to know.

"I said show me." I anxiously repeated myself. "Show me how sorry you are . . . show me right now." The secret was out, so I lowered her hand to my stiffness below. "Because I want to show you more than I've ever wanted anything before in my life."

"Then *you* show *me*," she said and surprisingly moved her hand away.

Were we on the same page? "What do you want me to show you baby?" I had to be sure that we both wanted the same thing.

She said, "Show me that you forgive me."

I thought about asking her if she was truly up to what I wanted and the way I wanted it, but she didn't have to tell me twice. My hands slid down to her waist, unbuttoned her jeans, and slowly worked them down to her knees and then her ankles until she stepped out of them. One look at the silky red thong that housed her prized brown package made me want to drool, and as I took off her shirt and bra I think I did. I laid her on the bed with her legs spread and bent at her knees.

As I got naked my dick grew solid just looking at her body, and my mouth began to water, every taste bud I had wanted to be saturated by her juices. I crawled up the bed, between her thighs and greeted her fat juicy pussy with my lips. My tongue parted her gates and exposed the headquarters of her pleasure. I sucked on that swollen bump of flesh until she spewed cum all over my mouth. I wasn't done though, I French-kissed those pulp lips . . . my tongue tickled her within and my lips pulled on hers. Before I was complete I lapped up her juices, leaving only enough to moisten her tight slit for my entrance.

Panting from the beating I had already put on her below, Sarai said, "Now I'll show *you*."

"Nawh." I turned down her offer of a blow job. "I gotta feel you right now." My face was hovering over hers and my hand was on my meat rubbing it up against her wet hole. "Damn I want you girl."

As my dick entered her I felt both of our bodies inhale, exhale, and then tremble. Sarai didn't have to suck my dick, her warm snug pussy did it for her . . . it kept pulling me in with every thrust. It was as if she had a magnet within her walls . . . I was drawn to the back of her pussy and pushed far into her depth with each pump. She ground herself into me tauntingly, she knew just how good she was too. The feeling was overpowering, I nearly lost control, this couldn't be a two minute affair, so I rolled us over until she was on top riding me and I sat up to meet her. With her nipple in my mouth and my hands bracing her back I gave her as much dick as I possibly could. "Mel, shit, oh ooh, Mel, oh yes."

I won't lie, we started out making love, but five minutes into it we were straight up fucking and loving it. After she tired out herself on top of me I rounded her and plunged into her doggie-style. She tried to show off by backing it up on me, but one real good long deep stroke shut her all the way down. That was to show her that I was still the man . . . *her* man. I held her frail body in place and stuck her hard and fast from the back and as she screamed my pulsating dick became rocklike until it oozed sweet cream in her bowl. "Damn!" I panted. "Shit!" I was all smiles and so was she.

"There's got to be something else I need forgiveness for," she joked.

"I'm sure there is." I said.

We both fell onto the mattress sweaty and gasping for air. "You still have it, Mel," Sarai said as she rolled onto her side to be closer to me.

"Where was it supposed to go?" I asked, still trying to catch my breath.

"I don't know," she joked. "Thought maybe you left it at what's-her-name's house."

"*House* is the key word. That was a house." I rubbed her arm. "You are my home," I said. "And a real man always brings the best shit home because home is where the heart is."

"I missed you so much." She kissed my nose. "You always know the right things to say."

"It's not the right thing," I informed her, "it's the truth, baby."

"Okay, tell me the truth about this, then . . ." She paused and then continued: "Where do we go from here? Our apartment is gone, I'm dead broke, no job, no—"

"Sarai," I interrupted, "we might be homeless and penniless, but as long as we have each other, we have so much more than what others have."

"I love you," she said while rubbing my chest. "Thank you."

"For what?" I asked.

She answered, "For loving me."

"You never have to thank me for that." Suddenly I heard noise coming from the living room area.

"What was that?" she asked me.

I didn't think twice about it. "It's probably just the TV."

"I turned the television off." There was another sound, but this time it was closer. I could feel her body trembling; she was scared.

It was like a déjà vu of the night that changed our lives. We both sat up and looked at each other in the dim lighting. We had to be thinking the same thing . . . not again. "Did you lock the door when you came in earlier today?" I asked.

"Yeah, I think so, but . . ."

As Sarai spoke, the bedroom door swung open and the silhouette of a man walked in, the lights came on, and out from behind Nick jumped Nat. "When did my house become the Holiday Inn?" she asked jokingly.

"Nat!" Sarai yelled, relieved, and scrambled under the sheets. "You scared the shit out of me."

"Well, I hope it didn't come out on my sheets." She laughed. "What are y'all doing here?"

Sarai and I looked at each other and couldn't help but burst into laugher. We knew that no one would believe our story even if it were made into a movie. "It's a long story," Sarai said timidly, "but we kinda need to stay here for a while."

"Well, why don't the both of you put on some clothes, and since the hotel guests drink free, let's all have a glass of wine over this long story because I see that it obviously has a happy ending," Nat said as she closed the door, smiling.

"Well, we have quite a story to tell." I lay back down. "We can turn this stuff into a book."

"What should we title it?" Sarai giggled and suggested, "*Going Broke*?"

"No, that would be the first one." I laughed. "This is the sequel, so we'd have to call it *Dead Broke*."

"Who needs money when you have love?" she asked.

I held her closer to me. "Not me."

"Me neither." She said it and I believed her. "Me neither."